Dead Beat

Candy Justice

For William
Who has a great
journalism career
ahead of him!

Candy

DEDICATION

Dedicated to my darling husband, Bob Willis, who died in January 2018.

He was always loving, encouraging and touchingly proud of me.

ACKNOWLEDGEMENTS

A big thanks to the nearly 100 readers and friends who voted in the Facebook poll as we tried to decide which to choose of the two fantastic *Dead Beat* book covers designed by the multi-talented Jonathan Capriel. And thanks to Don Peters for his in-depth analysis of all the feedback from readers and friends. It helped make a hard decision easier. And as always, a huge thanks to my editor, Kat Leache, for her eagle eye, wisdom and sense of humor. I want to thank those who read my first Britt Faire mystery, *Pre-Marital Murder*, and left reviews on Amazon and Goodreads, and if you also enjoy Book 2, *Dead Beat*, I would be most grateful if you again post your reviews or send me a personal message making comments or asking questions. I love hearing from readers.

I am currently writing Book 3 in the Britt Faire series, *Last Night at Water's Edge*, which takes place in Memphis and the Mississippi Gulf Coast. My deadline for finishing *Water's Edge* is August 1, with a publication date of September 1. *Pre-Marital Murder* and *Dead Beat* are now both available as e-books and trade paperbacks — both can be bought from Amazon. Book 3: *Last Night at Water's Edge* will also be published as both an e-book and trade paperback and can be bought through Amazon.

SPOILER ALERT

If you are about to start reading *Dead Beat* (Book 2 in the series) but haven't read Book 1, *Pre-Marital Murder*, be advised that *Dead Beat* contains an element that will spoil the suspense of Book 1. So if you think you will ever read *Pre-Marital Murder*, I suggest you do it before reading *Dead Beat*.

WRITER'S NOTE

While most of the characters in *Dead Beat* are entirely fictitious, the character of Lettie Nolan is based loosely on my dear, late friend Jo Evelyn Grayson. The mention of Allan J. Rawlinford near the end of *Dead Beat* is entirely (not loosely) based on a real person and his connection to Britt is exactly my relationship with the real Mr. Rawlinford. Look for him again in more detail in a future Britt Faire mystery. And finally, the details of the real-life Memphis serial killer George Howard Putt in 1969 and his victims are entirely factual. History always remembers the names of famous serial killers, but rarely does history remember and honor the memory of their victims. This is my attempt to rectify that in my own small way.

Candy Justice

CHAPTER ONE

During those two terrifying months, I was glad I had quit piano lessons in the third grade.

Ironically, I heard about the first death during a jazz brunch at Miss Cordelia's with Logan. Usually I get my murder news from Jack, who is a homicide detective, but not this time.

Logan Magee lives in Harbor Town, a beautiful residential community in the middle of the Mississippi River on Mud Island, which thankfully doesn't fit its name. One end of the island is a city park reached by monorail from downtown Memphis, and the other end, accessible by a small bridge, is a collection of apartments, condominiums and drop-dead gorgeous homes with incredible views of the river. Logan lives in one of those top-of-the-line houses, despite the fact that he appears to be a penniless doctoral student at the University of Memphis. Until recently, he was a very successful international investment expert and obviously invested his own money well. There aren't many 34-year-old single guys living in houses like this.

You're probably wondering if Logan and I are dating, but don't ask, because I don't know. All I can say is we spend a lot of time together, but so far it's Platonic. He's fresh off a broken engagement — his excessively beautiful blonde fiancée is about to marry his best friend. And I have my own romantic baggage, so...

Anyhow, Logan often wants me to come out to Harbor Town for the weekend jazz brunches at Miss Cordelia's, the little grocery store at the core of Harbor Town's commercial center, which consists of a pizza place, a day spa, a dry cleaner and a Montessori school. It's all manufactured charm, of course, like the rest of Harbor Town (until 30 years ago, the island was nothing but trees, grass, a small landing strip and mud.) But manufactured or not, when you're out there, it really does seem like a wonderful fantasy world.

This warm Sunday in late October, we had just gotten our food — seafood strata with mimosas — and Logan caught me in the middle of my first bite with the news.

"Did you read the paper this morning?"

"No, it's still in the wrapper in the driveway, and I didn't even check the online headlines. I slept late. Why?"

"So you haven't heard about Saundra Barkley being murdered near Beale Street?"

"That's terrible. Was it a robbery?" I work at the local daily newspaper, so I am usually among the first to know these things, but I was off that weekend and decided to take a one-day break from news. I didn't even check Twitter. I wondered why Jack hadn't called to tell me. Maybe he was working on the case and was too busy.

"They didn't take her purse, and there was no sign of sexual assault. Somebody just walked up to her and stabbed her in the back with a steak knife between 3 and 4 a.m. Saturday morning when she was walking back to her car alone. She was unconscious but alive when they found her, but she died on the way to the hospital."

"Did they mention suspects or witnesses?"

"No, other than asking anybody who might have seen anything to come forward — the usual."

I guess you could say Saundra Barkley was a has-been R & B singer, but she was still a local celebrity. And anyone anywhere who was alive in the sixties or listens to oldies radio stations, remembers the Charlettes. For a short time, they were the biggest girl group outside Motown. Their first hit, "Sweet Honey Baby," went to the top of the charts in the mid sixties and really made some money for Memphis' Stax Records label.

Before they could have a second hit, the Charlettes were killed in a small plane crash in Louisiana — you know, the same old story of performers trying to get to an out-of-town gig in bad weather. Saundra was the only one of the Charlettes who didn't die — she got a bad case of food poisoning the day they were supposed to leave, so she didn't go with the other girls. She wasn't the lead singer, so they could do okay without her. Some of the bodies were never recovered from the bayou they crashed into.

The odd thing is that a few years later, a similar thing happened to another Stax group, the Bar-Kays, an all-male group that backed up Otis Redding and went down with Redding in a plane crash on their way to a show in Madison, Wisconsin, in 1967. Just like the Charlettes, one of the Bar-Kays, James Alexander, survived because he wasn't on the plane that crashed. He took a commercial flight later. Another Bar-Kay, Ben Cauley, was the only person on the plane to survive the crash.

Of course, the loss of Otis Redding was a great musical and personal tragedy and dominated the headlines, but the death of the Bar-Kays seemed extra sad to me when I heard years later that they were just a bunch of talented high school kids, who could only perform on weekends because they had to be back in school on Monday.

The Bar-Kays regrouped and continued to perform, but the Charlettes, I guess because they had only had one hit, were finished.

But Saundra Barkley managed to get a solo career out of the deal. Nobody expected it, but she wrote a great song, "Baby Gotta' Leave," and recorded it, and it sold more than the Charlettes' big song did. After that hit, she dumped Stax and signed with Motown.

I'm not saying she had a huge career after that, but she did okay — two duets with Marvin Gaye and touring with some of the other big Motown acts like the Temptations, or was it the Four Tops? Anyhow, she did okay for herself, and when that gradually came to an end, she came back to Memphis, where she managed to stay in the public eye, at least sporadically.

Saundra's latest gig has been teaching vocal music at the University of Memphis. She wasn't a full-fledged professor, but she taught on an adjunct basis and never failed to mention being a "music professor" any time she was interviewed and left the impression she had a Ph.D., which she did not. And any time there was a rock 'n roll retrospective on TV, she managed to get interviewed. She was still beautiful and told great stories. Depending on whom you ask, Saundra Barkley was either a professional survivor or an opportunist. "Nice person" was never part of the description.

And now she was dead, stabbed with a steak knife near Beale Street, Memphis' most famous music street. In the early 1900s, the days of W.C. Handy, the joints were jumping on Beale with blues and ragtime. In the 1920s and early 30s, Beale Street specialized in gambling, prostitution, violence and liquor, which were all illegal, and cocaine, which was not. Cocaine could be bought legally in drug stores on Beale and from patent medicine salesmen.

Many consider Beale Street the birthplace of the blues, which, of course, it was not, literally speaking. The blues was originated by poor black musicians in the nearby Mississippi Delta, but their sound migrated to Memphis, where the blues was embraced by both black and white people of every social status. And W. C. Handy brought the blues to the world by writing and publishing sheet music of his famous songs like "Beale Street Blues," "Memphis Blues," and "St. Louis Blues."

During the 1920s and 30s, the Beale Street clubs and saloons, especially the Palace Theater, were the place to see Ma Rainey, the first really famous female blues singer; singer and native Memphian Alberta Hunter; comedian Butterbeans and his wife, Suzy; and Bessie Smith, who did her last show on Beale Street just hours before she died following an automobile accident in North Mississippi on September 25, 1937.

White Memphians had always loved the blues, and Boss Crump, who was white, used the W.C. Handy band during his campaigning for mayor. During the Jazz Age, the Palace on Beale was host to Midnight Rambles, beginning at 11:30 p.m. on Thursday nights for white patrons only.

By the 1950s, things were tamer on Beale, and it was the social and entertainment heart of black Memphis. Even many middle-class, church-going black parents would allow their teenagers to go to Beale sometimes. A white kid from the projects, Elvis Presley, sneaked off to Beale whenever possible to hear performers like B.B. King and Phineas Newborn Jr. do blues, jazz and R & B.

Then after becoming virtually deserted during the 60s and 70s, except for a few pawn shops and A. Schwab Dry Goods Store, Beale Street became a music mecca again in the 1980s with clubs and restaurants and live blues, jazz and rock n' roll played by professional musicians inside the clubs and amateurs outside on the streets and in Handy Park.

And the Memphis Police made sure Beale and most of the downtown area were free of prostitutes and free of most of the more serious criminals so that the young locals and tourists of every age would feel safe there. So murders like Saundra Barkley's were rare these days.

As soon as Logan and I finished eating and parted company at Miss Cordelia's, I called Jack to ask for the low-down on the murder. As it turned out, he was working on the case, but couldn't tell me much more than Logan had. Before they chalked it up to random street violence, they were talking to everybody they could and had found that Saundra had a lot of enemies, none of whom seemed likely to have killed her.

Personally, Jack said, he was leaning toward the theory that she was murdered by someone who knew her, someone who wanted to be sure everyone knew she was not murdered randomly.

"Why do you say that?' I asked.

"Well, it wasn't a robbery or her purse and jewelry or car would have been taken," said Jack , who sounded like he was eating in his office. "And most people who would want her dead would go out of their way to make it look like a random robbery to throw the police off. But I think whoever killed Saundra Barkley wanted to send a message that she had been murdered for a reason. Maybe it was a warning to somebody else even."

I'm sure you're wondering why a homicide cop would tell me, a reporter, all this off-the-record stuff. We've known each other professionally for years and have developed mutual respect, but it's also a personal relationship. I'm not saying we're exactly a thing — I'm not sure what we are. I'm not in a big hurry to find out.

CHAPTER TWO

The next morning I was sitting at my desk in the newsroom staring out the window when my mother called from Florida, where she and Dad took early retirement a few years ago. She was upset about Saundra Barkley's murder and wanted to know if they had arrested anybody yet. Mom grew up with that music, and she loved the Charlettes and Barkley's duets with Marvin Gaye. I told her all I knew, which wasn't much, and then we chatted about Dad and what she had heard lately from my sisters.

After we hung up, I went back to thinking about how I now have the perfect job. For the past two years, I've had what I thought was the perfect job, but it turned out I was wrong. My old job was only first runner-up to the most perfect job.

For nine years I was a newspaper reporter — first general assignments, then covering cops and then settling into covering criminal courts for several years. I liked all of that, but then two years ago, I was made a columnist. A dream come true. City Lights has been the name of the column for many years, and I took it over from a venerable old guy, a Memphis institution, who finally retired and then died of a heart attack 12 days later. Nobody was surprised. He could take any amount of deadline pressure and professional stress, but his heart couldn't hold up under the strain of boredom.

So I had a tough act to follow. I used the column to write

about anything I wanted to, but mostly I used it as a platform to discuss the plight of the homeless and other disadvantaged Memphians. And I had a lot of fun jerking the chains of various politicians and greedy land developers.

Then one day a few weeks ago, the editor called me into her office. As I made that long walk across the newsroom to her office, my vision was blurred, my pulse raced. I was sure the editor was going to fire me or at least complain about my column. I have this thing about authority figures — I always expect the worst. Never mind that my stock had gone way up a couple of months ago when I broke a huge international story.

Instead of firing me, she told me what a good job I was doing and that she'd like to "expand the scope of my work." I immediately interpreted that as a plan to restrict my freedom and give me more work to do. But she wanted to give me more freedom and more money. The editor said my new title would be Editor At Large, which meant I could write a column as often or seldom as I wished, and I would also write in-depth feature stories or investigative pieces when I wanted to. The only catch was that she wanted me to do more social media. I am notorious among the online people in the newsroom for often "forgetting" to use social media. I told her I was okay with that as long as I didn't have to express my opinion but could just use social media to promote my writing, which is what they want most anyhow.

So now in light of Saundra Barkley's murder, I was rolling around ideas in my head. Should I do a story on the impact on the music scene? But how much impact could there be at this stage of her career? How about a story on whether Beale Street is becoming dangerous again? No way — that wouldn't be fair and would be sensational. One murder does not constitute a trend.

Then it hit me. How about a story on how the Charlettes' plane crash changed Saundra Barkley's life? I read somewhere that people who are the only survivor of some disaster or accident either feel guilty or special for the rest of their lives. So that's what I wrote about.

At first I was going to interview others who had been lone

survivors of something, but then I decided instead to just concentrate on Barkley. I talked to her sister, who said that Saundra always felt "blessed, not guilty" about not being on the plane with the other girls. It was just God's mercy that Saundra was spared, the sister said.

But everybody else I talked to said Saundra Barkley always felt special because she wasn't killed in the plane crash like the others. The words these fellow musicians, friends and university students used to describe Barkley's attitude included "anointed," "singled out by fate," "arrogant," "chosen by God" and "better than everybody else." Many of them asked not to be quoted by name, because they hated to speak ill of the dead.

Her producer at Stax Records, Stewart Linton, said the first time he saw her after the plane crash, he expected her to be grief-stricken and falling apart about how close she came to dying herself. "Instead," he said, and he didn't mind being quoted by name, "she was upbeat. If she was upset, she didn't show it. She said people were saying her singing career was over, but she would show them, that she had a lot more talent than they were giving her credit for. It was all about her."

The now elderly mother of one of the other Charlettes told me that she was shocked and hurt when Saundra came to the funeral home for visitation and said she felt God had spared her because He had something special in mind for her.

"Can you imagine saying that to a grieving mother?" the elderly lady asked me. "It was like saying God didn't have anything special planned for my baby or the other girls."

I tried to figure out if Saundra Barkley was always so self-confident or if it was surviving the plane crash that brought out this in her. There was no consensus. Some said she always had faith in herself, others said she changed completely after the crash.

It was a hard story to write, since most of the opinions of Saundra Barkley were negative. I wondered if anybody I was talking to had hated Saundra enough to kill her. There were plenty of people who seemed not to like her, but hate? The most bitter among Barkley's acquaintances were people who had worked at Stax with her. After all, they had taken a chance on her as a solo, and then when her first solo record was a big hit, she dumped them for the more prestigious Motown label. Then the death of Otis Redding, their hottest star, a couple of years later, must have made it all a double blow.

None of them seemed to be shedding tears over Saundra's death, but I still couldn't imagine any of them hating her enough to kill her, especially after all these years. When I said that to Jack, he said, "Never underestimate the power of hate to smolder for many years and burst into flames when you least expect it."

CHAPTER THREE

Jack called later that week and suggested I meet him on the deck of Central Barbecue for lunch. It was still warm and perfect for eating outside, and I was glad to see him.

Cops aren't really my type — I've been telling Jack that for years. I still use various lame excuses like, "We're pals. I don't want to ruin it with a romance."

I still say cops aren't my type, but I like Jack — I can't help it, and he's a sexy guy, not good looking like Logan, but he's got something. Anyhow, I told Jack a couple of months ago that I needed a little space — I hate myself when I use clichés like that. In this case it wasn't an excuse to get away from him. I just meant I needed him to just keep being my friend and give me time to figure out if I want more. And he's done that, but thank goodness he hasn't gone away altogether.

He was waiting on the deck when I got there — a big plate of barbecue nachos and two beers waiting. Of the hundreds of barbecue places in Memphis, there are some others that have barbecue nachos, but Jack and I think Central has the best. Chopped pork barbecue on the chips with barbecue sauce, cheese sauce and two kinds of grated cheese. Yum.

"Hey, kiddo," he said, standing up and giving me a little sisterly hug. "Dig in."

I did.

"Are ya'll still working 18-hour days on the Saundra Barkley murder?"

"We're slacking now — I haven't worked longer than 12 hours a day since we started concentrating on three suspects."

"Let me guess, one of them is her ex." I had learned years ago when I was a police reporter that cops always suspect husbands and wives and exes first when there's a murder, and too often they're right. "I've never understood why people kill their spouses when it's so easy to get a divorce."

"They don't kill their husbands or wives because they want to end the relationship. They kill them because they hate them. And yeah, you're right, one of the three suspects is her ex-husband. They've been divorced more than 20 years, but everybody says they never stopped hating each other. She always told people her ex hated her because she was more successful than him, and he always told people he hated her because she's a bitch."

"Is he a musician, too?"

"Yeah, a trumpet player, Dewitt Starks, works sporadically, never could give up his day job."

"I'm inclined to believe his assessment of Saundra. I haven't been able to find anybody who seemed to really like her, except a couple of her students and her sister."

"Don't be so sure about them. They're probably lying."

"And who are the other two main suspects?"

"Well, there's this crank, Ray Taggart, they call him Slick, who's been telling anybody who would listen for the past 40 years that the one hit solo record Saundra had was written by him. Says he gave it to her for the Charlettes, and later on after the crash, she recorded it herself and claimed she wrote it. He never got credit or a dime out of it."

"Do you think that's true?"

"Nobody seems to know, but it's possible. And the third suspect is one of her old record producers?"

"The guy from Stax who I quoted in my story?"

"Yeah, Stewart Linton. He got fired right after Saundra dumped Stax for Motown, and he always blamed her, but some of the folks I've talked to say that wasn't why he got fired. It was because he was drinking too much and not showing up for work."

"So all the suspects are in the music business, huh?"

"At the moment it's just those three, but that could change, of course. We've just started questioning them."

"How did you locate them so quickly?"

"Britt, there are a lot of musicians in this town, but they all seem to know each other, and some of them love to dish the dirt on the others."

"I always thought there was a lot of camaraderie among musicians."

"There is, but still they know the down-low on everybody else, and they like to gossip, so it made it easy to find out about Linton and Taggart. Apparently, those two have been griping about Saundra for so many years, it's..."

"Like a broken record?"

"Yeah, something like that. Sorry, kid, but I got to go back to work."

"Keep me informed, Jack."

"Don't I always? I don't have to say, do I, that what I just told you is off the record, reporter girl?"

"For now."

I know you think I'm using Jack, and I am, but that doesn't mean I don't like being with him. He really is pretty cute.

CHAPTER FOUR

This time Jack gave me the news. A Memphis rapper had been murdered in the early morning hours outside the Plush Club, a Beale street venue used mostly for special events, like boxing, parties and rap performances.

I was sitting at my desk in the newsroom about nine when the call came.

"Which one?" was my first question.

"You mean you know one rapper from another? I thought you were a jazz girl."

"I didn't say I'm a big rap fan, but I'm not totally clueless about hip-hop artists like you are. So who was murdered?"

"He goes by Mutha Boy — his real name's Donté Washington. If you want to know more, come over to the office. In fact, we kind of need your advice."

"*My* advice? The cops need *my* advice? That's a first."

"Anyhow, can you come over now?"

"Sure, I can't wait to hear how I figure in this."

"Britt, no kidding, it's really important you not mention this to anyone until after we talk."

"Get real, Jack. Do you think the paper won't find out about this with or without my help?"

"Trey will be all over it any minute when he sees the police report, I know that, but, well, anyhow, for once trust me and don't argue. You'll understand when you get here."

I was so anxious to hear what Jack and "we," whoever "we" was, had to say that I paid the outrageous fee to park in the lot across the street from the Criminal Justice Center, better known as 201 (its address), instead of my usual habit of driving around until I found a metered space on the street.

When I walked into the office, Jack wasn't alone. The police director, the head of homicide and a public relations guy were there. Wow, what a "we." Jack spoke first after offering me a chair.

"Britt, I know this is out of the ordinary."

"*That* is the understatement of the year," I said. "Please go on. For once I'll try not to interrupt. Unless I have to."

Jack smiled, the others didn't. Jack was outranked by everyone in the room, except the PR flack, so I guess he was doing the talking because they knew he and I were friendly.

"Britt, can we talk off the record?"

"I'm not sure, Jack. This is a very big story."

The police director spoke up.

"We aren't in any way trying to suppress the news story, Miss Faire. That would be impossible anyhow. We're just asking that you help us with a difficult decision, and we're asking that you not tell anyone that we consulted you on this."

Now Jack's boss in Homicide, Walter Raines, joined in.

"Besides that, the only thing we might ask you to keep off the record is a couple of details of the murder that might jeopardize the investigation."

"If that's what those details really are, I don't have a problem with that. All reporters hold back some things, if the cops ask nice and make a good case for it really interfering with the investigation, but..." and I turned to the PR guy, Todd Hartfield, "but you all know as well as I do that the cops sometimes use that excuse to hold back information for non-legitimate reasons. I won't be a part of that."

"We wouldn't ask you to," Raines said.

"I assure you, this is all legitimate," the police director added.

I looked at Jack and saw a look on his face I could trust. Jack would never draw me into something he knew I couldn't ethically be a part of.

"Well, let's hear it," I said. "I'm on the edge of my seat." And I was.

"I told you on the phone, Britt, that a rapper had been murdered a few hours ago outside the Plush Club."

"I assume then there were witnesses?"

"No, not to the murder, but there were a couple of witnesses to what happened just before. The rapper left the Plush Club about 3:45 with his entourage of three. I guess he's not a big enough star for a full posse. Then he said he forgot something and went back in. He said he'd meet them in the parking lot. He didn't say what or who he forgot. Anyhow, the others were milling around in the parking lot laughing and talking and finally somebody realized the rapper should have been back by then, so a couple of the guys went to look for him. They found him by the back exit, on the ground..." Jack paused, I guess knowing how I would react to the next bit, "And he had a well-placed steak knife in his back."

Predictably, I gasped. "So we've got a serial killer on our hands."

"Not necessarily," the police director said.

"How can you say that — two musicians killed on Beale Street in one week, both stabbed with steak knives, and it's all a

16

coincidence?"

"Britt," Jack said, annoyed, "will you let us finish before you draw your conclusions."

"But..."

"Please, Britt," Jack begged.

"We made a big mistake when Saundra Barkley was murdered last week, Miss Faire," Raines said. "We normally hold back a few details of any murder from the public, because we don't want copy cat murders to occur. I'm sure you know there is always a danger of someone hearing about a murder and using the same methods in an unrelated murder to cover their tracks."

I nodded yes.

"I don't know if I'd call it a mistake, Wally," the police director said.

"It was pretty much unavoidable in this case," Jack said. "With Saundra Barkley, there were so many people around when the cops and the paramedics got there, and she had fallen forward, so all the witnesses saw the knife in her back. So we couldn't keep that information from the public to protect against a copycatter."

"So didn't Mutha Boy's friends see the knife in him?"

"No, because he was lying on his back. His eyes were wide open, so they knew he was dead, and they all freaked. They didn't try to pick him up or roll him over, they just called 911. They were taken aside for questioning while the medical examiner was examining the body and the scene. Nobody was allowed near the body this time."

"So, what makes you think it might not be a serial killer?" I asked, looking at Jack.

"Well, to begin with, the diversity of the victims. True they're both black and both musicians, but they're on opposite ends of the spectrum. She was 68 and a has-been do-wopper who lives in the suburbs, and he is a 24-year-old rapper still living in the hood, who's had only one fairly successful CD."

"None of those factors mean they weren't killed by the same person," I protested.

"You're exactly right, Britt," Jack said. "But those factors are part of a reasonable doubt at this early stage, combined with how well publicized the crime scene was with Barkley."

Suddenly I looked at the PR guy and had a terrible idea.

"Is this all about money? Are the powers-that-be worried that a serial killer stalking Beale Street will run off all the tourists and hurt business downtown?" I looked at all of them, but settled my gaze on Jack, because I knew I'd know if he lied to me.

"Britt," Jack said, "I give you my word of honor, and you know that means something, that money is not the big factor. I'm not saying it's not a factor at all, but I swear it's not the main concern. Can you imagine the panic that would occur throughout the city if they thought a serial killer was on the loose?"

"But doesn't the public deserve to know this, so they can protect themselves?"

"But what if it's not a serial killer, and we cause this panic for nothing," the police director said.

"What are you suggesting?" I asked, looking from man to man.

"We're trying to buy time, a few hours, maybe even a few days to investigate the rapper's murder."

"I hate the way you keep calling him this impersonal term, 'the rapper.' Nobody ever called Saundra Barkley 'the girl group singer'," I said with emotion. "It's dehumanizing."

"I'm sorry. Miss Faire is right," the police director said. "I want the victim referred to as Mr. Washington from now on." He looked meaningfully at the other three men.

They were just trying to appease me, but I didn't call them on it. At least this young man would get a little respect in death one way or the other. Because of his young age and his new-found, but not fully realized success, his murder seemed so much more tragic to me than Saundra Barkley's. How hopeful he must have felt about his life up until that very moment when a knife was plunged into his back.

"So, let's go back," I said. "How is it that a few hours or a few days will help?"

"For one thing, Britt, it will give us time to interview people who knew the... knew Mr. Washington to see if there are any obvious suspects. Maybe there was an altercation at the club earlier in the evening, maybe somebody had been threatening him, maybe he had a messed up personal life. And time will give us a chance to see what the forensic people can tell us. We know from the height and angle of the stab wound that Saundra Barkley was murdered by someone between 5 foot 9 and 6 feet tall. We'll compare that to Washington's wound. There are just so many things that need to be determined before we can say with any certainty that both of these murders were done by a serial killer. Even if they were both killed by the same person, it may not be a serial killer, as such. It could just be somebody who hated them both. We'll look for connections between them, a common enemy."

"Okay, I buy that it would be good to be sure before unleashing panic on the public, but what was all that stuff about needing my advice. What does this have to do with me?"

"This is the part you won't like," Jack said, "but hear us out."

Suddenly, I understood.

"You want me to turn, you want to make me into a spin doctor," I said, pointing to the PR guy, Hartfield. "That's his job, not mine. No way I'm going to help you come up with a disinformation campaign, also known as lying."

Before anybody else could say anything, I stood up and walked, almost ran, out of the room and headed down the hall toward the elevators. Jack ran after me, calling my name. I whirled around on him, furious, but he pulled me into an empty interrogation room before I could spew my venom in front of anybody else.

"How dare you put me in that position! How could you, Jack? I thought you were my friend. I'll never trust you again." I saw that the last statement hurt him to the core, and I meant for it to.

"You have every right to be mad, Britt, but do I get just a couple of minutes to defend myself, two minutes before you write me off forever?"

I started to say no and leave, but decided to let him talk, not for his sake, but for mine. I couldn't bear to think Jack had totally betrayed me, all evidence to the contrary.

"You've got two minutes," I said, sitting down forcefully into a chair, my arms crossed in defiance.

"First, let me say I knew you would react this way, and I was counting on that."

"What?"

"I got a call about 4:30 this morning from Bowers, one of the other guys in Homicide. He woke me up to say Raines wanted me on this case, even though it wasn't my shift. In fact, I was supposed to be off today, my first day off since Barkley was killed. So I got over to the scene as quickly as possible, but before we were finished at the scene, Raines called on my cell and told me the director wanted to see me right away. I went back to 201 and was brought before the three guys we just met with in there. They were genuinely concerned about all the things they said to you — that wasn't a lie. And they wanted me to ask you to help us suppress the news for a few days, maybe give the PR guy some tips on how to throw off the press a bit, especially the TV people, who have a greater potential for creating panic than the newspaper."

"And you actually thought I would do that?"

"Of course not, Britt, don't you think I know you after all these years? I told them no way, but they were sure that they could be persuasive and that my presenting the case would sway you. They were giving me way too much credit for being able to influence you, and I told them so, but they thought I was being modest or something. Well, anyhow, I had no choice but to go along. They were sitting there when I called you, so there was no way I could warn you about what was going to happen."

"So you just did this big acting job to save your job?"

"Well, I *was* saving my job, but I was also telling the truth. I believe everything I said in there about the importance of being sure we're right before unleashing paralyzing fear on the public. Remember how embarrassing it was for the department and what needless fear we caused when we announced last year that that rich guy, what was his name, anyhow that he had been brutally murdered in his house at Southwind and then it turned out to be an accidental head injury. Half the people in Southwind had checked into hotels in different parts of town and one had put his house up for sale by the time we found out we jumped to conclusions."

"Yeah, that was real embarrassing for the MPD."

"Not just embarrassing, but irresponsible, causing all that panic when the guy just fell down the stairs and bled all over the place. Anyhow, Britt, I believed what I said in there about needing time, but I knew that wasn't really possible or that if we did pull it off, it would be without your help. I would have been so disillusioned with you if you had said yes."

"Would you really?"

"Definitely. Cops and reporters, even good cops and good reporters, are going to be at cross purposes sometimes, but I've always admired your ethics, and it would have killed me personally if you had gone along with this. And something good did come of this, Britt."

"What?"

"Because we are so close, I would have told you all that stuff confidentially as a friend, but this way you know it, and *they* were the ones who brought you into the loop, not *me*, so it's your decision how much you're going to tell your readers."

Thankfully, he didn't end with some guilt trip like, "And I'm sure we can trust you to make the right decision for the safety of the public."

My arms were no longer crossed and I wasn't angry with Jack any more, but I did have a tough decision to make. How much should I reveal to my paper? First I wanted to hear what the police director would have to say at a press conference scheduled for noon. Then I would decide what I would do.

CHAPTER FIVE

I don't know why all the police big-wigs thought they needed my help. The police director, coached I'm sure by the PR guy, did a masterful job of delaying all-out serial killer panic.

After reading a statement, the director said he would take a few questions, and naturally the first question from the press was, "Director, is there a serial killer on the loose in Memphis?"

The director was cool as can be. "That's a very reasonable question, and I can't give you a definite answer at this early stage of the investigation, but I can tell you that we do not believe this murder was carried out by the same person who killed Saundra Barkley. We have identified several likely suspects in the Barkley murder, and before you ask, no, I can't identify them yet, but we feel we are close to solving that murder. In the case of Mr. Washington's death, we are fairly certain his death is the result of a rivalry within the rap culture. I'm sure you all remember the murders of Tupac Shakur and Notorious B.I.G. a few years ago and the more recent murder of Nipsey Hussle."

"What makes you think that is true in this case?" another reporter asked.

"I'm not at liberty to share those details just yet, but it's no secret that rap musicians are often connected to gangs and that there are bitter, sometimes fatal rivalries among the different rapper factions."

It went on like that for several more questions, and by the time this hit the TV news, everyone had forgotten about Saundra Barkley, and the story was now that Memphis had had its first rapper rivalry murder. I had to hand it to them — the cops very skillfully steered the story away from a possible serial killer angle to the sexier rapper rivalry murder idea by implying that there was solid evidence pointing to that and that the Saundra Barkley murder was nearly solved, which of course it wasn't.

After watching the press conference, which was carried live on all the TV stations, I called Jack on his personal cell phone.

"Tell your bosses I said congratulations. They should get an Oscar and a commendation from the Public Relations Society of America."

"So you think the TV people fell for it?"

"Oh, definitely."

"What about your paper?"

"Probably not, but the TV stations have already solidified the idea in the minds of average Memphians that this is a rapper thing and nothing they have to worry about. The TV reporters will be doing man-on-the-street interviews asking leading questions like, 'Are you surprised that a rapper rivalry in Memphis would result in murders like those of Tupac Shakur and Notorious B.I.G.?'"

"We can only hope," Jack said.

"But it's a lie, Jack, and the director knows it."

"Who says it's a lie? We think there's a good chance that it *was* a rivalry murder."

"That is such a racist assumption to make."

"Racist? Have you ever noticed, Britt, that the police director is black himself."

"So what? He's still a middle-aged and middle-class man, who probably totally looks down on hip-hop music and assumes all rappers have rap sheets."

"Which they often do. Why do you think one of the record companies is called Death Row Records and rap is full of references to illegal activities? You get street cred by committing a crime."

"How can you generalize like that?"

"Okay, I won't generalize. I'll be specific. Donté "Mutha Boy" Washington's profession before he became a recording artist was neighborhood drug dealer."

"Was he ever convicted of that?"

"No, but both of his brothers are serving time for selling crack, and the cops in his neighborhood always knew he was doing it, too, but never got him for more than simple possession."

"That's guilt by association, Jack. Is that fair?"

"Maybe not, but crime really does seem to run in some families. Several years ago, the justice department did a national survey and found out that nearly half of prisoners had another close relative either serving time then or recently."

I wasn't sure how to argue with that, so I just silently resolved to do a story on the Memphis rap scene.

•••••••••••••••

I thought it would be hard to get good sources for my story, since I am a white, not-that-cool 33-year-old, but to my surprise I found that a lot of the Memphis rappers, DJs and producers were anxious to talk to me. They were upset about the cops saying Mutha Boy's murder was a rivalry slaying.

In the first place, they told me, Mutha Boy's career was on

the rise, but he wasn't famous or powerful enough to inspire a rivalry murder.

More importantly, my sources told me, that kind of stuff just doesn't happen in Memphis. Several referred to "hometown love." They pointed out how the biggest rap stars from Memphis, like Three 6 Mafia and Yo Gotti, still live here because they feel loved and appreciated in Memphis, and they "want to keep it real." I think it may also be that in Memphis, their Rolls Royces stand out from the crowd, and if they lived in New York or LA, little kids wouldn't follow them around asking for autographs. It's the old big fish in a little pond phenomenon.

Memphis' own style of Southern Hip Hop, which many consider the origin of crunk, goes back more than 20 years, but most older adults in Memphis didn't even know the city had a nationally known rap culture until the movie "Hustle and Flow" was made here, and members of Three 6 Mafia and Frayser Boy wrote a song for the movie, and the song won an Oscar. When the exuberant threesome accepted the award and shouted thanks to Memphis, I'm sure a lot of local Oscar watchers were surprised — "You mean those guys are from here?"

But now that they know, Memphians are only too willing to believe Mutha Boy's murder is a rap rivalry, because the alternative — believing that a serial killer is on the loose — is just too scary. And my story said that.

After all the people I interviewed told me the rivalry thing was complete BS, I asked each of them what their own theories were on the murder. I got a couple of interesting answers.

More than one person mentioned an incident a few months ago when Mutha Boy was auditioning female dancers, some of whom were under-aged. One 17-year-old girl's father and brother found out that Mutha Boy had pulled up her dress to see if she had the right size bottom for his show. The dad and brother threatened to kill Mutha Boy.

A couple of people suggested that Donté Washington may have been murdered by a dentist. That's right, you heard it right. It seems that the dentist, a white guy, had made the rapper a really great grill — a mouth apparatus of gold and diamonds — and Mutha Boy was sending a lot of other customers his way. The dentist, Dr. Arthur Kendelman, was so successful that he quit his regular practice and was doing nothing but grills or grillz, as they've been spelled since Nelly's hit single. Then Mutha Boy started demanding a cut and when Kendelman refused, Mutha Boy turned most of the dentist's customers against him. Definitely bad blood there, I was told.

My story came out a few days after the murder of Donté Washington, and Jack called to say that the cops already knew about the angry father and brother and were questioning them, but they didn't know about the dentist until they read my story. It's not the first time I've wondered, "If we reporters can dig these things up, why can't the cops?"

I was about to hang up when Jack stopped me.

"Oh, yeah, one more thing, Britt. We've got one more suspect, even though we don't have a name yet. I guess you didn't stumble on this. A witness who saw Washington come out of the Plush Club with his friends, the first time, before he went back in, said there was a girl, a white girl, 20 something, dirty blonde hair, in a wheel chair, who seemed to be alone. She asked Washington for his autograph and he blew her off, said he didn't have time, he was tired."

"And you think a woman in a wheelchair killed him because he wouldn't give her an autograph?" I was being intentionally obtuse, since we were obviously playing the I-found-out-more-than-you game.

"Highly unlikely, since the stab wound was between the shoulder blades and Washington is six-three, but the witness said the girl cried when the rapper was unkind to her. Maybe, just maybe, somebody else got mad about that."

"I can't imagine somebody killing another person over an autograph," I said, knowing full well I had tripped myself up with that one.

"Don't give me that, Britt. You know as well as I do that all it takes is booze or drugs or just hormones and some people will kill you over less than that. You've written plenty of those stories. Like the guy who killed another guy at a bar because he was a Steelers fan."

"Or like the father and daughter who were killed the same night, in unrelated incidents, him over a $5 bet and her over a parking space," I conceded.

"I rest my case," Jack said and hung up.

CHAPTER SIX

I called Logan on Sunday afternoon to see if he'd like to go down to Alfred's on Beale that night to hear the Memphis Jazz Orchestra. When it comes to shared interests, Logan and I are off the charts. With a few exceptions, we like the same music, the same books and movies. We both like to play board games and go to trivia contests at bars. We even both are devotees of extra crunchy peanut butter, although I'm a strawberry jam girl, and he's adamant about grape jelly. I don't like grape anything.

So it was an easy sell — well, no sell at all actually — to get him to say yes to Alfred's. The jazz orchestra considers this regular Sunday night gig their weekly rehearsal, so they take long smoke breaks and approach the whole evening's performance very informally, but the casual observer wouldn't know it wasn't an official performance.

Despite there being no cover, there is rarely a big crowd there — mostly, I guess, because it's Sunday night, which is a pretty dead night on Beale. Every other night, the street, which is closed to motor traffic every evening between Second and Fourth Streets, is jammed with people, streaming in and out of the clubs. This Sunday night the crowd was even sparser because of the news of two murders on or near Beale Street, but Logan and I weren't afraid because we look too square to be taken for musicians.

The second reason the jazz orchestra doesn't pull in a crowd is the most disheartening one — Memphis just isn't a big jazz town even though its jazz roots go back nearly a hundred years. You can see the city's slogans on the sides of city buses, "Home of the Blues" and "Birthplace of Rock 'n Roll." That's where the city's musical identity most lies, but that doesn't mean Memphis hasn't produced some great jazz talents — Phineas Newborn Jr., James Williams, Kirk Whalum, Harold Mabern, to name a few. And Jimmie Lunsford's jazz big band in the 30s was considered the swingingest dance band anywhere. But musicians mostly had to leave the city to make a living playing jazz. Those people are better known in New York than in their own hometown.

Those who stay find they have to do a little of everything to make it. As Joyce Cobb, a great local jazz singer reminiscent of Ella Fitzgerald, once told me, "I'd love to do nothing but jazz, but people won't let me. They want some blues and rock 'n roll thrown in, too, so that's what I give them."

Still jazz does have its followers in Memphis, and Logan and I are among them. Always before, we had just listened to the big band and had drinks or dinner, but this night Logan surprised me by asking me to dance. There are always a few dancers on the floor, but never a crowd unless a busload of European tourists or a ballroom dancing class are there.

Our first dance was a slow one, "Angel Eyes," and when the next number was an upbeat number by Count Basie we stayed out there and did a respectable swing, which my grandmother always calls jitterbugging.

Halfway through the swing number, Logan said, "I knew you'd be a good dancer."

"How could you know that?" I challenged.

"I could tell by the way you walk that you'd be a good swing dancer."

"Do I shake my booty when I walk? I hope not."

"No, you just move well."

When we went back to our table, Logan asked me how I

learned to dance to that kind of music.

"I was about to ask you the same thing."

"My mother taught me," he said. "That's one of those weird things that happens when you're an only child."

I smiled because I could imagine vivacious Maggie Magee teaching little Logan how to dance. I knew Maggie before I knew Logan, so I fully appreciated Logan's mom's spunk and attitude toward life.

"That's typical of you, Britt. I ask you a question, and I end up answering one. How do you always manage that?"

"Just being a good reporter. Well, anyhow, I developed an affection for big-band music when I was a little girl and my parents took me and my sisters to the Skyway of the Peabody where the Glenn Miller Orchestra was performing. I learned to dance standing on my daddy's shoes. Then a college boyfriend and I took ballroom dance lessons."

"Glenn Miller? How old are you? I could have sworn you were in your 30s and not in your 70s."

"Very funny. Glenn Miller may have died during World War II, but his orchestra has continued to tour all these years, with younger musicians, of course, but playing the same music and arrangements. They always come to Memphis once a year, and I usually go."

"Can I go with you next time? I'd love to hear them."

"It's a date." I immediately hated myself for using that word, but Logan didn't recoil or anything, so I guess it was no big deal.

"You never cease to amaze me, Britt — you're a delightful anachronism sometimes."

"Delightful anachronism," I said in my best southern belle accent. "Why, suh, you'll turn a girl's head with such sweet talk."

There was a momentary look of hurt on Logan's face, and

that made me feel terrible.

"You're making fun of me," he said, "but I meant it as a compliment. I guess I'm no wordsmith and certainly not a poet."

"I wasn't making fun of you. I have the unfortunate habit of making a joke when I'm unsure of myself."

"See, that's what I'm talking about — you never cease to amaze me. How many women would admit something like that?"

"Was that a bad thing to admit? Should I have kept that confession to myself?" I wasn't joking. I was suddenly unsure of myself again.

"I love the way you say those disarming and honest things. I've talked about you to my therapist."

"Talked about me to your therapist? That doesn't sound good. Does he think I'm the root of your problems, even though you've only known me five months?" This time he knew I was joking, and he laughed.

"No, so far he hasn't pinpointed you as my problem. What I meant was I've told him that I admire your way of communication — self-effacing humor, but not truly putting yourself down, and honesty without spilling your guts to everyone who'll listen."

"I didn't know you were in therapy. Is it because of all you went through this past year?"

"Well, believe it or not, I'm in therapy because I feel so good."

"Okay, and what do you do when you feel bad?"

"What I mean, Britt, is that it doesn't seem natural for me to feel so happy after that horrendous year and after having my fiancée break up with me and plan to marry my best friend. It seems like a normal person would be traumatized and depressed, but I'm not."

"Why do you think that is?"

"I don't know. I guess that's why I'm going to a therapist, just to be sure I'm not stuffing my feelings. When you grow up in a family where a fatal hereditary disease hangs over everybody's head, you either live in a constant state of fear and depression, or you get good at avoidance. So, I guess I'm just getting a psychological check-up."

"But you had the test and found out you didn't have the gene. Do you think you'll find that you're in denial over Caroline marrying Ben."

"Or maybe I'll find out I really am fine with it, and that I really am as happy as I seem."

The band played another slow song, "Embraceable You," and Logan pulled me gently back to the dance floor. This time he held me close and didn't talk. Instead of the usual light touch on my back, Logan's right arm was firmly wrapped around me, his left hand held my hand close to his chest and his face was pressed against mine. I needed a cold shower for more than one reason when we finished.

CHAPTER SEVEN

When Logan and I left Beale Street that Sunday night after the jazz orchestra's performance, it was still early, so we walked over to the Peabody lobby and had a drink. The Peabody's famous ducks were already back on the roof in their luxury apartment, having spent the day in the lobby fountain.

Watching the ducks march out on a red carpet from the elevator to the fountain each morning and back again in the afternoon is a big tourist attraction, but I prefer the evenings there. It's not exactly quiet, but it's a laid back crowd, and I love just being there in the lobby that Tennessee Williams wrote marked the beginning of the Mississippi Delta.

Logan and I talked about the two musician murders and both said we weren't sure any more whether it was a serial crime or a strange coincidence. At times when we were not talking, we would pick up bits and pieces of other conversations about the same thing. I guess because the victims had both been musicians, most people didn't feel too threatened by it.

"Even though I'm not a musician," Logan said as we walked back to his car, "I find myself glancing over my shoulder when somebody comes up behind me."

"I'm a little spooked by the murders, too," I said. "Maybe we shouldn't have parked in the parking garage. It's so deserted this time on a Sunday night."

Then we both laughed at our paranoia. Logan drove me home to Midtown — I live in the Cooper-Young district, which is only about 10 minutes from downtown. As we pulled up in front of my house, I glanced at my front door and saw what looked like a note wedged between the unlocked screen door and doorframe.

"What could that be?" I said to Logan. In this day of texting, e-mail, cell phones and answering machines, nobody ever leaves a note on your door anymore.

"I'm curious, too. I'll walk to the door with you."

As we read the note silently together, we both gasped, almost in unison.

In pencil on lined notebook paper were these words:

Sandra gotta leave

Mama's Boy too

I know whose next

Guess who

I looked at Logan and he said, "Could it be a joke?"

"I sure hope so, but I can't think of anybody I know who would make a sick joke like that. We've got to call Jack, and let's not touch the note anymore in case there are finger prints on it."

I called Jack from my cell phone, and he said he'd be right over. Logan and I sat on my porch steps and waited for him. Jack jumped out of the car and bounded toward us. I could see on his face that he was surprised or maybe sorry to see Logan was with me. They are on friendly terms, but still. I didn't owe Jack an explanation, but I gave him one anyhow.

"We just came back from hearing the jazz orchestra downtown, and this note was wedged in the door."

Jack took out a handkerchief and picked up the note and read it.

"Britt, think hard — is there anyone who would do this as a joke, anybody?"

"I've been wracking my brain. I don't think so. Do you think it's real?"

"We can't afford not to assume it is. Crime Scene is on the way over to check for fingerprints around the door, and they'll bag the note and test it. We'll get a couple of uniforms over here to question the neighbors to see if anyone saw somebody leave the note. We'll have to wake them up, but we can't take a chance by waiting until tomorrow.

While we waited, Jack sat down on the porch steps with us, and we analyzed the note. I pointed out that the "gotta leave" part was a reference to Saundra Barkley's only solo hit, "Baby Gotta Leave," the one Slick Taggart says she stole from him.

"Well, he or she misspelled Saundra's name and Mutha Boy's and put "whose" instead of who's," Logan pointed out.

"The 'whose' is probably just a grammar error," Jack said, "but I'd bet that the names were misspelled intentionally. Maybe to give the impression he didn't know them personally, or."

"Or," I interrupted, "he misspelled them to show his disdain for Saundra and Mutha Boy, kind of a passive aggressive put-down."

"But murder isn't passive," Jack said. "Still you could be right, disrespecting them even in death."

"If the killer is still wanting to put them down, even in death," Logan asked, "doesn't it indicate he hated them personally, as opposed to picking them at random?"

"That's a possibility," Jack said. "What worries me most is

that he's telling us there will be another murder."

"Now, do you think your bosses will tell the public that a serial killer is at work?" I asked.

"I don't know what they'll do, but I know what *you* need to do, Britt. You need to write a story tomorrow about this. I meant it before when I said we shouldn't panic the public unnecessarily, and I meant it when I said I thought the two murders were unrelated, but this is different. Regardless of what the MPD PR guy might say, it's time to tell the public so they can protect themselves. It would be irresponsible to hold this back, even on the chance that it's not real."

"That's what I planned to do. Glad to know you agree."

"I'm going to call the director now and wake him up. I'll tell him you're going to do the story and advise him to give you a quote rather than refusing to comment. I hope he'll take my advice."

I scrambled around for paper and pen while Jack called the police director. After they talked, he put me on the phone with the director, and he gave me a quote: "We have no idea at this point whether this note is genuine, but we cannot afford to ignore the possibility that these two murders may be the work of a serial killer. I want to assure the public that every available police officer will be assigned to the case, but until we solve these crimes, I want to urge the public to take every precaution. Make sure doors are locked, walk in groups to your cars at night and take no chances."

It was a good quote, but I asked him one more question, "Director, do serial killers usually leave notes?"

"Usually not, but it's not unheard of," he said. "I have never had to lead an investigation of a possible serial killer, but I was a patrolman during the last serial killing in Memphis, the George Howard Putt murders in 1969, and I hope and pray Memphis won't have to deal with another Putt."

Then the director asked me a question, "Any idea why the killer, if that's who wrote the note, would send it to you?"

"I can only guess that it's because I wrote stories recently about both Saundra Barkley and Donté Washington."

"Well, be prepared for the killer continuing to use you as a contact. That's usually how it works."

After I hung up, Logan said something that hadn't hit me during all the analyzing of the note and talking to the police director.

"Britt, what bothers me most is that a serial killer knows where you live."

That was a sobering thought, but I couldn't let myself worry about that right now. I had to get to the paper and write my page-one story and figure out how to do it without being sensational. I hoped I would get a copy editor who would use the same discretion in writing the headline.

When I got home almost two hours later, the crime scene investigators had come and gone and Logan had gone home, but Jack was still sitting on my front steps.

"I wanted to make sure you got inside safely," he said. "I've already searched the house to make sure it's safe. Please don't accuse me of smothering you, Britt, but don't forget to turn on your security alarm."

I just smiled, gave him a long hug and went inside.

CHAPTER EIGHT

I was proud of the way our paper handled the story. Our editor and managing editor, who were at home when I called the night metro editor to say I was coming in to write the story, both came back to the paper to have some input on how the story was presented.

We all agreed that we would honor the police director's request that we describe the message of the note, rather than print it word for word. I wrote that the note referred to the deaths of Barkley and Washington and forecast another murder, but my story didn't say the note came to my house; it didn't tell what kind of paper and writing instrument were used; it didn't say that the note was written as a poem; and it didn't mention that Saundra and Mutha Boy were both misspelled. This way, it would be easier for the police to distinguish future notes from copy-cat notes.

To my relief, after much debate about whether some suggested headlines were "insipid" and others "tabloid screamers," the editor and managing editor, in consultation with the news editor and me, chose a good middle ground: "Murders of two musicians near Beale may be work of same killer." A smaller subhead said: "Note of unknown origin predicts another murder." It seemed to say there *may* be a serial killer here, but don't panic just yet. We decided not to put the story online until about the time people would be reading the print edition, so that the TV people wouldn't seem to beat us on our own scoop.

But for all our good intentions, the TV stations in town made up for our self-control by going berserk with high-pitched promos for every newscast the next day. "Serial killer stalks Memphis." "Memphians shutter in fear with serial murderer on the loose." "Are musicians the only Memphians in danger from a serial killer?"

The day after that, the TV stations were still carrying on with fear tactics, and by that time our paper had had time to put together a background piece on the last time Memphis experienced a serial killer.

The summer of 1969 will be remembered by many for the first moon landing, Woodstock, Chappaquiddick and Hurricane Camille, but Memphians remember it as a summer of fear. Just days after the Manson Family murders in California, a middle-aged Memphis couple — Bernalyn Dumas, a nurse, and Roy Dumas, a tax examiner, were found murdered in their Midtown apartment, just a few blocks from where I now live. It was later discovered that George Howard Putt, 23, entered the apartment to burglarize it, but noticed a photo of Mrs. Dumas, which reminded him of his mother, so he stayed around to kill and sexually mutilate her when she got home from work. He strangled her in one bedroom and her husband in another.

At first the Dumas case was handled as a double murder committed during a robbery, but eleven days later, a few miles away, 80-year-old Leila Jackson was found strangled to death in her boarding house.

Putt's next victim, just five days later, was 21-year-old Glenda Sue Harden, a downtown secretary who was last seen headed to her car after work at 5 p.m. Her body was found in a park south of downtown the next day. She had been stabbed 14 times.

Police told the public, "We are faced with a cunning sex killer." Even though the last victim was stabbed, police began to suspect a connection, which was never proven, between the Memphis murderer and the Boston Strangler, who killed 13 women in 1964. There were many similarities between the two killing sprees.

Twelve days later on Sept. 11, 1969, Putt killed for the last time. His victim was 59-year-old Christine Pickens, a dental receptionist, who was celebrating her birthday that day. Neighbors heard her dying screams from her apartment as she was being stabbed 20 times, and one neighbor chased the killer, firing a pistol but missing Putt. Police joined the chase and Putt was arrested a few blocks away.

Putt, 23, who was abused and neglected as a child and who began committing crimes when he was 11 years old and had been charged with attempted rape twice by the age of 16, had killed five people in 29 days. He was given a 497-year sentence and died at the age of 69 in 2015 in a Tennessee prison hospital of natural causes.

After I read the story about the Putt murders, I hoped and prayed we weren't in for five murders this time. Ironically, that is exactly the number of murders that would occur before Christmas.

CHAPTER NINE

"I hate to say I told you so." The voice on the phone was Jack.

"No, you don't — you *love* saying, 'I told you so.'"

"Well, anyhow, Britt, according to the Tennessee Bureau of Investigation, we don't have a serial killer on our hands."

"Well, I hope they're right, but what do they base that conclusion on?"

"First of all, the TBI and most other law enforcement agencies don't consider two murders a serial crime. A serial killer is defined as someone who kills three or more people at different times."

"Well, thank you, Merriam-Webster, but practically speaking, every serial killer had only killed two people at some point. Is that all you have to prove your point?"

"I wasn't trying to prove a point. Do you think I would have sat outside your house night before last to make sure you got in safely if I hadn't agreed with you that it was a serial crime?"

When I didn't answer, he went on, "No, in fact, I was so convinced it was a serial murder that I called the TBI today to ask for a profiler to be sent here to help us. They almost laughed in my face. It seems that criminal profilers are only sitting around waiting for cases on TV. The TBI does have profilers they use when needed, but they can't justify sending someone here until it's officially, by their definition, a serial crime. You know how tight the state budget is these days."

"So when we have a third murder, they'll send somebody?"

"Not necessarily. The guy I talked to said this case seems fishy to him."

"Fishy? Now there's a good solid, clinical word for a crime fighter to use."

"Anyhow, Britt, he said there were a lot of things about this case that don't add up to serial killer."

"Like what?"

"I'll tell you if you'll stop interrupting me. First of all, this killer kills the victims in public places and just leaves them there. Most serial killers like to work in private or at least at deserted public places, so they can torture or sexually abuse their victims. Which brings up another thing — most serial killers are sex killers of some kind, and this one doesn't seem to be, unless he just gets off on killing people without doing anything overtly sexual to them."

"Most are sex killers, but not all, right?"

"Right, but there's more. Most serial killers are white and kill white people like Putt did, but here both victims are black. And most serial killers kill one gender, and we've got a man and a woman."

"Anything else?"

"Most serial killers target vulnerable groups like prostitutes, old ladies, women walking alone at night and children. Instead we've got a 6 foot 3 young, healthy man and a woman who is anything but vulnerable, according to everybody who knew her. And most serial killers choose victims randomly, not target one profession like music. Prostitutes being the one exception."

"All this 'most' stuff tells me nothing. Can't this be one of the exceptions?"

"What are the chances of a serial killer being the exception in all those categories, Britt?"

"I don't know. All I know is that human beings can't be fit into neat little categories."

"That's more true of normal people than deviants."

"By very definition so-called normal people should be easier to generalize about than crazed killers," I said.

"Well, in the first place, most serial killers aren't crazy, and despite your logic, serial killers have been studied extensively, and there are definitely common characteristics."

"I know, Dr. Freud, they all had unhappy childhoods and weren't loved by their mothers."

"Well, you can joke, Britt, but it's true. This guy at TBI told me that one study showed that one hundred percent of serial killers had neglectful or abusive childhoods. Half of them had at least one criminal parent — I told you crime runs in families — and I think it was 70 percent that had family histories of alcohol and drug abuse."

"So did this guy at TBI say anything besides that we don't have a serial killer here?"

"Well, he told me some of the characteristics you can expect of a serial killer, if that's what this is — generally speaking they are white men."

"Yeah," I interrupted, "that assumption is what got them in trouble with the Beltway Snipers. They kept looking for one white man while two black men kept shooting people. And the victims were both black and white, male and female, young and old, and they weren't sex killers — so much for generalizations."

"Do you want to hear what else he said or are you going to keep lecturing?"

"Go ahead."

"They're usually ages 25 to 34, with at least an average IQ and often nice looking and/or charming."

"So just for the sake of argument, let's say that we do have a serial killer and that one of the suspects in these two murders is the serial killer for whatever reason. Do any of them fit this description?"

"Well, let's see, in the Saundra Barkley case, you've got three main suspects — her ex-husband is black and the other two are white. All three are middle aged, not 25 to 34."

"The ex-husband and the record producer, Linton, probably both have average or above IQs, don't you think? But Slick Taggart, who claims Saundra stole his song, sounds like a low-brow, from your description."

"But the ex-husband, Dewitt Starks, and Taggart aren't suspects, if this is a serial killing."

"Obviously Starks wouldn't be, but why not Taggart?'

"Because he was in police custody for questioning the night the rapper was murdered. So if this is a serial killing, it isn't Taggart, but if the two cases are separate, he could still be the killer of Barkley."

"What about the murder of Donte Washington?"

"The suspects there are the dentist, Dr. Kendelman, who is white and the right age and IQ, but doesn't seem to be connected to Saundra Barkley."

"Doesn't *seem* connected, but you never know. Maybe she stiffed him for a fee for a root canal or something," I said. Jack didn't laugh.

"Then you have the father and brother who said they'd kill him for fondling the girl. They're black, intelligent, and the brother is in his early twenties and the dad is in his forties."

"And don't forget the girl in the wheelchair and whoever might have been defending her."

"Well, we know nothing about that mystery person, and there is certainly no reason to believe he would also kill Saundra Barkley, but believe me, we're looking for connections between both victims and who they knew and who hated them."

"What did the TBI say about the note I found on my door? Doesn't that point to a serial killer?"

"It might just point to somebody who wants to feel important by taking credit or blame for murders he or she didn't really commit." Jack said. "Somebody who gets a sense of power from frightening people."

"Don't get me wrong, Jack, I don't *want* this to be the work of a serial killer — I just have a bad feeling that it is."

"Frankly, I don't know what to think anymore, but if there are more deaths and more notes, I guess we'll know."

CHAPTER TEN

I had heard all kinds of rumors since my story about the note from the alleged serial killer had come out in the paper. In my neighborhood, because it's not far from downtown and because a lot of musicians live there, there seemed to be a fair amount of concern about a serial killer "stalking the city," as the TV people continued to describe it. But I wasn't sure people in other parts of the city and county were reacting that way.

Midtowners and Downtowners are usually the least fearful of Memphians for two reasons — there isn't that much crime here, contrary to the opinions of most suburbanites, and the kind of people who are drawn to live in Midtown and Downtown are of the tolerant and tough urban variety.

In the suburbs of East Shelby County — Germantown, Collierville, Cordova and Bartlett, there always seems to be a lot more fear of the known and unknown — that's why they live out there, often in treeless subdivisions, to get away from crime, city schools and people different from them.

But, of course, you can run, but you can't hide. And unless somebody figures out how to build a big electrified fence around the suburbs, criminals will find their way there — some already live there, also contrary to conventional suburban wisdom. Like the medical school professor arrested in his suburban home with ecstasy, meth and cocaine, all ready for his Labor Day Sale. As to getting away from the "different" people, some of the different people eventually move out there, and then the not-different people have to move further out into the suburbs.

Anyhow, I imagined that the people in the suburbs, due to their pre-disposition for fear and because of the fear tactics of the TV stations, were probably shaking in their boots at the thought of a serial killer "stalking the city." Even if you aren't in the city, technically, this was too close for comfort.

And I wondered how the people in low-income neighborhoods in North and South Memphis were reacting. Crime is with them their whole lives, so maybe they don't think too much of the serial killer scare.

But I was only speculating about most of this, so I decided to take the pulse of the city and county and write a story about it. Just making some random calls to people around the area and asking if they were afraid was too anecdotal and too leading. Instead, I decided to spend some time in various parts of town and just try to blend in and listen. No questions asked.

First I spent two days riding city buses, which would sample the opinions of   low-income people and the elderly. Unlike a bus or subway in cities like New York or Chicago, where people of various socio-economic levels ride and mostly mind their own business, in Memphis it's different. Memphis doesn't have a subway or light rail system, and the transit authority buses are too few and inconvenient to be ridden by anyone who could afford a car.

I got on the bus at the MATA main station downtown and rode all over the city, necessarily transferring many times, but that was good, because that caused me to have to sit endlessly at bus stops with others. As I suspected, Memphis bus riders don't sit quietly like they do in large northern cities. On every bus I rode, there were some who kept to themselves with earphones on or just staring out the window, but many more chatted with whoever was sitting near them.

To my pleasant surprise, I found that the bus riders were their own community of regulars who knew each other by face, if not by name. So much so that it wasn't unusual for a bus driver to wait at a bus stop a few seconds longer than scheduled because a regular was not there yet. Several times breathless people would run half a block toward the bus while the driver and passengers waited patiently. Nobody complained, because next time they might be the ones running late.

To my utter astonishment, one time the bus driver actually got off the bus and walked across four lanes of Central Avenue traffic to help an elderly lady cross the street to get on the bus. He even carried her Dollar General shopping bags for her. I wanted to write a letter to his supervisor commending him for his kindness, but realized I might get him in trouble.

As regulars got on and off the bus at various locations, there were waves and greetings of hello or goodbye from other regulars or from the driver.

As I rode around the city those two days, I found that people from low-income neighborhoods were taking the serial killer threat seriously, even if they weren't musicians. As one woman said to the man across the aisle, "Some folks would just as soon kill you as look at you, and a serial killer even more so." All those around her agreed with nods and "Damn right" or "Yes, Lord."

If it was after dark, passengers would caution each other to be careful as they walked from the bus stop home. One woman said to another, "Walk in the middle of the street if you have to, so somebody can't jump out of the bushes and grab you."

I not only learned a lot from my two days of bus riding, but I also enjoyed the camaraderie. Enjoyed it much more than the following days in East Memphis and suburban Shelby County.

I made an appointment to get my hair done at an upscale hair salon in Germantown and listened not only to my hairdresser, but to other customers nearby. I heard nothing about the serial killer, so I finally asked my hairdresser if she was worried.

"Not really," she said. "Those things just don't happen out here."

"Have any of your customers the last few days been talking about it?"

"Some have, but mostly they just say that they're gonna stay away from downtown for a while, and they darn sure aren't going to let their older kids go downtown to Beale Street or to a basketball game at FedEx Forum. And forget downtown concerts."

"But they don't seem fearful that the serial killer could kill somebody out here?"

"No way. Why would this serial killer come out here — we don't have any nightclubs or anything? The closest you'd come is somebody playing piano in a nice restaurant."

The next two nights I went to several bars in East Memphis and suburban Shelby County, with Logan along to protect me from pick-up attempts. The bars included sports bars, bars connected to restaurants and neighborhood bars, and the story was the same as the hair salon. Only about one in 10 people we talked to showed any concern at all about the serial killer targeting someone in their neighborhood, but many swore off downtown until the murders were solved.

"I'm not even buying my season tickets for the Tigers or the Grizzlies until I know this sicko is behind bars," a well-dressed middle-aged man said to Logan.

His friend on the other side of him said, "Hell, Bill, you aren't going to let some pervert murderer come between you and basketball, are you?"

"I'll just sit on this stool and watch them on TV if it comes to that," Bill said. "It's not the same, but it's better than getting killed downtown."

A number of the people we talked to said all this serial killer stuff confirmed that they made the right decision to live out East. Although nobody came out and said it, I think the fact that both victims were black added to the sense of safety in the suburbs, where the majority of people are white.

Even in Southeast Shelby County and the Hickory Hill area of Memphis, where there is more racial diversity and which are widely regarded as having more of a crime problem than the Northeast and due East parts of the city and county — even those people seemed quite smug about living so far from downtown where the killer roamed.

So much for my theory that suburbanites were more fearful by nature than urbanites.

After five days of gathering information informally about people's fears or lack of them, I wrote a story, which also included analysis by several psychologists and a criminologist, who said that it is true that serial killers who do all their killing in one city tend to do it in one part of the city. George Howard Putt, Memphis's last serial killer, was cited by two of my expert sources — all his victims were killed in Midtown or Downtown.

The day after my story came out, I went to my car after eating dinner with my friend Vicki at Molly's LaCasita in Midtown and found a note under the windshield wiper of my car. The lot behind the restaurant is small and dark and not visible from the main street, Madison, and unfortunately there are no security cameras in the parking lot. I got into my car quickly and locked the doors before reading the note. Again in pencil on notebook paper, it said:

I'm walking in Memphis

And Bartlett and Germantown

And Collierville and Cordova

And everywhere

CHAPTER ELEVEN

My hands were literally shaking when I tried to dial Jack's number, so much so that I had to make three tries before I punched in the right numbers. When I told Jack what I had found on my car, he sounded really grim.

"This isn't good, this isn't good at all," he said without his usual reassuring confidence. "Are there still a fair number of cars in the parking lot at Molly's?"

"It's nearly full."

"Good. That's the safest place for you to be until I get there. Keep your doors locked and don't open your door or windows for anybody, even your best friend, understand? I'm coming, but I'm not going to drive into the parking lot. I'll call you when I get close and will tell you what to do, okay?"

The wait seemed interminable, so I called Logan to tell him what had happened. He offered to come over, but I told him to let Jack handle it.

"What about tonight, later?" Logan asked. "You aren't going to go home alone, are you?"

"What choice do I have? I can't go into hiding just because a possible serial killer is using me to communicate."

"Britt, things are different now. The first note being left on your house is creepy, but there are lots of ways he could have found out where you live with all the Internet directories out there, and you could get a person's address from various public records, but what happened tonight means he's following you. He knew you were eating at a certain restaurant at a certain time."

"Stop, you're scaring me to death," I said.

"Come out to my house and stay for a while. As you well know, I've got three unoccupied bedrooms and a good alarm system."

"Logan, that's really sweet, but I can't just move in with you until this guy is caught, which might never happen. Some serial killers kill over a 20 or 30-year period. I can't live in fear."

"Okay, how about this compromise — just spend this one night over here, and we'll figure out a long-term plan tomorrow?"

"That sounds reasonable. I'll call you after Jack leaves."

A few minutes later, Jack called. He said he was on Madison in his own car parked in front of the Blue Monkey, which is next door to Molly's.

"Drive down that side street that connects the parking lot and Madison," he said. "Drive home and let me follow you from a distance, so I can see if anyone is following you. If nobody is, I'll come in to your house, but wait in the car for me to get there. Take Madison to Cooper and then turn left onto your street."

We did just that and when we got to my house, Jack was convinced nobody had followed me, so we both went in. While we were talking, the crime scene van arrived and bagged the note and checked the windshield and wipers for fingerprints. When we were alone again, Jack told me of his concerns.

"I'm worried about you," he said. "This guy is stalking you."

"Isn't that too strong a word? Stalking sounds like he wants to hurt me. I think he is just using me to communicate and doesn't want to use the post office or telephone or e-mail for fear of being traced."

"But you've got to admit leaving notes at your house and at a public parking lot is pretty risky behavior, potentially more risky in terms of a witness seeing him leave the note."

"Not really. I live on a small, quiet street without much traffic, and that lot behind Molly's has a handful of parking places and is on a dead-end street."

"Granted, but the main point is that he couldn't know you were at Molly's unless he was following you."

"Unless he works at Molly's or was a customer there tonight by chance and just recognized me and decided to seize the moment. My picture was in the paper and on TV quite a bit in August, so a lot of people recognize me now unfortunately."

"I don't believe in coincidences," Jack said, "but I'll talk to the manager of Molly's and question the staff when I leave here, near closing time, see if anyone seems suspicious or maybe somebody took a smoke break out back and saw somebody leave a note on your car."

"Jack, did my article about how people in the suburbs aren't worried about the serial killer cause him to send this note? Will he kill somebody out there to prove I was wrong? I'll never forgive myself if that happens."

"That doesn't sound like you, kiddo. You and I have talked a million times about how cops and reporters have to do their jobs and can't feel responsible when some nut does something in response."

"It sounds good in theory, but now that I may be responsible directly for some innocent person in the suburbs being targeted at random by a serial killer, I don't feel so sure of myself."

"Stop that," Jack ordered, but with a kind voice. "You are not responsible directly or otherwise. The killer and only the killer is responsible and don't forget that."

"I'll try."

Jack gave me a reassuring hug and moved on to the next order of business. "Now, we need to get you somewhere else for the night. Please don't argue."

"For once I won't. I already thought about that. While I was waiting for you at Molly's, I arranged to stay with a friend tonight."

"Good. I'll follow you there before I go back to Molly's and talk to the staff. I'll hang back again and see if anybody follows you. Where are we going?"

"To Harbor Town," I said, trying not to sound sheepish.

"Logan is the *friend* you're staying with?" Jack asked, putting a sarcastic emphasis on the word "friend." "Well, that's cozy. Are you two a romantic item now?"

"Oh, Jack, don't be silly — you sound like a jealous high school boy. I told you in August that I wanted to stay friends with you and Logan and nothing more until we all sorted some things out."

"I don't need to sort anything out — I know how I feel about you."

"Okay, well, good for you, but I *do* need some time to think, and there's no guarantee that I'll ever be more than friends with you *or* Logan. This thing tonight is just practicality. Logan has three extra bedrooms and a connected garage that I can drive right into without having to walk from my car to the house. And a good alarm system. That place is like a fortress."

"As much as I hate for you to spend the night at Logan's house, I do feel better about your safety with a man in the house — forgive me if I'm being sexist."

"You *are* being sexist, but I had the same thought. If this guy is watching me, I don't want to draw his attention to one of my female friends. Well, let me get a few things together and you can follow me out to the island. I promise to pack a long flannel nightgown, along with my chastity belt."

"Listen, smart mouth, there's one more thing we need to discuss — are you going to write a story about the note tonight?"

"I don't know. I don't want to, but I have to tell my editors in the morning and let them decide. I can't deal with this tonight. Besides that decision shouldn't be made without all the editors talking about it."

"Why can't *you* decide — it was sent to *you*, not to the paper?"

"Jack, you know better than that. It didn't come to Britten Faire, average citizen. It came to Britten Faire, newspaper reporter. That takes it out of my hands. I'll let you know what they decide tomorrow."

After I packed an overnight bag, we left. We had a plan which would make it look like I turned right onto Cooper and that he was going in the opposite direction, but he circled around and again followed me from a distance. When we got to Harbor Town, Jack called me and said it looked clear, and I called Logan to say I was almost there and that Jack was following me.

As I pulled into the driveway, Logan's garage door opened for me. I loved the safe feeling as the door shut behind me, but I felt bad for Jack, who I knew had mixed feelings about watching me disappear into Logan's space.

CHAPTER TWELVE

Logan was waiting inside the garage for me and took my bag into the house.

"Didn't Jack want to come in?" he asked. If Logan ever feels threatened by Jack's relationship with me, he never lets on. Maybe he doesn't care enough about me to be jealous.

"He was going back over to Molly's to interview the staff, to see if anyone might have noticed someone putting a note on a car. Also, there's always a chance that it's somebody who works there or who was a customer there and just happened to see me and seized the moment. I hope so, rather than the alternative."

"That somebody is following you. That, Britt, is a really scary possibility. I'm really worried about you," he said as we went into the kitchen. "Let's go upstairs, and I'll give you the pick of the bedrooms."

Logan's house, like all those on primo river-front lots in Harbor Town, makes maximum use of the location. Each house is very different architecturally except that they all feature either porches, balconies, even widow's walks and big windows — whatever it takes to give as many rooms as possible a view of the river. Logan's Victorian has a wrap-around porch on two sides on both floors, so that the living room, kitchen and three of the four bedrooms upstairs have not only river views, but outdoor seating with a view. The master bedroom is one of those, and I naturally picked the other bedroom that faces the river directly to the west and provides a beautiful view of the sunsets.

The prime property in Harbor Town looks west across the river to Arkansas. The east side of the island gives a view of the Pyramid Arena that is now a giant sporting goods store and the Memphis skyline, but on the western side, the view is pastoral. Downtown Memphis is built on a river bluff, so buildings and parks are right on the water — the bluff protecting them from flooding, but on the Arkansas side there is no bluff, so a deep, undeveloped wetland is what you see from that side of Harbor Town. Sitting on Logan's porch, it's hard to believe you are in a city, the only clue being the lighted Hernando Desoto Bridge nearby. Another, older bridge connects Tennessee and Arkansas on the south end of downtown.

Logan ushered me into the bedroom I chose, which was large with high ceilings, decorated in white and hunter green. I thought, but didn't say, "I could get used to this." After putting my things down, Logan led me out onto the second-floor porch, which was also accessible from his bedroom. The porches are deep, allowing for a table and chairs and two cushiony armchairs with a table and lamp between them. The lamp was on, but he switched it off when we sat down to enjoy the cool, but not cold early November night.

"Shall we talk about a long-term plan for your safety now or wait until later?"

"Let's get it over with."

"I'm not trying to mother you or anything, Britt, but I would feel better if you would stay here for a few days, since you can drive straight into the garage and have direct access to the house. I'll give you your own key and garage door opener. Don't worry — you can come and go as you please."

"I'm tempted, but it's so hard for me to give in to this fear thing."

"You'll forgive me, Britt, but that sounds like false pride. I'm not trying to scare you more than you already are, but Britt, what if the killer knows where you live and knows where you were going to eat tonight because he knows you."

"Don't say that! You're scaring me to death. But maybe I *will* take you up on your offer at least for a couple of days until I feel a little braver. Just a serial killer being on the loose and knowing where I live isn't enough to really scare me, but the possibility that he is following me or might know me — well, I won't lie — that freaks me out big time."

"It should. You can't count on a psychotic killer to act rationally. Just because you're not a musician, you can't be sure he hasn't fixated on you. He might decide to kill the messenger."

"Logan, stop — you've made your point. No more of that kill-the-messenger stuff, okay?"

Logan smiled apologetically and put his hand on my arm for a moment. "Sorry, Britt, I did go too far. I just didn't want you to take the risk too lightly."

"Well, if I was taking it too lightly before, I'm sure not now. It's not just what you said. I can't tell you the chill that went up my spine when I walked toward my car alone and saw that note tucked under the windshield wiper. I knew without picking it up who it was from. And tomorrow we'll have to decide whether to publish the note or not."

"Why would you? Wouldn't that just be giving the killer what he wants?"

"It would, which is the down side, but it would also warn people in the suburbs not to be so foolishly confident that it can't happen to them."

Logan went into his bedroom and got us Diet Cokes and a can of cashews from the mini-bar. "Who will decide, besides you?"

"I'm only a small part of the decision-making process. This is a top management decision now."

"Leaving you out doesn't seem fair."

"Are you kidding? I *want* to be left out of this decision. The first note was a no-brainer, except for what details to leave out, because it was the first real indication that a serial killer might be at work. But this decision is a no-win situation."

"How?"

"Don't you see? If we don't publish at least the gist of the note and then he kills somebody in the suburbs, everyone will be furious that we didn't warn people. But if we do publish it, and he kills somebody out there, we'll always have to worry that he did it to prove he meant business when he wrote the note."

"Man, that is a dilemma. What do you think the editors will decide?"

"I really don't know, but I know one other issue that will go into the decision that they won't be proud to talk about, and that is we want the killer to keep communicating with us, so we have the exclusive. If we don't publish it, the killer could start communicating with the TV stations. Not only would we lose the exclusive, but then we'd all have to suffer the overexposure the TV stations would give it."

"So you think the editors will go with publishing the note?"

"Probably, but I know they won't make the decision lightly."

"I remember how much journalistic debate went on when the Unabomber said he'd quit killing people if a couple of national papers would print his letter," Logan said.

"The newspapers agonized over whether they would be giving in to a serial killer by publishing the letter, but..."

"But it was the right decision," Logan finished my thought, "because the letter was read by Ted Kaczynski's brother who recognized his brother in it and turned him into the authorities."

"Their decision was vindicated by the fact that the

Unabomber was caught, but this case is different. Our killer isn't promising to stop the killings — he's promising to continue them, and I can tell you, Logan, I will be absolutely consumed with guilt if somebody in the suburbs is killed, because I'll always feel that my story about lack of fear out there inspired him to kill somebody else."

"I'd hate for you to blame yourself, but I'm sure I'd feel the same way if I were in your position."

Suddenly, paranoia kicked in, and I felt strongly that somebody was out in the darkness watching us talk in the moonlight, maybe even somehow listening.

"I'm kind of tired, Logan, can we call it a night?"

We stood and he kissed me on top of my head. "Goodnight, Britt. No nightmares, promise?"

"I wish I could make that promise."

"Well, there are good locks on all the doors and windows, and I have a fool-proof security system."

"Famous last words" were my final cynical words for the night, but I smiled at Logan as I went into my bedroom.

"I'm right next door if you need me," he said as I closed my door slowly. "Just put your lips together and whistle, or better yet, bang on the wall."

CHAPTER THIRTEEN

I decided to stay a couple more nights at Logan's. It was like staying in a luxury hotel, and most of all, sleeping there really did make me feel safe.

The second night, I didn't even see Logan. He had an evening tennis match, and I had dinner at Amerigo with Lisa, Elinor and Phyllis, longtime friends of mine. They wanted to know all about the Barkley and Mutha Boy murder investigations and were full of advice on ways I should be cautious.

By the time I got to Harbor Town, Logan was in his bedroom, but not asleep. As I passed his door, he said goodnight but didn't come out. I suspect he was trying to show me that he wouldn't be overly protective if I would agree to stay on for a while. But I also suspect that he intentionally waited up for me. That was sweet.

As anybody who knows me even a little can tell you, I guard my independence fiercely — I don't like to be mothered or smothered. My cousin William describes me as "psychotically independent," but that's not exactly true. Sometimes I am very touched when somebody cares enough to protect me, like Jack waiting on the porch for me that night of the first note and Logan waiting up for me this night. I wish they weren't both so sweet — it confuses me.

The third night I stayed at Logan's it was like grown-up

summer camp. We brought in ribs, potato salad and beans, which we ate on the upstairs porch, and then we adjourned to the kitchen and played board games until late. Logan suggested inviting Jack to join us, but I told him that Jack is not a board-game person. We played Trivial Pursuit and then Sequence.

At bedtime we went back out onto the porch outside our bedrooms. Bundled up in warm robes, we talked about weddings. I asked him if his best friend, Ben Spurrier, and Logan's former fiancée, Caroline Crawford, had set a date for their wedding yet.

"Ben said they're looking at dates in the summer — they've decided against a big wedding like Caroline and I were going to have. Just family and close friends."

"Are you really going to be Ben's best man? Won't that be awkward?"

"I don't think it will be as awkward for the three of us as it will be for everybody watching, so a small wedding is a good idea. I don't think any of us wants to be a Jerry Springer show. Why shouldn't I be Ben's best man? He's been my best friend since kindergarten, and he was gracious enough to agree to be *my* best man, even though he was secretly in love with Caroline. It might be a little weird to switch roles, but not painful for anybody this time."

"You're more civilized than me. I couldn't even go to Drew's wedding, much less be in it, not that I was asked or anything."

Like Ben and Logan, Drew and I were best friends from an early age. But Drew and I ruined everything by getting married. The marriage lasted three weeks, just long enough to effectively destroy our friendship. Then he met Liz, and they were married in September, and I lost my best friend forever. It's not that we don't still care for each other — it's just that male-female friendships can be difficult when one friend gets married, especially when your opposite-sex friend is also your ex-wife.

"Does it still hurt?" Logan asked.

"I'm over the divorce. It's like the marriage never happened.

It's Drew's friendship I miss, but I'll get over that, too, eventually."

On that note, we went to our bedrooms. The next morning, I woke up certain I needed to move back home. These three days at Logan's place had been fun and safe, but I guess my independent streak kicked in, and I felt kind of silly for hiding out from the guy leaving the notes, who might not even be a killer.

•••••••••••••••

I had been back at my place without any problems for two days, and it had been five days since I had gotten the Walking in Memphis note on my car. With each day, I felt less guilty about the possibility that my article about lack of fear in the suburbs would inspire the killer to kill somebody out there.

But just as I was feeling better, the call came from Jack.

"I just wanted to tell you before you heard from someone at the paper that we've had another murder," he said.

Of course, the first question in my mind was, "Where?" but I was afraid to ask, so I asked the other journalistic questions, "Who, what, when and how?" There was no point in asking "why?"

"When did it happen, Jack? Was it a musician? Was it a steak knife in the back?"

"Yeah, knife in the back. I guess you could say he's a musician. Name's Larry Carpenter, and he was murdered apparently about 4 a.m. as he was walking from his car to his house."

"What do you mean, you guess he's a musician?"

"He's an Elvis impersonator."

I almost laughed but caught myself when I remembered this is a human being who has been murdered, no matter that he has a goofy profession. I didn't have to ask the dreaded question.

64

"Carpenter was coming home from a gig at one of the Tunica casinos. I really hate to tell you this, kid, but he lives in Germantown."

There was a long silence, and then I said, "It's all my fault."

"Don't be ridiculous, Britt. You know better than that. It's the fault of a murderer, who decided for whatever reason, to go around killing musicians, who he probably doesn't even know. I'm sure he planned to kill other people anyhow. At the most, your story may have made him choose somebody from the suburbs, but so what? A murder victim is a murder victim. A Germantown guy's life isn't more valuable than a downtown guy's."

What Jack said made some sense, but I wasn't ready to let myself off the hook.

"If anybody's to blame, it's probably your newspaper for running that *Walking in Memphis* note. I hope that wasn't your decision."

"No, but the note came in response to my article about how everybody in the suburbs felt safe. Well, enough self-flagellation. I can do that later. What else do you know about the guy?"

"Not much. We just got the call a couple of hours ago. A lady walking her dog about 6 this morning saw him lying in his yard and called 911."

"So he lives alone?"

"Yeah, the neighbors say he and his wife are separated, that the wife has gone back to Sweden or Switzerland where she's from. One neighbor said Sweden, another Switzerland. She must be rich, because I can't imagine an Elvis impersonator making enough money to buy a house like that."

"Maybe he's got family money, and she killed him while they were still officially married, so she'd inherit."

"We already thought of that, but she's been back in Europe for almost three months. I called her as next of kin — one of the neighbors had a number for her — and granted, she didn't sound heart-broken over his death, but if she can prove she was overseas last night, she's not a suspect. Of course, she could have hired somebody to kill him, but somehow I don't think so. Besides, spouse murderers always act shocked and grieved, hoping to cover up their crimes. It's actually in her favor that she didn't act grief-stricken."

"What did she say?"

"Just that she wasn't surprised."

"Did she say why not?"

"She said he would do anything for money, especially lie, and that he spent time with some people who were of 'the criminal element.' We'll talk to her more later."

"It's always possible, Jack, that somebody this guy cheated or who hated him for some other reason saw the article about the latest note and decided to kill him and make it look like the serial killer did it."

"Could be, or maybe we've got ourselves a certifiable serial killer."

CHAPTER FOURTEEN

Because I felt I had been an accessory in the latest murder, I vowed not to write about this murder, to leave it to other reporters. But I couldn't do that, of course.

What people outside of journalism don't seem to understand is that we reporters don't want bad things to happen — but when they do, we want to be part of the action. We can't stand to be left out of covering the big story.

An older reporter at our paper, Charlie Chisenhall, told me that he was in the newsroom that August afternoon they got word that Elvis Presley had died. A cub reporter was sent over to Baptist Hospital to see if it was true, because they had gotten erroneous reports of Elvis' death several times in recent years and didn't take this one seriously.

Once Elvis' death was confirmed, the whole newsroom came alive and people started working on various Elvis stories for the next day. Several people were working on the lead story, but there was also a need for a story from the entertainment writer about Elvis' career; the medical reporter did a story on possible cause of death; the fire reporter tried to find the paramedics who transported Elvis to the hospital; the police reporter got the cops' side of it; and various general assignment reporters were sent to Graceland and out among the public for reactions.

And, of course, that was just the beginning. By the next day, reporters from throughout the world were swarming our newsroom, using our facilities to send back their stories (that was in the days before laptops and cell phones, so professional courtesy to out-of-town colleagues prevailed).

Anyhow, this reporter, Charlie, told me that just his luck he was the education reporter and was working on a big story about the Board of Education at the moment. He was dying to drop the story and work on the Elvis story, but his editor told him they had to have some non-Elvis news in the paper the next day, and he was elected.

I really felt for him as he told the story. Everybody else was doing the exciting breaking news, and Charlie was stuck writing a story that nobody would read.

So that's a long way of saying that I couldn't stay away from the serial killer story. It's asking too much of a mortal reporter.

What especially drew me into this story was the big house in Germantown and what the wife said about his lying and hanging out with criminals. Unless Larry Carpenter had money from some other source, I couldn't imagine his being able to afford a big house in an affluent suburb. I mean let's face it, being an Elvis impersonator is a pretty cheesy profession and not that lucrative except during the summer tourist season, which climaxes the week of August 16 with what tourists call "Elvis Tribute Week," but the locals call "Dead Elvis Week."

Amazingly, people from all over the world build their vacations around the Candlelight Vigil at Graceland and other contrived activities. So during that week, an Elvis impersonator can get a good bit of work, but not enough to buy a big house in Germantown. There are some modest homes in Germantown, but Larry Carpenter's house was not one of them. Public records showed that he had bought the house three years before for almost three quarters of a million dollars, which buys a lot of house around here.

Some people quoted in the initial story, which I didn't write, said they thought he got his big money from performing at the casinos in Tunica, Mississippi, which is about an hour southwest of

Memphis. I didn't buy that. The casinos didn't do that many Elvis shows, not nearly enough to finance a house in Germantown.

Besides, Larry Carpenter isn't the only Elvis impersonator competing for those gigs, some reportedly much better than Larry.

Elvis impersonators fall into two categories — either young, sexy Elvises with guitars or old, fat Elvises in polyester jumpsuits, the latter category being by far the most common. Then there are two sub categories — those who lip sync to Elvis CDs and those who are real musicians themselves.

Carpenter, who at age 57 had no choice but to impersonate old Elvis, barely qualified for the latter sub group. He did his own singing but wasn't that great, by all reports. His saving grace apparently was that he bore a striking resemblance to the King and could work himself and his female audience members into a sweat with his jumpsuit moves. He billed himself as, "The Sexiest Elvis Alive." Humble, too.

I decided to find out more about Larry Carpenter and the source of his healthy income. I wasn't getting anywhere talking to his neighbors and people who employed him, and he didn't seem to have friends, only acquaintances.

Then a break-through came quite by accident. I decided to take a Backbeat Tour, a 1950s bus that tours various music sights while a guitarist sings rock n' roll music from a stool in the front of the bus. I was going to see if any of the Elvis tourists had heard about the murder and what their reaction was. I was just looking for a little color for my story, but found a valuable source.

I was sitting in front of a couple who had that European tourist look about them. I turned around and asked a couple of innocuous questions to break the ice, stuff like, "Is this your first trip to Memphis?" "Yes." "Did you come for Elvis or other reasons?" "Mostly for Elvis. We've wanted to come ever since we heard Larry Carpenter speak in Paris."

I was only half listening until I heard Larry Carpenter's name, and they didn't say they saw him perform his Elvis act — they said they heard him *speak* and in Paris?

"And now tragically," the man said, "we find Larry has been murdered."

"Where did you hear Larry Carpenter speak? I know it was Paris, but what kind of gathering was it?"

"It was an Elvis convention," the woman said. "We were told that Larry travels the world talking about his close friendship with Elvis. We were planning to go on his Elvis cruise in the Greek Islands next year."

I told them that I had no idea he was close friends with Elvis.

"Oh, yes, he and Elvis lived in the housing project together and were in the same class at Humes High School. They were very close. And later when Elvis was famous, he never forgot Larry — he gave him a new Cadillac for Christmas one year, and Larry was always invited when Elvis would have a private showing of a movie or rent an amusement park for the evening."

"He had wonderful stories to tell about his times with Elvis, things you never read in the books about Elvis," the woman added.

"We were surprised that you can't buy Larry's book here in Memphis or at the Graceland gift shop," the man said. "It is only available in Europe and Japan, we found out."

So that's how Larry Carpenter could afford a house in Germantown. He peddled his friendship with Elvis to anyone who would buy. There was only one little problem: Larry Carpenter was 57, and if Elvis were alive today, he would be 82, so they could not have gone to high school together. I guess a lot of Elvis fans attending Larry's events weren't very good at arithmetic.

CHAPTER FIFTEEN

I called Jack because he is a certifiable Elvis fan, and I wanted to see what he knew about the friendship between Elvis and Larry.

"Close friend? You can't be serious. He wasn't a close friend."

"How do you know? You may like Elvis' music, but you're no Elvis scholar. Couldn't Elvis have had a younger friend you didn't know about?"

"Tell me exactly what these tourists said."

I only got so far as the stuff about living in the projects with Elvis and being in the same class at Humes High School before Jack interrupted me.

"See, that shows you he was a liar. He couldn't have been in Elvis' high school class. Too much age difference."

"I figured that one out on my own, Jack, but maybe they were really friends, and Larry just exaggerated to impress girls. He made a fortune giving speeches in Europe about his friendship with Elvis, and he even wrote a book about it, but the tourists told me that the book was only available in Europe and Japan."

"Because," Jack said, "he knew if he told those stories here, there would be real friends of Elvis', like George Klein, who would expose Larry as a liar."

"I guess he just killed time between Elvis conventions and cruises by doing his Elvis impersonator act. The real money was in lying. Maybe that's what Larry's wife meant when she said he was a liar."

Jack said he was going to call the wife again and talk to her about all this, and I said I was going to get on Amazon and see if I could find that book by Carpenter since it couldn't be bought in an American bookstore.

•••••••••••••

Jack and I met for Mexican food about seven. He had been working 16-hour days since Carpenter's murder, and he went on strike long enough to have dinner with me, but he passed on his favorite, margaritas, just in case somebody else got murdered before the night was over. Carpenter's murder had elevated this to a serial killing spree by anyone's definition, and Lt. Jack Trent had been named to lead the investigation.

"Did you find the book?" he asked as he crunched a salsa covered chip.

"It wasn't hard. I paid to have it FedExed to me, so I should get it tomorrow. I can get some great quotes for my story."

"You know, don't you, there will be people who'll accuse you of speaking ill of the dead?"

"I'm not really comfortable doing that in some cases, but this time, who cares?"

"Well, lying about knowing a celebrity isn't a crime, and he wouldn't be the first."

"But he made so much money lying, and besides, as far as I could find out, he didn't have close friends or family here, so I'm not hurting grieving loved ones or anything by printing the truth. What did his wife say? Did you reach her?"

The waiter interrupted us, so I ordered chicken flautas and Jack ordered his usual cheese and onion enchiladas.

"It seems she met Larry while he was giving an Elvis lecture in Stockholm. She had been an Elvis fan all her life and had always dreamed of going to Memphis one day and visiting Graceland. She went up to him after the lecture, and he immediately invited her up to his room for a drink. She was young at the time, 29, and he was 53, and he seemed like a glamorous older man to her. And she kept saying how much he looked like Elvis and how charming he was. She said it was like Elvis came back to life and chose her."

"I can't believe she fell for all that."

"Well, anyhow, she went on with him to his next lecture stop in Norway, and then to England, and they got married before heading back to Memphis two weeks later."

"What a fool."

"She thought she had a real catch in Larry, and she was really impressed with his house — he had just moved into the Germantown house a few months before. She also told me that Larry even published his own Elvis magazine, also only available outside the U.S."

"How long before the bubble burst?"

"It happened gradually, she said. She started asking questions that he never seemed to have a good answer for, like why he didn't mention his close friendship with the king in his nightclub act in the Memphis area and why wasn't his book available in the U.S. and why didn't he ever get interviewed by people doing articles or documentaries on Elvis? All he would say was that Europeans and Japanese appreciated Elvis more than his hometown folks, and that he didn't want to exploit his friendship with Elvis."

"Which, of course, obviously wasn't true, considering he'd made a fortune exploiting his so-called friend without a second thought."

"Well, finally, he admitted to her that he made it all up to make a buck, and she was furious. She said she was already disillusioned with him, and with that confession, she lost all respect for him."

"And she thought she knew him so well after a two-week courtship," I said sarcastically. "Is that when she left him?"

"No, she hung in there as long as the money flowed freely, but when he got into a lot of gambling debt and they were in danger of losing the house, she packed up and went back to Sweden."

"But none of that explains why the serial killer picked Larry Carpenter as his last victim, except that he lived in the suburbs."

"Britt, you keep looking for reasons, but most serial killers pick victims at random and don't have rational reasons for killing."

"*Most* pick victims at random, Jack, but *some* know all or at least some of their victims, like the BTK Killer in Kansas. I just have a feeling in my gut that the killer knew all three of these victims."

The waiter served our dinners, and we changed the subject to football.

"Can you believe Ole Miss beat Alabama?" I asked. Even murder couldn't compete with SEC football for the rest of the meal. After all, this is the South and it's fall.

CHAPTER SIXTEEN

I had meant to ask Jack about the knives the night before, so I called him at the office.

"I keep meaning to ask you about the knife that killed Carpenter — was it the same kind as the other two?"

"None of the three have been identical. They're all standard steak knives you see in nice restaurants, you know, the big kind, not those little serrated things you get when somebody gives you a set of steak knives for a wedding gift."

"Have you ever gotten a wedding gift, Jack?" What a weird way for me to ask what I've always wondered. I've known Jack Trent for six years, but only in recent months have we had personal conversations. Before that it was friendly business talk only. I'd always wondered about his past.

"Are you asking me if I've ever been married?" Jack said with a laugh.

"Yeah, I guess I am."

"Well, the answer is yes. Now do you want to know about the murder weapons or don't you?"

Obviously, Jack didn't want to talk about his former marriage, so I dropped the subject. For now, but not forever.

"So what about the knives?"

"Well, as you know, none of them have finger prints on them, and as I said, they're not identical, so we've been to all the restaurant supply houses and identified which restaurants use which knives. Then we checked their lists of employees — waiters, busboys, cooks and dishwashers, especially — to see if anybody has worked at more than one place."

"Let me guess, a lot of people have worked at a lot of the restaurants."

"Of course, that's the way of the food industry, but it was worth a shot. And we are talking to all of them, and three interesting names showed up — the brother who threatened to kill Mutha Boy. His name is Jason Brownell. Anyhow, he worked as a waiter at two of the restaurants that use knives like that. And Dewitt Starks, Saundra's ex, works in the kitchen at one. And Slick Taggart has been a dishwasher in several of them."

"It could just as easily be somebody who was a customer and slipped a knife in a pocket or purse or somebody who went directly to the restaurant supply house and bought them. Several of those places let the public purchase individually," I said. "I buy drinking glasses from Lit myself. Hey, Jack, is the Tennessee Bureau of Investigation lending a hand now that we've had three murders, and it's officially a serial killer?"

"They're sending somebody in a couple of days, a woman named Irene Ringold, from Nashville."

"It should be interesting to hear her take on all this, huh?"

"Yeah, it would be nice to catch this guy before he kills somebody else."

"You *will* tell me everything she says, won't you?"

"Only if you promise not to print it?"

"You're no fun, Jack, no fun at all."

•••••••••••

I was still thinking about the steak knives and about Larry Carpenter when I remembered I was supposed to go by my friend Tricia's apartment to pick up a book she was lending me. Her little brother, Michael, who is in college, was there when I got there, and he began asking me a lot of questions about Mutha Boy's murder.

"Are you a rap fan, Mike?"

"Of course," he said, as if it's a given. I had heard that 75 percent of rap CD's are bought by white kids and young adults, and I guess Mike was evidence of that.

"So what's your take on this serial killer, if that's what it is? Do you think Mutha Boy was killed as part of a rap rivalry?"

"Well, I've heard the various theories on why he was murdered, but I have my own theory."

"And that would be?"

"I think his producer killed him."

"What motive could his producer have? If Mutha Boy doesn't keep recording, the producer doesn't make money."

"You would be so wrong about that, Britt. Mutha Boy has had one successful CD, but I hear that the other stuff he's done is pure crap, and they're starting to think this is it."

"A one-hit wonder?"

"They wouldn't call it that, but yeah, that's the idea. Anyhow, since his future isn't bright, they would make more money off him dead than alive."

"How's that?"

"When Tupak and Biggie were murdered, their producers dug out some stuff that was too crappy to release while they were alive, but because they were dead, the stuff sold like everything."

"Interesting theory," I said, not convinced. I changed the subject by asking how Memphis rap is different from other rap. He pulled out his I-Pod to illustrate the differences for me. We listened to several cuts, which weren't familiar to me, but then we got to one that sounded familiar. Then I heard it. Throughout the cut, I could hear bits and pieces of a song from the sixties.

"That's Baby Gotta Leave and that's Saundra Barkley singing it," I said, incredulous.

"A lot of rappers do that, you know, sampling or biting somebody else's stuff. Rap on one hand is very original and spontaneous, but at the same time derivative."

"Who is the rapper doing this?"

"That's Mutha Boy."

CHAPTER SEVENTEEN

I couldn't wait to tell Jack what I had found out about the connection between Mutha Boy and Saundra Barkley.

"That means," I said, "that Slick Taggart, the guy who claims he wrote Baby Gotta Leave, had a motive to kill both of them, her for stealing his song, Mutha Boy for making more money off his song."

"You're forgetting one little thing, Britt — opportunity. Slick Taggart was in police custody the night Mutha Boy — now you've got me calling him that, too — the night Donté Washington was murdered. Taggart couldn't have killed him. Besides, I really think this Taggart guy is just one of those loose canons who goes around bragging and trying to get attention. I knew a guy in college who claimed to have written one of the Rolling Stones' songs, even though he would have been 10 years old when the song was written, but he always stuck to his story. Said he was a child prodigy, and they took advantage of his age and naivete to steal his song. And it seems like every best-selling writer gets accused of plagiarism."

"Okay, okay, you've made your point, but I still think there could be some connection between Mutha Boy and Saundra Barkley, even if that connection isn't Slick Taggart."

"Well, if you figure it out, let me know, Britt. You know I'm always open to your ideas, even though you're not always right."

"When exactly is that profiler or whatever she is coming to town?"

"Next week, the Monday before Thanksgiving."

"Maybe she can shed some light on how all this stuff connects, if it does. Hey, Jack, speaking of Thanksgiving, what are you doing for the holiday?"

"Well, if nobody else gets killed before next Thursday, I'm going to see my mother in Paris."

"France?"

"Tennessee."

"I hear it's pretty up there around Kentucky Lake. Is that where you grew up?"

"Not really."

"Not really? You sort of grew up there? What does 'not really' mean?"

"I swear, Britt, a person can't have a simple conversation with you without being interrupted and interrogated. I'm surprised you don't carry a dangling light bulb with you at all times."

It's a common complaint of Jack's against me, but he rarely says it with any real anger. I think most of the time he just finds this habit of mine slightly annoying, maybe even a bit endearing.

"Yeah, like cops aren't just as bad as reporters about wanting to pin down the exact truth. Anyhow, how did you not really grow up in Paris?"

"Well, my dad was in the service, and we moved around a lot when I was a kid. We lived in Germany for two years and a bunch of places in the U.S. After Dad retired, we moved to Paris, Tennessee, and I graduated high school there, but it never really felt like home. No place ever has, except I guess Memphis now."

"You said you were spending Thanksgiving with your mom. Does that mean your dad passed away?"

"He died a couple of years ago, and Mom stayed on in the house."

"A couple of years ago? I knew you then — why didn't you tell me when it happened?"

"That was when you were trying to get over your three-week marriage. I figured you had your hands full without me dumping my problems on you."

"That's what friends are for."

"Well, I don't make friends easily, and when I do, I'm not likely to run to them with my problems."

"That's sad, Jack. It's probably because you moved around so much."

"Sure it is, Dr. Freud. It doesn't take a shrink to figure that out. When all you ever have are temporary serial friendships, you don't depend on friends too much. Hell, you don't even join clubs or try out for the football team when you know you'll probably be moving on in a year or two. But sad? That's girl talk, Britt. Don't waste your sympathy on somebody who is perfectly happy with his life, who has everything he ever wanted. Well, almost everything. Gotta' run, kiddo. Talk to you tomorrow or the next day."

He hung up before I could interrogate him about his mysterious former marriage. As to that having-almost-everything part, I wasn't about to go there.

CHAPTER EIGHTEEN

"I hate country music" was my reply to Logan when he called on Friday morning.

"But, Britt, bluegrass isn't country and western music. It's old time mountain music, and it's great. How many times have you listened to bluegrass played live?"

"Well, I guess never, but if it's not country music, it's a first cousin, and I'm sure I wouldn't like it."

"I thought reporters were supposed to be open minded and seek out all the facts before they came to a conclusion."

"Nice try, Logan, but I don't think my personal musical taste falls under the Society of Professional Journalists Code of Ethics. What exactly is this thing you want to take me to?"

"I never knew this until my mom's next door neighbor told me about it, but every Friday night out on the town square in Collierville, all these bluegrass musicians gather informally and play for five or six hours. They usually have stopped for the winter by now, but the weather has been so unusually warm this fall that they aren't quitting until Thanksgiving. This is the last one until spring. Come on, Britt, give it a try — it'll be fun."

"Well, okay, if you promise not to stay the whole time."

"I'll make a deal with you — we'll stay one hour and after that it's your call when we leave. Deal?"

"Okay, what time?"

"I'll pick you up about five and we'll eat some barbecue at the Germantown Commissary on the way out there."

•••••••••••••

Stopping at the Commissary to eat was a good idea — not only are the ribs good, but it breaks the 45-minute trip from Midtown Memphis to Collierville. Collierville is one of the few Memphis suburbs that is a real town, not just a bedroom community.

It used to be a charming, sleepy little town on the eastern edge of Shelby County until about a hundred thousand city dwellers decided to ruin it by moving out there with their shopping malls and overpriced tract houses. Now it's a nightmare of traffic and commercial encroachment. If I had lived in Collierville all my life, I'd really be ticked off about all this. As it is, I don't care. That's just 100,000 fewer people we have to deal with in the city.

But once you get past what seems like endless miles of shopping and fast food restaurants on the western side of Collierville, you get to old town Collierville, and it's like a different world — pretty old houses and small churches and a charming historic town square. And this Friday night in November was cool, almost warm.

I wasn't surprised to find a bluegrass band playing in the gazebo while the audience stood around listening. There *were* about 10 musicians in the gazebo, but they weren't facing the audience. They were standing around in a loose circle facing each other, like they were playing for their own enjoyment, totally oblivious to the 40 or so adults, kids, and dogs around them listening.

Around the grassy town square, that scene was repeated several times — groups of musicians gathered around facing each other while spectators listened and peered over the musicians' shoulders for a closer look into their exclusive club. Around the bandstand, the audience was mostly in lawn chairs, but those around the other groups mostly stood.

Logan knew immediately that he had me hooked. I was fascinated by both the music and the odd arrangement. The music, provided by various violins, or I should say fiddles, and guitars, mandolins, banjos, upright basses and even one harmonica, was infectious. Lively and folksy, but not loud. Not at all annoying like country music. And even though each group was playing a different song, sometimes just yards from another group, the overall effect was not at all discordant. Very much to the contrary, in fact.

"You like it, admit it," Logan said.

"Don't be smug," was all I said, but my smile told the story. I led Logan from group to group soaking up what seemed to me to be a very pure art form.

I couldn't understand all the words of the songs, but I caught various phrases like "Why did I leave my plow on the farm and take that job in town?" and something about how loving you puts "nails in my coffin." And, of course, there was lots about The Promise Land and streets of gold and "backsliding 100 proof."

"I admit it *is* different from what I think of as country music," I told Logan, and of course, he said, "I told you."

Our part of Tennessee, the west, is not big country-music territory. We leave that to Nashville in the middle of the state. And I guess bluegrass is more a product of mountainous East Tennessee.

"I think it's because bluegrass is mostly acoustic," Logan said, "not a lot of those steel guitars and such."

"And it's not as whiny sounding, like country music, even though the lyrics are similar."

What fascinated me most was the people playing and singing the music. About half of them were what you'd expect, old codgers in suspenders and gray-haired ladies with tight beauty-shop curls. But the rest of the musicians were really diverse, except for race — every one was white except one tall, middle-aged woman playing a bass. An unlikely bunch was mixed in with the stereotypical bluegrass folks. One of the fiddle players was a handsome, beefy fireman and next to him another fiddler, a wispy young girl who looked more like a symphony violinist. One of the banjo players I recognized as a Criminal Court judge in Memphis. Another of the bluegrass musicians was a stock analyst that Logan knew.

And the best part was the way the event was so fluid. The musicians just moved around the square playing with whichever group took their fancy at the moment.

"Which one of the musicians is your mom's neighbor?" I asked Logan.

"That's her there playing the bass, Lettie's her name."

"The one black person?"

"Yep, she warned me this event was going to be lily white, except for her. I guess bluegrass just isn't a musical form embraced by black people, generally speaking."

We were in the suburbs, which are dominated by white people, but there are some black people who live out there. But not on that night in that place. I told Logan I thought it was the only time, other than when I went to Maine, that I had ever been in an almost entirely white public gathering.

Memphis is 60 percent African-American for two reasons. In the 1870s there were several yellow fever epidemics that wiped out much of the white population of the city, but killed many fewer black people, whose African heritage gave some of them an immunity to the disease. Then in the first half of the 20th Century, Memphis was the land of opportunity for poor black people on farms — people who didn't want to go as far as Chicago or Detroit to improve their lives.

The mayors of Memphis and Shelby County were both black at one point in recent years, as is the police director and many other leaders, and Memphis, and to a lesser extent the suburbs, are racially quite mixed. So it was a bit of a shock to be at a musical performance that was essentially all-white.

"I wonder how your friend feels being the only black person here," I said.

"Let's ask her later." And we did.

When things were breaking up about midnight, Lettie found us in the much dwindled crowd. Logan introduced us, and Lettie hugged me, like she had known me forever.

"Maggie tells me you're cool," Lettie said, "but I knew that anyhow after what you did for Maggie and Logan last summer."

"Hey, Lettie," Logan said, "we were wondering how it feels to be the only black person here tonight."

"Am I? I hadn't noticed," she joked. "I know black people aren't supposed to do bluegrass, but I do, so sue me. Some of my friends give me a hard time about it."

"How did you get interested in it?" I asked as Logan helped her zip her bass into its soft carrying case.

"The man my daddy worked for at a hardware store taught me how to play bass — I had to stand on a stool to reach the neck. He was a bluegrass picker, so that was the first kind of music I played. Always had a soft spot in my heart for bluegrass ever since."

"But that's not all she plays," Logan said proudly. "Lettie plays in jazz groups and plays blues and a little rockabilly and has had some great gigs with famous singers who come to town and hire local musicians."

"You mean you actually make a living playing?" I asked, incredulous. "No day job?"

"That's right, not even music lessons."

"I'm impressed. Not too many musicians can say that."

"Well, piano players and bass players, if they're versatile, can make a living, because everybody needs a rhythm section. And, Sugar, I am nothing if not versatile."

"Talented, too," I said.

"Thanks, Baby Doll," Lettie said as we walked toward our cars. "I would really love to talk some more, but I got to get up early tomorrow. I promised Virgil I'd come out and pick with him tomorrow. He lives over in Fayette County and used to play with us on Friday nights, but he's got a bad arthritic hip — he's getting up there in age — so he can't come much any more. But picking is Virgil's lifeblood, so I promised him I'd go over and we'd make some music tomorrow. Wanna come?"

"I'd love to," I said without hesitation.

"I'm in," Logan said. "We'll just swing by and pick you up. What time?"

"Pick me up about nine and that should put us at Virgil's by 10:30."

CHAPTER NINETEEN

It rained during the night, bringing in a cold front. We woke to a sunny day, our first really cold day of the season. Dressed in bulky sweaters and jeans, the three of us loaded up the bass in Logan's BMW and headed to Fayette County, which is even further than Collierville. But we had a lot of fun talking on the way out there.

Anybody who knows me well can tell you that I have an obsessive side to my personality. When I discover something new that interests me, I am insatiable to know and experience it all. If I discover a new author I like, I immediately read all of his or her books. Same with music and many other things, so I had lots of questions for Lettie. I have been accused a few times of "interrogating" people.

"Was last night a typical crowd, Lettie?" I asked. "This must be the best kept secret in town."

"Well, bluegrass isn't everybody's cup of tea, but those who like it, like it a lot. I think you're on your way to being one of those people. But to answer your question, we never have a huge crowd, but the attendance has definitely been down since the serial killer started his stuff."

"I can see why the musicians might be scared," Logan said, "since the killer is targeting musicians, but why would the spectators be frightened?"

"I guess some of them might be afraid the killer will decide to expand his repertoire and include music lovers," Lettie said. "Most of the people there last night were the pickers and their families. Not too many others."

"Lettie, mom tells me you're a great singer, so why didn't you sing last night?"

"And how would Maggie know such a thing — I've never sung for her?"

"She said she hears you singing around the house when the windows are open or when you're working in your yard."

"I do like to sing, and I do it sometimes with the jazz or blues groups I play with and in my church choir, but I don't have the right kind of voice for bluegrass. I sing with my mouth open, which won't do."

Logan and I both laughed and asked her what she meant.

"Didn't you notice how the people who were singing last night did it kind of tight-lipped, just barely opening their mouths and sang sort of through their noses? When I sing, I open my mouth and belt it out. So when I do bluegrass, I just pick my bass and keep my mouth shut."

"Tell me about this old guy we're going to visit today?" I said.

"Well, his name's Virgil Palmertree, and he lives in a little rundown shack out in the sticks with his boy, Travis, who everybody calls Bud. Bud's about 60 and never went to school. Virgil says Bud is a little slow and says it right in front of Bud, who doesn't seem to mind or maybe he's just used to it. Bud's Virgil's only child and Virgil's wife died about 20 years ago. So it's just the two of them. It nearly killed Virgil when he had to stop picking on Friday nights at the Collierville Square. He lived for that, and so did Bud."

"That's so sad, and you're so sweet to go all the way out there and play with him," I said.

"Well, I can't go every Saturday, but more often than not, I get out there. Virgil plays a mean banjo, and Bud's real good on the harmonica, so we have a lot of fun."

•••••••••••

When we drove up the dirt driveway to Virgil's house, he was waiting for us on the porch, sitting on a pillow in a rickety cane-bottom chair that looked like it might collapse any minute. His leathery face, reddish brown from 80 or 90 Tennessee summers, didn't change expression, but he shifted around in his chair in an excited way.

As we got out of the car, Virgil shouted through the screen door into the house, "Turn off that teeeveee, Bud, and get out here. Lettie's here and she brung some other folks. And bring my banjo, will ya?"

Bud, who looked like he'd never missed a meal, ambled out onto the porch carrying his daddy's banjo. Around Bud's belt were 8 or 9 small leather cases, probably intended for knives, but in this case holding various harmonicas.

"Hey, Miss Lettie," Bud said, breaking into a big grin. "Who's your friends there?"

"Virgil, Bud, I'd like you to meet Britt and Logan."

"Those both sound like boys' names," Bud said with a smile.

"You're right," I said to Bud. "I've had to put up with this boy's name all my life. My whole name's Britten Faire. Britten was my mother's last name before she got married."

That was probably more information about me than Bud or Virgil needed or wanted, but Bud smiled sweetly.

"You two pickers?" Virgil asked.

"No, sir," Logan said, "but we sure do like to listen. Hope

you don't mind us tagging along with Lettie."

"You're welcome anytime, boy," Virgil said. "Lettie, you gonna take that bass out of that contraption and play or we gonna jaw bone all day?"

Lettie just laughed and unzipped her case. In no time, they were playing, "Will the Circle Be Unbroken." Several songs later, they did a number I remembered from last night, and I sang what words I remembered with them, "Late at night, do you ever think of me, do you ever think of me late in the night," which might not have been the exact words, but it was close enough. I tried to remember to keep my mouth almost closed when I sang, and Lettie and Logan were about to bust a gut laughing at me. Virgil and Bud seemed pleased that I was joining in without invitation, which seems to be the way of Bluegrass musicians.

They played for more than an hour until Virgil started looking a little tired. Lettie took the cue and said we needed to be going back "to town." When we left, I hugged Bud and Virgil, getting the first smile of the day from Virgil.

"My wife was a mighty fine woman," Virgil said. "And I weren't never unfaithful, but I don't think she'd blame me for taking hugs from young girls when I can get 'em, and that ain't often, I can tell ya."

We all laughed and waved goodbye as we got into the car.

•••••••••••

As we turned from the dirt road that lead to Virgil's house onto the paved county road, I turned in my seat to talk to Lettie and noticed a dusty old Buick behind us, back too far to see the driver. I didn't think too much about it until we turned into a little country restaurant to eat lunch and the Buick turned, too.

"I think somebody's following us," I said. "That car has been behind us ever since we turned onto this road, and now it's turning in at the restaurant, too."

Lettie and Logan laughed, but not unkindly.

"Poor Britt," Logan said. "You're so stressed out by getting stuck in the middle of this serial killer thing, that it's making you paranoid."

Lettie explained that this was the only place to eat within miles and it was no wonder that we all had turned into the same restaurant. Still, I watched as the man got out of his car. He was medium height and thin and in his 40s, I guessed, with the pale skin of a city dweller, not a farmer or country person. He walked toward the restaurant as we were getting out of our car and held the door for us as we walked in ahead of him. He sat down at the counter, which was an L shape. He was facing our table.

Under my breath, I said to Logan and Lettie, "That guy is looking right at me. He gave me a kind of creepy smile just now."

"Probably cause you're a pretty, young girl," Lettie said.

Just as I was about to give in to full paranoia, the man's cell phone rang. He answered it and soon after, put his menu down and started walking out. He left the building without a glance in my direction, got into his car and drove off toward Memphis.

We settled down, me feeling a bit foolish, and ate a great lunch of smothered pork chops, turnip greens, squash and corn bread. As we were headed back to Memphis after lunch, I asked Lettie something I hadn't thought to ask earlier.

"Lettie, since you're a professional musician, I'd like to know what you think about all this serial killer stuff. Do you think the crimes are random, like most serial killings?"

"I'd be surprised if they were totally random, and don't ask me why I know that. I don't *know* it — it's just intuition. As many musicians as there are in this city, it's still a pretty intimate community, almost everybody knows everybody else, at least to speak to or at least by reputation. There's a lot of camaraderie and generosity among music people, but there are also plenty of grudges, jealousy and hard feelings, even hate, out there to make somebody kill those three people for a reason, not randomly. And that, Baby Doll, is exactly what I think is going on."

CHAPTER TWENTY

The Monday before Thanksgiving, Jack called me and made an offer I couldn't refuse.

"Britt, how would you like to sit in on the meeting with the profiler from Nashville?"

"Are you kidding? I'd love it. How did you swing that?"

"Well, you know there'd be strings attached, but I thought you might be willing to overlook that in this case."

"What kind of strings?" I said, suspecting ropes instead of strings.

"Well, I suggested letting you sit in on the profiler session, and everybody immediately said no, no press allowed. Then I reminded them that you aren't just a reporter, you are a principal in the case since the killer communicates with you and it might be helpful for you to be a part of the mix."

"So far, I'm with you. What are the strings?"

"Well, the police director agreed with me, and then Raines came around, but they both say only if you don't do a story…"

I interrupted him with some protestation that that wasn't fair to ask a reporter not to write something like that and not fair to the public.

"Britt, will you stop interrupting me? You'd have to hold off on the story, but not forever. They know you or any reporter could go out and interview some shrink and ask him to profile the killer, so they've got no problem with you doing the story. They just want you to wait a few days, a week tops, for us to digest what the profiler says and come up with a plan for how to use that information. Then you get to break the story exclusively. How does that sound?"

"I can live with those strings, if you promise I get the story first."

"They don't want the TV stations to get it first any more than you do. They know you'll put it in proper context, so if you get it first, maybe the TV guys and others will follow suit."

"Well, it's a nice idea, but whether it influences TV or not, I'll take the deal. When will the profiler be here?"

"She's here now going over the reports from the medical examiner and homicide and asking a lot of questions. Stay near the phone, and I'll call you when she's ready to talk to us. We won't start without you."

"Great, and Jack, thanks, you're a real pal."

"Which is exactly what I don't want to be to you."

"I didn't say you were only a pal — I meant you were a pal to set this up. Don't be so sensitive."

"Well, that's a first — a homicide detective being accused of being overly sensitive."

We both laughed and hung up.

Irene Ringold didn't at all look like her name. I had expected a scholarly looking frump. Instead, the woman seated at the end of the conference table was an extremely attractive middle-aged woman with shoulder-length, thick salt-and-pepper gray hair, a great figure and beautiful smile. Jack and I were on one side of the table and the police director and head of Homicide were on the other.

"First," Ringold said after the introductions, "I want to make it clear that I am not here to offer a panacea. I think the Beltway Snipers reminded us that profiling is not a pure science, but rather a helpful tool sometimes in identifying who might have committed a crime. Statistically we're usually right, but that doesn't mean it always helps in apprehending the perpetrator. And too much reliance on profiling can cause us sometimes to overlook viable suspects, who don't fit the profile."

I jotted down notes — they wouldn't let me record the session — because that would make a great quote for my eventual story.

"That said, let me tell you my impressions after looking at the facts of this case. First of all, this is a tough one. A lot of things don't fit the things we know statistically and anecdotally about serial killers."

She went on to talk about some of things we'd already heard from the Tennessee Bureau of Investigation guy Jack talked to on the phone.

"Most serial killers are sex killers, but this one is not. Most kill in private in order to fulfill some sick ritual, but this person kills quickly in public and runs. Most serial killers are white men and kill white people usually of the same gender, except for snipers who seem to be more random in picking their victims. Our killer here has killed two black people and one white, one woman and two men. Our killer has targeted people who all share the same profession, which is very unusual unless that profession is prostitute or topless dancer. Most serial killers kill over a long period of time with months or years between victims. Ours has killed three people in a month."

"George Howard Putt," Raines said, "our last Memphis serial

killer, killed five people in 29 days."

"And we must consider the possibility that our present killer lived in Memphis then and was somehow inspired by Putt, but that would make our killer at least middle aged, and most serial killers are 25 to 34 years old. Putt strangled his early victims and stabbed the later victims, I believe."

The cops all nodded yes. Jack asked the question we'd all been wondering about.

"Ms. Ringold, what do you take from all these atypical factors?"

"The first possibility is that it is not a serial killer at work here at all, but someone who killed Saundra Barkley for a reason, who was followed by two copy cat murderers, who had their own reasons for wanting their victims dead and saw this as a good opportunity to make it look like a serial crime. That would take attention away from suspects with motives in the individual murders of the rapper and the Elvis impersonator. This is possible because there were so many witnesses to the immediate aftermath of Barkley's murder, and it was widely reported that she was killed with a steak knife similar to those commonly found in restaurants. The knives in the second and third murders were also the kind commonly found in restaurants, but weren't identical to each other or to the Barkley knife. And the press also reported that Barkley was stabbed in the back and what portion of her back."

"But," Raines said, "It never got out in the media that the medical examiner had said the killer in all three was between 5 ft. 9 and six feet tall."

"A height that takes in probably half the male population and a lot of women, too," Jack said.

"Good point," Ringold said. "Now, let's look at the evidence in favor of it being a serial killer, not copy cats."

"The notes," I said.

"Exactly, Ms. Faire. By the way, I hope these officers have

thanked your newspaper for not publishing all the details of the notes."

"I don't recall a thank you," I said, smiling at the three men.

"The newspaper acted very responsibly in the matter," the police director said in his usual formal manner.

"I studied both notes — it's awfully helpful when killers send notes. And I studied the newspaper coverage of them, and key aspects were never made known to the public, like the type of paper used and type of writing instrument. So the similarity there makes me lean toward the serial killer theory. The first note was a poem, which might indicate the killer was a songwriter, but it was a pretty basic poem that anyone could write. The second note was not a poem, but both of the notes used references to song titles, *Walking in Memphis* and Barkley's song, *Baby Gotta Leave.* And both notes predicted another murder."

"What," Jack asked, "do you make of the notes being delivered in person, first to Britt's house and second to her car in a restaurant parking lot?"

"Well, it tells me that the killer is bold and feels invisible or at least not vulnerable. That's in keeping with he or she killing in public. Probably the killer feels empowered by doing something so bold and not getting caught. Our killer is a risk taker, and not all serial killers are."

I asked her if it was unusual for a serial killer to send notes and to do it through an intermediary like me.

"Most serial killers don't send or leave notes, but it's not rare either. It does indicate a fairly intelligent killer, one who plans his crimes, instead of killing on impulse, as most do. When they do send notes, it's often to the press, rather than the police — that part's not unusual," she said and then paused and looked at me with what I was afraid was pity. "But Ms. Faire, you do need to realize that it is very, very unusual for the serial killer to know where the reporter lives, and that part about leaving a note on your car really is alarming. It means he was watching you, at least that day. This may be just another sign of his in-your-face boldness, but it also could indicate he's becoming obsessed with you personally. Be careful, Ms. Faire, be very careful until this guy is caught."

Irene Ringold was scaring me to death, so I changed the subject. "What about the bad grammar and misspelling in the first note?"

"Well, at face value that would indicate, of course, a person of little education, but an intelligent killer would go out of his way to disguise his education by intentionally misspelling words and writing with pencil on cheap notebook paper, so that really tells us little. I know none of you wants to hear this, but we'll know a lot more after he kills again. Next time he's bound to supply a few more pieces of the puzzle."

"Ms. Ringold," I said. "Earlier you talked about two possibilities, either it was a serial killer picking random victims or three killers targeting people they have a motive to kill. Isn't it possible that the two could be combined? Could it be a serial killer with a different motive for each victim?"

"That would be unusual, but not unheard of, and frankly that would be ideal — if anything about a serial killer is ideal — because we could look for something or someone who is connected to all the victims. That's why I would suggest investigating each murder the same as you would if it were a single murder, just in case. And again, Ms. Faire, be very careful in your personal comings and goings. Don't take for granted your own safety. It's possible — not likely, but possible — that the killer is an acquaintance of yours who is killing people just as an excuse to seem important to you and feel close to you."

I felt Jack tense next to me, and he grabbed my hand under the table.

CHAPTER TWENTY-ONE

I didn't want to let on to anybody just how much Irene Ringold had upset me with her implication that the serial killer could be someone who knows me and is killing people to impress me or feel close to me. I tried to distract myself by getting busy with preparations for my parents' arrival for Thanksgiving. They were driving up from Florida on Wednesday and staying until Saturday.

Both of my sisters were supposed to join us for Thanksgiving, but my youngest older sister, Libby, who lives in Nashville, called on Monday night to say she couldn't make it. Her new boyfriend talked her into spending the holiday with his family. She was hoping that I would break the news to Mom and Dad so she wouldn't have to feel guilty when she heard the disappointment in their voices. Let me rephrase that — the disappointment in my mother's voice. Dad wouldn't be nearly that subtle — he'd complaint that they see little enough of her as it is (true); that it is inconsiderate to cancel at the last minute (true) and that he's glad she's got a boyfriend (false), but doesn't see why she can't be away from him for three days.

"No way I'm going to do your dirty work for you," I said.

"Please, Britt, do me just this one little favor. I'd do the same for you."

"No, you wouldn't, and besides, I would never ask you to."

"Well, only because you haven't had a boyfriend in this century."

"Was that snarky remark supposed to soften me up to help you?"

"I'm sorry, Britt, but you know how they are."

"Yeah, I hate it when parents want to see their children on Thanksgiving."

"Don't be so self-righteous, Britt. You've missed several holidays over the years."

"Only when I had to work holidays during my early years at the paper. Even when I had a boyfriend, I never cancelled Christmas or Thanksgiving with the folks to be with him."

"Well, that's just the difference between us — you live for work and I live for love."

"Love? You've only known this guy for what, two weeks? How could it be love already?"

"I wouldn't expect you to understand, Britt."

"Well, I'll quit trying then. Libby, you'll have to call Mom and Dad yourself."

"Well, I won't. I guess when I don't show up, they'll just worry until you tell them why I'm not coming."

And with that, she hung up. I couldn't wait to see my oldest older sister, the nice sister, Jill, whom Mom and Dad were going to pick up in Jackson, Mississippi, on their way up from Florida. Jill is a widow and has a son, Ryan, and a demanding job as a pediatrician and a dog and a cat to take care of, but she still manages to slip away occasionally to visit her family.

To get ready for the family, I had called Freddy, the man who does my yard work on the rare occasions I care about such things. I believe in cutting grass, for obvious reasons, but I don't believe in raking leaves, for obvious reasons (obvious to me anyhow). I thought

I would get the leaves raked this week, though, in honor of my family's visit. If the leaves were left covering the grass as they usually are this time of year, Mom would say sadly that it's too bad I don't have a husband to do that for me, and Dad would say I am a big, healthy girl and should do it myself.

I'm not frail by any means, but I wouldn't describe myself as big and healthy either. That sounds like one of those Wisconsin farm girls of Scandinavian descent or one of those women who spends her vacations hiking and camping. My idea of roughing it is staying in a bad hotel, and the closest I come to the great outdoors is sitting on the porch when the weather is not too hot and not too cold.

So with the fam coming on Wednesday, I asked Freddy to come over on Tuesday and rake the leaves and haul off the bags, so Dad wouldn't tease me about having the leaves raked just because he and Mom were coming. I took off Tuesday to clean the house and buy the groceries Mom told me to get for her Wednesday night cooking session.

Freddy is a nice guy, in his mid 20s I think and not very well educated but a hard worker and pleasant to deal with. I always give him lunch while he's working and pay him more than he asks for his yard work.

He was sitting at my kitchen table eating a ham sandwich and drinking a Dr. Pepper while I unloaded groceries.

"So what does your family do to celebrate Thanksgiving, Freddy?" I said, making small talk while he ate. "Does your mom cook a big turkey like this thing here?" I slapped the frozen bird before me.

"No, ma'am, Miss Britt," he said, brushing his sandy hair away from his face with a mayonnaisey hand.

"None of that yes ma'am and no ma'am stuff, Freddy. Like I've told you before, I'm not much older than you, so call me Britt."

"Yes, ma'am. I mean, okay. It's just that my mama taught all of us boys to be respectful of ladies, even if they aren't older than us.

And I definitely respect you, Miss Br…, I mean Britt."

"She sounds like a good mother."

"She is, well, she was. She passed away when I was 17, so to answer your first question, my mama won't be cooking a turkey. Instead, me and Daddy and my brothers usually cook a couple of frozen pizzas or make a pot of chili and drink beer and watch football on TV, just like we do on Christmas."

"Well, traditions come in all shapes and sizes. My family often goes down to Oxford, Mississippi, for the Ole Miss-Mississippi State football game and eats our turkey and dressing outside in the cold or rain before going over to the stadium. Are all your brothers still living at home?"

"Three of us brothers and none of us married."

"I have two sisters and none of us are married either."

"Maybe you and your sisters could marry me and my brothers."

I looked at his face to see if he was kidding, and I was pretty sure he was, but just in case, I changed the subject.

"How much longer do you think the yard work will take, Freddy?"

"Oh, about another coupla hours. You ought to call me over more often, and I ain't saying that to get more money either. I take a lot of pride in shaping up that bad looking yard of yours. I'd practically do it for free just to take pride in it and just to see that smile you always have when you look at what I've done."

Thankfully, my phone rang before I had to respond to Freddy, and he wiped his mouth on his hand and went back to his rake.

CHAPTER TWENTY-TWO

Thanksgiving morning we began getting our moveable feast ready to go. On alternating years when Ole Miss and Mississippi State play football at Oxford, where Ole Miss is, our family has always cooked a full, hot Thanksgiving meal and found a way to transport it to Oxford, which is about 80 miles south of Memphis. Once there, we set up portable chairs and tables and eat our turkey and dressing, rice and gravy, sweet potato casserole and lots of other good stuff and then head over to the football game.

You're probably picturing my crazy family eating alone on campus or in the Student Union, but there are thousands of others who do the same. The Grove, a 10-acre park in the middle of campus, is the place where Ole Miss fans picnic before games, and Thanksgiving is no exception. Most games bring about 50,000 people to The Grove, but Thanksgiving there is a somewhat smaller crowd.

What most schools call tailgating is taken to incredible heights at Ole Miss. The Grove on game day is a sea of red, white or blue canopies and under them are well-dressed people eating from silver chafing dishes beside floral arrangements and candelabra. My family has always been into quality of food more than presentation, but we're not totally slouches either.

Mid South weather being what it is — unpredictable — we sometimes have our Thanksgiving meal with nothing more than light sweaters for warmth, and at other times we have to eat wearing gloves and heavy coats. This year it was pretty cold after a fall that alternated between warm and chilly.

On Wednesday night, we had a fun evening of cooking and catching up. Then on Thursday morning, we packed everything up and took off for Maggie Magee's house, which is near Rhodes College and not too far from my house. Maggie, Logan and Lettie were waiting for us there with their food contributions. None of them have any connection to the two schools that would be playing that day, but Logan and Maggie thought it would be a fun adventure, and Lettie was invited to take the ticket we'd bought for my absent sister. Libby never did call, by the way, so she got her way, as usual — I had no choice but to tell Mom and Dad why she wasn't coming, but I also told them how manipulative she was about it.

So the eight of us climbed aboard a huge antique orange motor home that Dad had borrowed from a friend for the trip from Florida, a vehicle I felt compelled to disassociate myself from.

"Dad, why on earth did you bring this monster? You and Mom certainly didn't have to have something so big, and we could have taken two cars to Oxford."

Dad, with Ryan riding shotgun, was unrepentant.

"Don't be silly, Tootsie Roll, this is a lot more fun — everybody together."

That's right, you heard it correctly. My dad's pet name for me — one of them —is Tootsie Roll. Our family is used to it, but Logan and Lettie both burst out laughing.

"Is that because you're so sweet?" Maggie asked sincerely.

"Or," ventured Logan, "because you were skinny and brown when you were a kid?"

"Sounds more like a nickname for me," Lettie said, still laughing.

"There is no rhyme or reason to it," I said. "We are just a

nickname family. What can I say? Some families are and some aren't."

"Like what other nicknames do you have?" Logan asked as the big orange thing pulled onto Interstate 55, south toward Oxford.

"Well, I call her Sweet Pea," said Mom.

"You call *me* that," said Jill.

"Well, I call all of you girls Sweet Pea sometimes. And Daddy calls Britt Bitsy sometimes. And he calls Jill and Libby Snooks and Teeny."

"Dad's nickname is Bod. All of his childhood friends call him that," I said.

"It started because I was tall and thin and lanky like Ichabod Crane in *The Legend of Sleepy Hollow,* but later on it became a joke about my body."

"You know, like, 'Dad doesn't have a great bod. He's got a Faire bod," Jill added. "Mom's nickname is Totsie."

"And we," I said, "call Mom and Dad variations of those names — Daddakins, Dadbo, Momsy, Mommanator. You get the picture."

"Yeah, I sure do," Logan said. "I feel kind of unloved because my parents never gave me a nickname."

"We called you Logey and Baby Boy," Maggie said defensively.

"Those are terms of endearment, not nicknames. Now Tootsie Roll — there's a nickname," Logan said, shooting me a sideways grin.

So the next 15 minutes was spent trying to come up with a nickname for Logan. I think we settled on Logamatic, because he hated it most.

After the nickname conversation had run its course, we

somehow got back into the serial killer debate. I thought we had exhausted it the night before when my whole family ganged up against me, but, of course, it came back to take a bite out of an otherwise nice Thanksgiving Day.

"Maggie, Lettie," my dad said, "what are you two ladies doing to protect yourselves with this serial killer on the loose?"

"Well, I'm not doing anything much different," Maggie said. "I was always careful about going out alone at night and locking up good when I'm home. And Logan checks on me real often. But I do worry about Lettie, with her being a musician and all."

"Don't worry about me," Lettie said with a wave of dismissal. "I'm not well-known enough to be one of the victims. Everybody's heard of Mutha Boy and Saundra Barkley."

"Well, everybody hasn't heard of that other guy," Maggie said.

"Well, everybody's heard of Elvis, and I think they killed him to be symbolic," Lettie said. "But don't worry, I'm taking precautions. If I have a gig, I get somebody to walk me to my car and when I get home, I call Maggie on my cell phone and she watches from her window to make sure I get in okay."

"Well, that's good," my dad said, now able to move on to his intended subject. "I just wish Bitsy was as smart. Don't you think she ought to come back to Florida with us until this killer is caught."

"As I said before, Dad, you can't really expect a grown woman, a reporter no less, to run off scared to Florida with my mommy and daddy."

"You don't have to be sarcastic, Sweet Pea," my mom scolded. "Daddy is just thinking of your safety and our peace of mind."

"Don't worry, Totsie," Logan said, "I'll keep my eye on her for you. I've offered her my spare bedroom. My house has locks like Fort Knox and a garage that opens directly into the house, but she won't take me up on it."

My sister gave me a knowing raised eyebrow.

"I promise I'll be careful. I really will, Dad, but a person can't live in fear. It'll paralyze you."

Maggie apparently decided it was her job to take the pressure off me.

"Well, I don't blame you for not wanting to stay with Logan, Britt. What with his dangerous past, and besides, I thought he was going to grow up to be a serial killer. I read an article about how most serial killers when they're kids like to kill animals, and I got really worried about Logan."

Maggie was trying to be funny, but nobody was laughing.

"Not that story again," Logan said with a sigh.

"As I said, I was worried, but my husband said that all little boys like to kill things."

"It was ants, Mother. We put a firecracker in an ant hill. We weren't dismembering dogs and cats."

"Still, I'm relieved you turned out so well."

•••••••••••••

When we got to the Ole Miss campus, Dad dropped us and all the food and gear at the Grove and went to find a place to park the Orange Monster, as we all called it by then.

Thanksgiving Dinner al fresco was fun and afterwards we headed over to the game, which Ole Miss won 38 to 7. Logan and I shared a lap blanket at the game and several times he rested his hand on my leg. Even with his gloves and my wool pants, I still managed a little thrill when he touched me. Then I would think of Jack and feel a little guilty.

Driving home that night, the group was a little sleepy as we thawed out. Ryan fell asleep in the bed in the back of the Monster, and Mom rode up front with Dad. The rest of us sat in the kitchen/dining area and were pretty subdued until Dad cranked up the motor home's sound system to play his latest batch of golden oldies.

"Do you know how hard it was to get this Dave Clark Five CD?" Dad said. "They just don't sell these things in stores. I had to buy it from a German dealer who got it from Australia."

We all laughed at the idea of Dad working that hard to buy one CD, and before we knew it, we were all singing along to "Glad All Over" and "Catch Us if You Can."

It was a totally fun day — Libby's loss. When Mom and Dad set sail for Florida two days later, taking Jill and Ryan back to Jackson on the way, I felt sad, but I was ready to get some privacy and quiet back.

Sunday morning I wrapped my robe around me tight to stay warm and went outside to get the New York Times, which I only take on Sundays. Hurrying back inside I saw what I had missed on the way out — a piece of paper clipped to my mailbox with a clothespin. I should have remembered not to touch it, in case there were fingerprints, but instead I grabbed it, opened it and read from a piece of notebook paper:

"Wish I could've gone with you, Britt, on your little trip to Oxford, but I like my sweet potato casserole with those little marshmallows on top, not the way y'all fix it. I like to sing along to the oldies as much as the next one."

CHAPTER TWENTY-THREE

I was still in my nightgown and robe when Jack got to my house 20 minutes after I called him. I couldn't stop shivering even though the house was warm. Jack slipped his arms inside my robe when he hugged me.

"It's gonna be okay, kiddo," he said in a surer voice than I'm sure he really felt. "Let's look at the note and talk about it before I call Crime Scene."

We sat down at the kitchen table and drank coffee as we reread the note.

"How could he know all that, Jack? This note scares me more than all the others put together. It's like he was in the motor home with us, but that's not possible, is it?"

"I can't imagine there being any space in a motor home, even a big one, where a grown man could hide. No, it had to be some other way. How well do you know this woman musician who was with y'all?"

"You're not suggesting that Lettie is the serial killer?"

"How do you know she's not?"

"For one thing, I just know. There's no way it could be her."

"How can you be so sure, Britt?"

"I just know it. Besides, if it were her, why would she incriminate herself by writing a note about things that only people in the motor home could know? Because we know her the least, she'd be the first to be suspected, like you did."

"Okay, then, who in the bus would want to make it look like Lettie was the murderer?"

"Nobody, Jack. It was just my family and Logan and his mother."

"Could there be bad blood between Lettie and Logan's mother?"

"You're not saying that Maggie Magee wrote the note to try to incriminate her next door neighbor? Why on earth would she do that?"

"I don't know, Britt, but you have to ask every possible question if you're going to come up with every possible answer. Logan knows what the general public doesn't know, that the notes are written on notebook paper with pencil. Maybe he told that to his mother or her neighbor."

"This is stupid and ridiculous. There are other possibilities."

"Okay," Jack said patiently.

"What if somebody followed us down to Ole Miss? On game day, I-55 is crowded with football fans headed for Oxford. We were so busy talking and laughing, we wouldn't have noticed somebody following us. And in the Grove, it's wall-to-wall people. Anybody could have been nearby and seen what we were eating."

"That would explain him writing about the sweet potatoes," Jack said. "You don't even have to be that close to notice whether sweet potatoes are covered in marshmallows or not. But what about singing the oldies? Did y'all do that in the Grove?"

"Of course not. That was only in the motor home and only

on the way back."

"Were you singing loud enough for a car next to you on the interstate to hear you?"

"I'd like to think so, but I don't see it. The windows were closed because it was cold and those big honker motor homes are well insulated, so I really don't think anybody in a car next to us could hear us singing."

"How he or she knew this stuff doesn't bother me as much as something else, Britt. "

"I know what you're going to say. This note means the killer, if that's who wrote it, is getting more interested in me personally."

"Yep, that's what I was going to say, and that worries the hell out of me, Britt."

"It doesn't thrill me either."

"The only thing worse than having a serial killer on the loose is having a serial killer obsessed with you."

"Don't say it that way — you're scaring me to death. "

"Maybe you need to be scared, so you'll take more precautions."

"Like taking Logan up on his offer to stay at his fortress of a house?"

Jack suddenly looked like he'd had a shocking revelation.

"Britt, is it possible that Logan wrote that note?"

"Jack," I said angrily. "I can't believe you'd let your jealousy of Logan get in the way of your good judgment. You're saying Logan is the serial killer?"

"No, of course not. I'm asking if it's possible that Logan wrote the note, so you'd come live with him until this is all over."

"Do you really think that little of Logan?"

"If he did it, I'm sure he did it because he fears for your safety, like I do. Maybe he just thought it was the only way to get you to stay some place safe. That's all I'm saying, Britt."

"No matter how much Logan wants me to stay at his house, he would never scare me with a note like that and take a chance of throwing off the investigation with a bogus note. I can't believe you'd even suggest such a thing, Jack."

With that I headed for my bedroom. "I'm going to get dressed. Let me know when the Crime Scene guy gets here."

CHAPTER TWENTY-FOUR

I was really mad that Jack would suggest that Logan might masquerade as the serial killer and write a note to try to drive me to stay at his house. I tried to tell myself that Jack, as a homicide detective, has to consider every possibility, but I was still mad.

The final straw was getting a call from Lettie saying that she had gotten a visit from a homicide detective named Lt. Trent, who was not only asking about the Thanksgiving Day events, which everyone in the motor home might expect to be questioned about, but also asking about her whereabouts on the days of the three murders and if she knew any of the victims.

"I told him I knew Saundra back in the day," Lettie told me. "She formed a trio for a while and I was her bass player. But we hadn't been in contact since. She was pretty hard to work with, so I didn't even go to her funeral."

"You didn't tell me you knew Saundra when we were talking about the murders."

"Baby Doll, I know just about every R & B or jazz singer in Memphis. If they've performed live over the years, I've usually played with them at one time or the other. I've been at this for nearly 30 years. As far as I know, I'm the only female bass player in town, upright bass anyhow, so that makes me a novelty, I guess. I get more work that way."

"I know the detective who questioned you."

"I know you do. Maggie told me you did — that's why I called you," Lettie said and then laughed. "Baby Doll, does that detective really consider me a suspect?"

"I don't think so, Lettie. Did you hear about the note that I found on Sunday morning on my door?"

"Was it in the paper?"

"No, the editors decided it wasn't one that directly pertained to the murders, so they agreed not to run it. I just thought maybe Logan might have told you. I called him last night and told him about it," I said, relieved that Logan was keeping what I told him in confidence. "Anyhow, Lettie, this is confidential, but the note may have been from the killer, and it mentioned things that only someone inside the motor home would know."

"Like what?"

"I promised the police I wouldn't tell anybody the details."

"Well, if there was a note like that, I can see why they consider me a suspect. It's a joke to think of me as a murder suspect, but look at the choices here. Either your family wrote the note or Logan or Maggie. Since I'm the only one in the music business, I'm the logical one to blame."

"I'm sure Jack doesn't consider you a serious suspect after talking to you, but he had to check it all out anyhow, just in case."

"Well, that explains a lot," Lettie said. "It all makes more sense now."

"I hope you aren't going to worry about all this."

"Worry? No way, Baby Doll, or should I call you Tootsie Roll? I got better things to think about. Well, got to go. See you around."

Despite my defense of Jack to Lettie, when I hung up the phone I felt really mad at him. First he suggests Logan is cruel and manipulative enough to write the note and then he interrogates poor Lettie. So while I was angry, I phoned Logan and did something I knew immediately I would regret. Then I called Jack.

"Lettie Nolan just called me and said you accused her of being the serial killer."

"I did no such thing, and I doubt Ms. Nolan said that. That sounds like a Britt exaggeration. I questioned her like I have everybody else connected to these killings."

"You didn't question my family, and they were there just like Lettie and Logan and Maggie."

"You're being ridiculous, Britt. You're just mad because you know her. You've interviewed anybody you can get your hands on that might know something about the killer or victims, and you're just a reporter. As one of the cops investigating these murders, I have even more obligation to follow up on every lead."

"Do your accusations about Logan and Lettie have anything to do with your jealousy about Logan and me …" I couldn't think of what word to use. Not "dating" certainly, not "being friends," so I blurted out, "spending time together."

"Britt, do you really think I would let my feelings for you get in the way of an investigation as important as this?"

I felt foolish, but I had to tell him what I had done in a state of insanity and retribution a few minutes before.

"Well, I'll let you get back to work. By the way, I took your advice about protecting myself better, and my parents will feel better, too. I just called Logan and took him up on his offer to let me stay with him until this killer is caught."

There was a long silence on the other end of the line. Finally Jack said, "I *have* been worried about you. If moving in with Logan is what you think will keep you safe, then that's what you should do. Goodbye, Britt."

And Jack hung up.

CHAPTER TWENTY-FIVE

When I had impulsively called Logan to say I would accept his invitation to stay at his house until the coast was clear, he didn't sound surprised at all, as if he'd known all along that I would eventually see the light. That annoyed me because I like to think of myself as unpredictable and brave, what others in my life call stubbornly independent.

"When do you want to move in? Do you want me to help you bring your things over?" Logan asked.

"It's not like I'm moving in really," I said, wanting to make it clear I wasn't permanently running away from danger. "I'll just pack a suitcase and stay a few days until they catch this guy. I feel kind of silly really since…"

"Britt, you don't have to explain to me or anybody else why you're staying at my house for a while. I'm sure everyone who loves you will be relieved to know you're out of harm's way for a while."

"It's not like I'm really out of harm's way. I mean I'm not going to lock myself away in your house, cowering in fear."

"I can see you're sensitive on this subject. Forgive me if my terminology isn't the best, but at least at night when you're most vulnerable, you'll be here with good locks, a good alarm system, a connected garage and me to whack with my tennis racket anyone who tries to hurt you."

I told Logan that I felt like I should be braver than the average Memphian, since I'm a reporter, and he laughed.

"Oh, like you don't think other Memphians are getting better locks installed lately and taking all kinds of precautions, and they don't have as much reason to worry as you do, unless they're musicians. I invited my mother and Lettie to stay here for a while, too, but they refused, said they are looking out for each other."

"See what I mean, Logan, even Lettie, a musician, is braver than me."

"Britt, get real here. Lettie has less to fear than you do. She's just one of many musicians in the city, but you are the only person that the serial killer is communicating with and the only person he is stalking."

"I wish you wouldn't use that word."

"I know you don't like to think of it as stalking, and I didn't so much see it that way after the first note, but when he followed you to Molly's that night and left a note on your car, it became stalking, according to my definition. And that Thanksgiving note showed he is obsessed with you personally."

"Okay, Okay, you win. I'll go home after work and pack a bag and call you before I come to your house. Will you be home about 6?"

"I'll cook us some dinner. I'll cook spaghetti and open a jar of sauce. Pretty impressive, huh?"

"For you, yes. Too bad you're not one of those terribly modern men who cooks with roasted red peppers and sun-dried tomatoes and impresses all the women."

"I'll impress you by beating you at gin rummy after dinner. How about that?"

• • • • • • • • • • • • • • •

After our spaghetti dinner with salad straight from the grocery store salad bar and a good bread he got at La Baguette, Logan sensed, I guess, that I wasn't in a card-playing mood, so he suggested something from his vast collection of DVDs. So we watched three or four episodes of "As Time Goes By," that great British sitcom with Judi Dench and Geoffrey Palmer. I fall in love with stuffy old Lionel every time I watch it.

In some ways, Logan reminds me of Lionel, especially the way he dresses and his manner. Not that Logan is stuffy, but he has a conservative look and manner. He never goes too long without a haircut; he never skips shaving on a Saturday; he still wears all white playing tennis when almost nobody does that anymore; and he's much more likely to overdress than to underdress when he goes out.

Combine all that with his dark good looks, and he makes quite an impression. He's the kind of man other women look at lustfully when we're out somewhere. Sometimes it makes me feel proud that he's with me and not them, and other times it makes me feel that everybody is saying, 'What's *he* doing with *her*?'"

Jack, on the other hand, is not anybody that you'd stare at in public, unless you were thinking about how badly he was dressed. While Logan buys his clothes from Brooks Brothers and Oak Hall, Jack shops at Men's Wearhouse, which wouldn't be so bad if he had any idea about what goes with what. Jack always looks like somebody who pulls his clothes out of the closet while wearing a blind fold. As long as he doesn't leave the house naked, Jack is satisfied with his style.

But don't get me wrong — I'm not embarrassed to go out with Jack, even if his socks don't always match. Even when his hair is a bit shaggy and his clothes rumpled and mismatched, he has a confident, good-humored way about him that is attractive.

That night, my second time to move in temporarily with Logan, was supposed to be a casual, hang-out-at-home night, but

Logan wore khakis and a cashmere pullover sweater.

Before we went to our bedrooms about midnight, Logan, again reading my mind, said he wanted to make it clear that this night was special because I had just arrived, but from now on we'd just be roommates with nobody cooking for anybody else and each of us going our way.

"You mean we can never watch TV together or eat together again?" I asked teasingly.

"Well, sometimes, like we always have, but no more. You will just be my fiercely brave roommate most of the time."

I smiled and hugged him goodnight, and he kissed the top of my head.

"I'm glad you're here, Britt. I'm one of those people who love you and want you to be safe."

CHAPTER TWENTY-SIX

Logan was true to his word. He didn't hover over me or treat me like a guest. He didn't ask me to call him when I got somewhere or ask me when I would be "home." I went about my business, and he was busy with final research papers due for his graduate classes at the University. We just saw each other in passing, other than sharing a pizza one night.

Jack hadn't called me since I told him I was moving in with Logan for a while, so after a week I called him. Jack had taken me on a great picnic last summer to Mud Island River Park, and I had decided to return the favor.

"Trent, Homicide," he answered brusquely. I almost hung up.

"Hey, detective, want to go on a picnic with me?"

"Britt! Hey, kid, how are you?" He sounded so glad to hear from me that it made me feel ashamed for not calling him sooner.

"Would they let you out of your cage long enough to go on a picnic with me?"

"A picnic in December?"

"Well, we'd have to go early since it gets dark so soon, but it's warm enough for a picnic. It's 65 degrees out there."

That's a Memphis winter for you. Coats one day and shirt sleeves the next. I love it. A Memphis Christmas is much more likely to be warm than white.

"Do you mean go on a picnic today?"

"Yeah, or tomorrow, whichever is best for you. I'll bring the food this time, but you have to pick the spot. As long as there's a river view."

"Let's do it tomorrow about 4. I'll clear some time for it, and I know the perfect spot."

After we hung up, I went to Goldsmith's — it's really Macy's like every other department store in the country is now, but it will always be Goldsmith's to me because that's what my parents and grandmother always called it. I bought a nice picnic basket that had wine glasses and real plates and metal flatware. I'm no more of a cook than Logan, but I bought a nice bottle of red wine and the next day at my house, I made roast beef sandwiches and chocolate chip cookies, one of my few homemade accomplishments.

I go by my house everyday to take in the mail and check for serial killer notes. Then I picked up Jack outside his downtown office, and he told me to drive up Riverside Drive and turn right on Crump.

"Are you taking me to Arkansas?" I asked. Just before we got to what is referred to as "the old bridge," Jack told me to turn right and the exit took us under Crump and past a derelict motel. When Jack saw the puzzled look on my face, he smiled.

"I was hoping you'd never been here before."

The sign at the exit said, "Metal Museum." I had heard of it, of course, but never had been there and wasn't even sure where exactly it was, except near the old bridge. But within a block or two after we had passed the old motel, we came to the museum property. It was on a shady street with almost no traffic. To the left was what looked like either an Indian burial mound or a Civil War battlement. Jack said it was both.

"The two Indian mounds were built by the Chickasaws as ceremonial mounds in the 1500s, so nobody's buried there," he said. "One is hollow, so it was used for storing ammunition during the Civil War, and the other mound for gun emplacements — it was perfect for spotting war ships on the river."

"Good, I'm glad it wasn't a desecrated burial ground. I'd hate to have some angry spirits ruin our picnic."

"If ghosts intrude on our picnic, they'll come from the other side of the road," Jack said.

On our right, in addition to the Metal Museum, there were two historic buildings that Jack said were the only remaining buildings from the U.S. Marine Hospital built in 1884.

"It was built to care for long-term patients from the Civil War," Jack said, "but that was around the time of the Yellow Fever epidemics that nearly wiped out Memphis, and they ended up doing Yellow Fever research here. They say that some of the Yellow Fever victims from the morgue here still wander the grounds."

"How do you know all this stuff?"

"When I was a young uniform, I patrolled this area and I did some research on it at the Memphis Room at the Main Library. I was fascinated by the place as soon as I saw it, and you will, too, when you see the view."

Jack took the picnic basket from my car and led me onto the museum grounds.

"Shouldn't we pay or something?"

Jack said no, that people were free to look at the view or picnic on the grounds until dark every night when they locked the gates. So we did, and it was spectacular. The river takes a dramatic westward turn right at this spot, and it's a view like no other.

"They say this is the spot where Hernando de Soto first saw the Mississippi River in 1541," Jack said, "but that can't be proven, of course. The History Channel, nor Discovery, were with him at the time to document it."

There must have been a few people in the museum buildings, but there was nobody on the grounds, so we had the gorgeous view to ourselves. We set out our food and wine at the table in the wrought-iron gazebo that one of the artisans there built, I assumed. We talked a little about the investigation, but mostly we just talked about normal stuff, the kind of things people talk about when there isn't a serial killer on the loose. Jack never asked me how it was going at Logan's. I was wishing he would, so I could say Logan and I were living like roommates, not lovers. As we watched the sun set, Jack and I sipped our wine with our free hands touching, but not exactly holding hands in the truest sense of the word. Still, it was nice, very nice.

We were startled by the sound of someone walking through the dried leaves on the ground behind us. I grabbed Jack's hand instinctively, and he grabbed his gun instinctively.

"Excuse me, sir, ma'am, we're closing the gates now," said a 40ish man in jeans and sweatshirt.

I let go of Jack's hand, and he dropped his gun hand to his side, hoping I'm sure that the curator hadn't seen him draw it. We apologized for staying after dark and walked back to the car. It was dark and deserted and starting to get cold, and I was glad to get back to the lights and warmth of downtown Memphis a few minutes later. I dropped Jack off at his office, and I drove back to Logan's. When I came in the back door from the garage, he was sitting at the kitchen table eating a crunchy peanut butter and grape jelly sandwich with a glass of milk. I chatted with him for almost an hour, but didn't tell him about our picnic. I went up to my bedroom and read a mystery until I fell asleep. I dreamed about Hernando de Soto and yellow fever ghosts.

●●●●●●●●●●●●●●●●●●●

I woke up about 6:30 the next morning to my cell phone ringing. It was Jack.

"I thought you'd want to know that an old blues singer was murdered last night," Jack said. "The medical examiner thinks he died between 5 and 8 last night. And Britt, his body was found near the Indian mound across from the metal museum."

CHAPTER TWENTY-SEVEN

I got dressed and left the house quietly since Logan was still asleep. Besides, I was too shaken by Jack's call to talk to anybody else right now. I just wanted to get to 201 as quickly as possible and find out everything Jack knew. It turned out, that wasn't much.

"They called me at home a little after five and said that they had found a body with a steak knife in the back," he said.

"Who is it?"

"Churnin Rivers is the name he goes by. He probably wasn't born with that name, but the ID on him gave that name, so I guess it's his legal name."

"What kind of ID did he have?"

"A Medicare card was all. We ran the name through the computer and found he'd been in jail, out at the penal farm, released about six months ago. He's got a long record of minor stuff, like public drunkenness, marijuana possession, petty theft, nothing that ever kept him locked up long, no gun crimes."

"How did you find out he's a musician?"

"On all his court paperwork, he lists his profession as musician, so we checked with the musician's union, and they said he's not a member, but he's been playing blues trumpet and singing around town for at least 40 years. Never worked very steadily until that movie maker, what's his name, put the guy in that latest movie of his, the one that was made in Memphis."

"Churnin Rivers was in *Black 'n Blue*?"

"Yeah, that's the one. Anyhow, they say he's been getting all kinds of gigs since the movie came out. Recently, some rich guy flew him to Paris to perform for a birthday party."

"I assume you mean France, since Paris, Tennessee probably doesn't have an airport," I said. Jack smiled for the first time since I had been there, but it was a fleeting smile.

"Do you realize this guy was murdered a hundred yards from where we had our picnic last night, Britt? And probably while we were there or just after."

"Maybe he was killed somewhere else and brought there later and…"

Jack interrupted me. "I wish, Britt, but there were blood splatters where he was found. It happened there."

"The horrible question is, 'Did it happen there because we were there?' Or was it a coincidence?"

"What do you think?"

"It could be a coincidence," I said hopefully, but not very convincingly.

"Homicide detectives don't believe in coincidences, Britt, and we're right 99 percent of the time."

"Is somebody from our paper already working on the story?"

"Yeah, Jonathan has already come by."

"Will you call me if you find out more?"

"Sure, and I need you to take your car over to the police garage. I want them to search it for a GPS or other tracking device.

And write down your parents' phone number in Florida. I'm going to get the cops down there to search that motor home they borrowed for the trip. I should've thought of that sooner. It still wouldn't explain the marshmallows on the sweet potatoes or the singing to the oldies, but it will help us know if the guy is physically following you or not."

•••••••••••••••••

As I was driving away from 201, my cell phone rang. It was Logan, who had just gotten up and heard the news on TV.

"It's already on CNN," he told me. "Are you covering the murder?"

"No, the day cops reporter is doing that, but I'm going to write an in-depth profile on Churnin Rivers. But first I've got to drop my car off at the police garage to be searched for a tracking device. Can you pick me up there and take me to work?"

"Sure, and I can pick you up after work, too. I'm through with exams now, so I've got a lot of free time."

"Good. How would you like to rent *Black 'n Blue* and watch it with me tonight or tomorrow night?"

"Sounds good. I'm glad Jack is getting your car checked for a tracking device. It really creeps me out to think this guy was murdered so close to where you were last night."

"Me, too."

•••••••••••••••••

It wasn't until I was at work an hour later that I wondered how Logan knew I was near the Indian mound last night.

CHAPTER TWENTY-EIGHT

I stayed late at the paper working on my Churnin Rivers profile. I wasn't having much luck. For somebody who'd been playing around Memphis at least sporadically for 40 years, there wasn't much known about the guy, at least at first glance.

I called Lettie, who said she thought of him more as a drunk and dope-head than as a musician. She gave me some names of people who might have known him, but they weren't much help either. One said he never heard of Rivers until he showed up in the movie last year, so I got our movie critic, John, to get me an LA phone number for the writer/director of the film, Brad Billikan , who when I called him said that Churnin showed up for an open casting call in Memphis, reeking of booze, but he had that dissipated, down-on-his-luck-forever look that make-up and good acting just can't duplicate.

"Why try to re-create authenticity when it's sitting in front of you," Billikan said. "The only concern in casting him was that he might be too drunk to come to work or that he might OD before we could start shooting, but he was so perfect for the role, and we were all about keeping it real."

"When you paid him, did he insist on cash or did he have a bank and a home address?" I asked.

"Actually, he did ask for cash, but we told him studio

accounting doesn't work that way. We usually deposit salaries directly into the actor's bank account, but Churnin said he didn't have a bank, so we cut him a check. But we didn't pay him a penny until he had completed the shoot, and we had checked the dailies to be sure we were through with him. That was the only insurance we had that he'd show up. As far as what address he gave, I could check his payroll forms."

"Yes, please. I'd appreciate that. What was he like during the shoot?"

"Well, he was only in two scenes, so we only needed him for a few days, but he was just what we hoped for. Now that the guy's gotten himself murdered, I feel bad to say this, but we didn't want him to clean up his act for the film. We just wanted him to show up the way he normally is, which is high and beat-up looking, and Churnin Rivers did not disappoint."

"Did he get friendly on the set with anybody?"

"Not that I know of. He just showed up, played his trumpet and sang, and said a couple of lines."

"What did he sing?"

"I Feel Like Breakin' Up Somebody's Home."

"Your idea or his?"

"His. He said it was his signature song, so we went with it. It even ended up on the soundtrack."

•••••••••••••••••

Jack called to say my car was ready to be picked up and that they had not found any tracking devices on it. I had been hoping they would find something. Creepy though it would be, it was worse to think of him physically following me.

Logan took me to pick up my car. The whole drive back to his house, I kept looking in my rear-view mirror. Every car that came up behind me I thought was the killer, but then I'd slow down and they would pass me. I wondered if I was going to be paranoid from now until the killer was captured. Probably.

That night, Logan and I ate peanut butter and jelly sandwiches for dinner. He had bought strawberry jam for me during my stay. I was too tired to watch the movie, but he said it was no rush — he'd bought the DVD instead of renting it.

CHAPTER TWENTY-NINE

The next day, I went to the Memphis Musicians Union, which I knew was somewhere near my house in Cooper Young. Before I left Logan's, I did a quick Google search to get the exact address and saw that the union was established in 1873 and is the oldest musicians' union in the country. When I got there, I realized I had passed that little building many times, but never noticed that it was the musicians' union.

A grizzled guy, who said he was a jazz musician and president of the local, told me that this serial killer going after musicians was making everybody nervous, but not keeping them from taking jobs.

"Did you know any of the victims of the serial killer?" I asked.

"I knew all of them, but Saundra was the only one I knew well. We went way back."

"Did you like her?"

"I guess you could say I liked her, but I didn't trust her. Saundra was always taking care of Saundra and nobody else. She would do anything to get ahead."

"What about this latest victim, Churnin Rivers?"

"Nobody much noticed him until he got himself into that

movie. And all of a sudden, he's the hot thing. I can tell you there have been some hard feelings about that. Some of the other guys feel like they've paid their dues, and Churnin was getting jobs they should've had. Not that any of them would kill him or anything," the union president quickly added.

●●●●●●●●●●●●●●●●●●●●●

After I left the union, I went to the address that Brad Billikan's secretary gave me and asked if I could see Mr. Rivers' apartment. It was really just a room in a boarding house on Vance, and the landlady let me in. I knew Jack was going to be mad at me for getting there ahead of the police. I guess they hadn't found an address for him yet.

"I wondered when somebody, the cops or somebody, was going to show up," Myrt Washington said as we walked slowly up two flights of steps. "I've been trying, ever since I heard that Churnin was the killer's latest victim, to work up some tears for him, but I ain't had any luck so far. He was a hard man to feel sorry for — not that I would wish him dead, no Lord, wouldn't wish nobody dead. I guess there's somebody somewhere who loves him or at least hated to see him die."

"What made him so unlovable, Mrs. Washington?"

"Everything, baby, everything you can imagine. He was always drunk and usually smoking pot and probably worse, but I've had other drunks room with me. I don't mind long as they keep to theirselves and don't cause me no trouble. But he was nothing but trouble, nothing but trouble. Getting in fights, keeping his TV too loud, burning food and stinking up the whole house, saying real bad things to the ladies who live here, calling them "ho" and worse. I never heard him say a pleasant word to anybody."

"Why didn't you kick him out if he was so bad?"

"Because he paid me six months rent in advance when he got

paid for that movie — and then kept up his rent every month when he got other music jobs because of the movie making him kind of famous. In that one way, he's the best renter I've got."

Getting up all those steps took a while since Mrs. Washington was overweight and had to stop every few steps to catch her breath. Then when we reached the top, she pulled a cigarette from the pocket of her flowered housecoat and lit up before she unlocked the door of Rivers' room.

The room smelled of body odor, booze and garbage that hadn't been taken out for a while, but it was surprisingly neat. There was a single bed, not made up exactly, but the bedspread had been pulled up over the pillow. I was careful not to touch anything and urged the landlady not to touch anything either until the police did their thing.

On the bedside table was his battered trumpet and an ashtray full of cigarette butts, and a nearly empty bag of marijuana was on the small kitchen table, along with dirty dishes from a meal.

"Did Mr. Rivers do a lot of cooking?"

"I don't know if it was a lot, but he did cook for himself. He told me one time that his wife died when the kids were still pretty young, so he had to learn to cook."

"Did his children or any other family ever come to visit him, or did he talk about them, like he'd seen them or talked to them recently?"

"Nope. As far as I know he didn't have a friend to his name, much less a family who wanted to be around him."

"Did anybody hate him enough to kill him?"

"Probably lots of folks, but I can't name any."

"Mrs. Washington, I appreciate your showing me around, and I want to give you a little something to compensate you for your time." I handed her a $20 bill, which she quickly tucked into her pocket, as if she thought I might ask for it back. "The police will be coming around in the next hour or so, and I'd appreciate it if you didn't mention that I came up here to the room."

"You got it, baby."

●●●●●●●●●●●●●●●●●●●●●

When I got to the car, I called Jack on his cell phone.

"Now, don't get mad, Jack, but I'm doing a profile on the latest victim, and I came around to interview his landlady."

"How did you find her? We haven't found an address for Rivers yet."

"I got it from the director of the movie he was in."

"Damn, why didn't I think of doing that? I'm slipping."

"No, you just have too many victims to juggle at one time."

So I gave Jack the address of the boarding house and told him I made the landlady promise not to touch anything.

"I just interviewed her, Jack. I didn't go up to the room."

"Don't give me that jive, Britt. Of course, you went up to the room. What did you find?"

"Nothing much. Bad smells, a beat-up trumpet, a little dope, but he didn't live in squalor like I had expected. I didn't touch anything. Sorry I lied to you about not going up there. Have you been able to find any next of kin?"

"Zip."

"Well, the landlady's no help either."

"Better go and get over to the boarding house with some crime scene guys. Thanks, Britt, even if you should've called us before, not after, you talked to the landlady and toured the premises."

I hung up and then went back into the boarding house. Mrs. Washington didn't seem surprised to see me return.

"One more question, ma'am. Did Mr. Rivers ever tell you what his name was before he changed it to Churnin Rivers?"

"No, he didn't volunteer it, but one time he got some mail that was addressed to Cleave Kellen or something like that, and I asked him about it, and he said it was his birth name, but Churnin Rivers was a better blues name, had a ring to it like Muddy Waters."

"Was there a return address on the letter? Was it a personal letter or business kind of letter?"

"Must've been personal, because it was written with an ink pen and was from somebody with the same last name. It was from down in Mississippi, some town I never heard of, something with the word coffee in it."

I thanked her and couldn't get out the door fast enough, hoping not to cross paths with the cops. I went to my house instead of to the office. I scooped up two days worth of mail from my mailbox and stuffed it into my tote bag and pulled the World Atlas off the shelf. As much as I depend on the Internet for research, there are times when you can't beat an old fashioned reference book.

I knew I had heard of a town called Hot Coffee, Miss., but my Atlas also listed Coffeeville, population 930. I turned on my computer and searched an Internet directory for Kellen or Killen and various other possible spellings from those two towns and found a Kelling in Coffeeville. When I called, a sweet voiced woman answered and said no, she wasn't related to Cleave Kelling, but his daughter, whose married name was Clara Turnbow, lived down the street. The lady even gave me Clara Turnbow's phone number. I love small towns. Everybody knows everybody and everybody's business.

When I called Clara Turnbow, a child answered the phone.

"Is your mom there?"

"She's at work. Oops, she told me not to tell strangers that I was here alone after school."

"You have a very smart mother, but I won't tell her you slipped up. Just do what she says from now on, okay?"

"Yes, ma'am." A polite child, too. Two points for Clara Turnbow.

"I'll call back later."

"Okay. She'll be home about 4:30."

When I reached her about 4:45, Clara Turnbow was understandably cautious about talking to this stranger, who claimed to be a reporter.

"I guess you're calling about the murder, but I don't know anything. We weren't in contact."

"How did you know your dad was dead?"

"I saw it on TV. If this had happened a few years ago, I wouldn't even have known it was him. Last time I saw him he was still going by his real name, Cleave Kelling. I hadn't seen or heard from him in 20 years — he left for good when I was 17. Then I recognized him in that movie and saw he was going by Churnin Rivers and tracked down an address in Memphis for him."

"How did you do that?"

"Simple. I just called the movie studio in California and told them the truth, that I'm his long lost daughter and I was trying to find him. They gave me the address. I guess the lady who answered the phone in bookkeeping just took pity on me."

"So did you reach your dad?"

"I wrote him a letter, telling him I had seen him in the movie and that I'd like to come up to Memphis to see him, maybe on Father's Day, and bring my husband and kids to meet him."

I heard her voice break as she said it. She stopped to

compose herself.

"He wrote back, one sentence on a postcard that just said, 'You only want to see me because I'm rich now.' That was it, that was all it said. Not, 'I'm sorry I went off and left you and your brothers.' Or 'I'm sorry I killed your mother.'"

Of course I was stunned by that last sentence, but I tried not to react too strongly. I've learned as a reporter that if you act shocked, people usually pull back and stop talking.

"Was he convicted of killing your mother?"

"Of course not — everybody knows it's okay to slap around your wife, especially if you're poor and black, and it's not murder when she falls and hits her head and dies of a brain hemorrhage." Now Clara sounded bitter. Who could blame her?

"How old were you kids when your mother died?"

"I was 15 and my brothers were 13 and 16. My oldest brother tried to kill Daddy when he did what he did to Mama. He broke a chair over him and hit him until my uncle stopped him. Daddy stuck around for a couple of years after Mama died. I guess, out of guilt, he tried to take care of us, but then one day he just left and we never heard another thing from him. Our grandmother took care of us after that. My brothers never forgave him and are probably glad he's dead, and I guess I ought to hate him, too, but he was all we had left and I just wanted to see him, see if maybe he'd changed. See if maybe he had started loving us."

"I feel bad for calling you at this hard time, Mrs. Turnbow. I hope I didn't make things worse for you."

"No, for some reason, it feels better to talk about it."

"I'm going to give your name and number to the Memphis police, because they need a next of kin. Your dad may still be due some money from the royalties on the soundtrack CD, and you might as well have it."

"I don't care about the money. I never did."

"I know that, but if there's a little inheritance, you might as well use it for your family. Take a vacation or start a college fund for your children. Tell them it's a gift from their grandfather."

"I'm glad you called," Clara said softly and then we said our goodbyes. When I hung up the phone, I cried. Not for Cleave Kelling, but for Clara Turnbow, who now would never have a chance to gain her father's approval and love.

CHAPTER THIRTY

I wrote my story about Churnin Rivers, painting a picture of a man living a friendless, empty life while two hours away in Coffeeville, Mississippi, lived his daughter, who wanted to love him despite all the ways he had hurt her.

It was a sad story and I felt down after writing it, even though I thought it was some of my best writing. I sent the story to the metro desk and left for the evening.

As I was about to walk out into the cold, dark December night, I did something very uncharacteristic of me — I asked the security guard to walk me to my car.

Driving home, I again found myself looking constantly into my rear view mirror and suspecting every driver who came near me of being the serial killer. Outside of Logan's house, there was a car that I didn't recognize, but nobody was in it, and it seemed unlikely that the stalker would be so bold as to park in front.

It was a relief to drive into the security of Logan's garage and walk straight into the kitchen. I could hear voices in the living room — Logan's and a woman's voice. I could only catch a few words, "Ben" and "I need to know" and the tone of both voices was very serious.

I didn't know what to do. It sounded like the kind of

conversation I shouldn't interrupt, but if I sat in the kitchen waiting for them to finish, it would look like I was eavesdropping.

The dilemma was solved for me when Logan and a beautiful blonde came through the door into the kitchen. It was Caroline Crawford, Logan's former fiancée, who was now engaged to Ben Spurrier, Logan's best friend since childhood. She didn't seem happy to see me.

"What are you doing here?" she asked coldly.

"I'm, I just got home from work," I said and immediately regretted my choice of words.

"Home?" She turned to Logan in an accusatory way.

Logan said with no defensiveness, "Britt is staying in one of my spare bedrooms until the serial killer is caught. He's been stalking her, so she doesn't need to stay at her house alone at night."

"I see," Caroline said and reached for her coat, which was on a kitchen chair. "You were protective of me once upon a time."

"That's Ben's job now," Logan said very matter-of-factly, but not unkindly.

"I'm sorry I bothered you, Logan."

"Don't be that way, Caroline," Logan said softly. He tried to hug her goodbye, but she pulled away and opened the back door, the one that led to the driveway, not the inside of the garage. He followed her outside to be sure she got safely to her car, but she never turned back nor said anything to him.

When he came back inside, I couldn't stop apologizing for my bad timing and bad choice of words.

"Oh, Logan, I am so, so sorry. I really screwed up big time. I had no idea Caroline was here or I would have stayed at work longer, but…"

Logan put his index finger over my lips to silence me. "It's okay, Britt, it's not your fault."

We both collapsed into kitchen chairs and he sighed.

"That was a very tense scene in there," he said pointing a finger toward the living room. "The doorbell rang and there she was with no warning."

"Is she having second thoughts about marrying Ben?"

"Not exactly, but before they actually set a date, she wanted to know if I still had feelings for her. I asked her to define 'feelings' and she accused me of side-stepping the issue."

"What issue?"

"Whether it is totally over between us or if we should try again."

"Whoa, that's heavy. Poor Ben."

"She said she's not in love with me any more, that she really loves Ben."

"Then why is she asking about a reconciliation with you?"

"She wasn't suggesting a reconciliation — she just wanted to be sure, I guess. I can understand her confusion, you know, with the strange way our relationship ended."

"Do you feel confused, too?"

"I guess you could call it that. I mean, how weird is it? Ben was secretly in love with her and then I stepped in and stole her away without even realizing that's what I was doing, and then he did the same to me when I was gone last year. You got to admit the whole thing is pretty strange."

"No argument there."

"Are you hungry?" Logan said, standing up. "I'm starving. And the cupboard is bare."

"Actually, I could really go for a Huey burger and cheese fries."

"Let's go then," Logan said, "I'll get my coat."

"Are you sure? What if he's out there watching?"

"Then he'll see us going into Huey's and getting our grease quota for the day."

•••••••••••••••••••

As far as we could tell, nobody followed us to Huey's or over to my house to pick up some things, so we were in a good mood when we got back to Logan's house. During dinner, I had told him about the investigation of Churnin Rivers and how I prided myself on sometimes being a step ahead of the cops. We decided to watch *Black 'n Blue* when we got back.

Some big budget films have been shot in Memphis in recent years — *The Firm* and other John Grisham movies and *Cast Away* and *Walk the Line*. *Black 'n Blue* was an independent film that didn't make a lot of money but had done very well at Sundance and gotten mostly great reviews nationwide.

Even though movie making isn't rare in Memphis, people here still flock to the movies to see local scenes and local people in them. As we watched *Black 'n Blue*, we did the same thing. "That's Rum Boogie." "I think that's those old apartments on McLean." "That guy has been in a ton of Theater Memphis productions." That kind of thing.

Then Churnin Rivers' two scenes came on, and we were mesmerized by his screen presence. Like the director had said, Rivers had something that no amount of make-up or good acting could duplicate. And of course, there was the eeriness of looking at a man on screen talking, laughing, singing — knowing he was murdered just two days ago.

Even though I had wanted to see the movie so I could see Churnin Rivers' part, the film was good, so we kept watching. Then suddenly near the end, I grabbed Logan's arm, which was near the remote. Go back. Did you see that?

"See what?"

"Go back to the last scene, the one at the club in Whitehaven."

We watched it again, and Logan this time saw what I had seen.

"Do you really think it's him?" Logan asked.

"I know it is. I've seen enough pictures of him. It's Larry Carpenter, the Elvis impersonator. So two of the serial killer's four victims were in the same movie."

"Maybe it's a coincidence."

"Jack says there are no coincidences when it comes to murder," I said, and then suddenly jumped up while looking at my watch. "Why am I just sitting here? I've got to call the paper. I've got to update my story for tomorrow before it's too late."

CHAPTER THIRTY-ONE

"When are you going to officially join the police force?"

I wasn't surprised that Jack had called — I had been expecting it since my story on Churnin Rivers came out that morning.

"I wasn't trying to make the cops look bad," I said.

"Yes, you were," Jack said without anger. "You love it when you show us up."

"Well, maybe I do, but it's nothing personal. I just like to do my own job well, and my job isn't just to sit around waiting for information to be handed out by the cops."

"But I give you stuff before the other reporters get it. You could at least return the favor."

"Okay, you're right about that one," I said a bit sheepishly. "You know I usually give you a heads up, but I didn't realize they were both in that movie until late last night. I just stumbled on it from watching the movie, and then I had to call the paper real quick and update my story. Speaking of which, you've got to give me credit for finding the next of kin for you and giving you the contact info, and it was before my story came out."

"Your story about the daughter was a real tearjerker." Again,

Jack said this straight, no sarcasm. I've always noticed that about Jack — he'll use the same insensitive words that other cops use, but it's okay, because he says it without sarcasm or perverse pleasure. "When the rest of us start to think we got bad parents," he went on, "all we have to do is read that story and all of a sudden, our dads are parent of the year."

I agreed and we talked about trying to have lunch or dinner soon. Before he hung up, Jack wanted to make one thing clear.

"Your story today, kid, was just good journalism, but I hope I can assume that if you stumble upon anything that's hard evidence, you won't make me read it in the paper."

I knew what he was thinking. "No, I haven't gotten another note, but if I do, you'll be the first to hear about it. I promise. Maybe he's going to use somebody else to communicate with from now on."

"I hope so. Well, talk to you soon, and we'll get something to eat tomorrow or the next day. Chinese sounds good, don't you think?"

"Yeah, great. See you then, Jack."

●●●●●●●●●●●●●●●●●●●●●●

The rest of the day, I worked on the Rivers/Carpenter story, trying to find someone who worked on the film who might know if they ever had any contact with each other during the making of the movie and if there was anybody who got angry with both of them. I came up with nothing. I guess every day can't be as charmed as the day before had been.

I left work before dark, so that I could go by home and check my mail. I still was paranoid about somebody following me, but I was relieved that my mail just contained the usual bills and junk mail. I picked up a few things I needed from the house and headed back to Logan's. He wasn't going to be home that night, so I was just going to eat cereal for dinner and spend the evening reading, but not until I paid my bills, which were overdue.

I cheated, of course. I don't have the self-control to pay bills when there is something fun to do. I love to read mysteries, but I'd sworn off them for a while. My life had been creepier than any mystery I could read, and I didn't want to add to my paranoia. So I looked through Logan's books until I found a Herman Wouk novel I had never read, something about an ad guy pushing soap.

Finally my conscience got the best of me, and I sat down to pay bills, but my Visa bill wasn't among them. I looked among the mail I had brought from home over the last few days and still couldn't find it. Then I remembered that one day I stuck my mail in my tote bag, so I went to my bedroom to retrieve it.

It was there, along with some other mail, which I glanced through, throwing away most of it without even opening. Then I saw the edge of notebook paper sticking out from the pile and my heart went cold. I unfolded the sheet — no way I was going to wait for Crime Scene to get there — and read:

Only sluts shack up with one guy and go on picnics with another guy.

•••••••••••••••••••

When Logan arrived home a couple of hours later, he looked surprised to see me on the sofa, in my terry cloth robe shivering like I was in the Arctic, Jack beside me, his arm around me.

The Crime Scene guy had come and gone and was headed to my house to again check the mailbox and surrounding area for fingerprints. I knew they wouldn't find anything — this guy was too smart. I had stopped pretending to be a feminist about this. The killer was a man, and everybody knew it, despite the lack of hard evidence.

We told Logan what was going on and he sat down in the armchair opposite us on the sofa.

"Maybe the fingerprint guys will get lucky at your house this time," Logan said.

"Don't count on it," I said.

"Well," Jack countered, "actually serial killers tend to get more careless after several kills. They say it's because the killer starts feeling more confident and like he can do anything and not get caught."

As if on cue, Jack's phone rang. He hung up after a brief conversation and smiled.

"See I told you. They got a good print off the mailbox this time. Maybe we'll have a match by tomorrow."

"If the serial killer has been arrested before," I said.

"He has — I can pretty much guarantee it," Jack said. "Very few serial killers go from a completely clean life to suddenly killing four people in two months. There are usually some minor offenses at least — it only takes one to get in the computer forever."

"You've become quite an expert on serial killers," Logan said with apparent admiration.

"Well, I talk fairly often to the profiler in Nashville, Irene Ringold. She's been real helpful."

"Criminal profiling is really a fascinating subject," Logan said.

"Yeah," Jack said, "But I'm trying not to get caught up in it too much. There are definitely patterns when it comes to serial killers, but if you trust that stuff too much, you could overlook the exception that is really the killer in a given case."

"Do you think this is an exception?" Logan asked.

"I don't know, of course, but I just have a gut feeling that all these musicians were killed for a reason and not chosen randomly, but I'll be damned if I know what that reason is. The FBI and TBI can profile all they want to, but I'm investigating all this as if each crime is individual and maybe in trying to find the reason one person was killed, I'll stumble upon a connection with the other victims."

While Jack and Logan chatted, I continued to shiver and was fighting back tears.

"Meanwhile, some psychopathic killer is obsessed with me and now thinks I'm a slut, who he probably thinks needs killing."

"He might like sluts and respect you for being one," Jack said jokingly, and it was obvious he immediately regretted his insensitive attempt at levity. I just stared a hole through him, and Logan looked uncomfortable.

"I'm sorry, kid," Jack said, putting his arm around me again. "That wasn't funny. But it is true that there is no reason to believe this killer would target you out of disapproval of your morals. Since he's one of the few serial killers that isn't a sex killer, he isn't likely to target you for what he perceives as sexual promiscuity."

I thought to myself bitterly that it would be ironic if I got murdered for being a slut when I hadn't had sex with anybody since my 3-week marriage. I was practically a virgin again. But I certainly didn't say that. My sex life wasn't Logan's or Jack's business.

"Well," Jack went on. "There are serial killers who target prostitutes for that reason or because they hate their mothers and so hate all women. But there is no pattern of that here. Only one of the victims has been a woman and none of the victims seems any more promiscuous than the general population. No, I think the music connection is the key to solving this thing."

"Maybe so, but I'm still worried about Britt," Logan said. "I can't stand the thought of some crazy killer stalking her and leaving her personal notes."

"I'm worried about her, too," said Jack. "Real worried. That's why I'm glad Britt is staying here at your house. No way she should be at home alone, and at my place, I'd never be there to protect her."

Oh, how touching, I thought sarcastically. They're competing to see who can show the most concern for me. I couldn't take any more of it, and besides my stomach was growling.

"I need comfort food," I said. "Pirtle's fried chicken and donuts."

Logan and Jack laughed and neither commented on it being almost 10 p.m.

"I'll go out and get the food, since I'm the only one of us who carries a gun," Jack said.

I said I was going to take a hot bath while Jack was gone, and Logan promised to restock the frig with beer and Diet Cokes.

CHAPTER THIRTY-TWO

Jack called me two days later to give me the bad news.

"We got a match on the fingerprint from your mailbox, but it was your mailman, not the serial killer."

"Unless my mailman *is* the killer," I said, sure I had an original idea.

"Don't think we didn't think of that, kid. He would have great access to your house and could leave notes without being noticed and could watch your house without attracting attention, at least during the day."

"But?"

"But he had an alibi, good ones, too, for every killing except one."

"Maybe he just arranged alibis to cover up his crimes." I was sounding more like a TV cop show every minute.

"That's always possible, but if he was going to do that, wouldn't he have gone on ahead and arranged an alibi for all the murders, not just three?"

"I guess so."

"But we did question him about what he might have seen. He said he noticed the note in the box one day. He thinks it was Wednesday morning. It's against postal rules to use the mailbox for hand delivered notes, but he decided not to report it. He said he hates to get people in trouble over something so little."

"I'm sure the serial killer will appreciate that. Did he see anything else?"

"May or may not be significant, but he said he did notice the same car parked down the street from your house two different days, an old land cruiser of some kind — he didn't know what kind, just big and old and rusty. A white guy in his 30s or 40s was sitting in the car. That's all he remembers, but I asked him to come downtown and look at the mug books and at pictures of the various enemies of our victims."

"When is he coming down?"

"He already did. No luck. How are you holding up?"

"I'm fine. I feel sort of silly for falling apart the other night."

"You had every right to fall apart, Britt. Don't be so hard on yourself."

"I think the fried chicken and donuts did wonders for me, but I'll have to lay off grease for a while."

"Are you working on another story about the killings?"

"No, I'm distracting myself with something totally different, a feel-good story. Have you heard about what the Humane Society is doing out at the women's correctional center?"

"What are they doing?"

"Well, they have this program where the inmates can volunteer to train dogs, so the dogs will be more adoptable. They screen the women and choose a few that then spend several months with the dogs, training them, loving them, taking care of all the dogs' needs 24 hours a day. Then when the dogs leave and are adopted, they encourage the new owner to write to the inmates and tell them how the dog is doing. Today they are graduating their first class of dogs, and I'm going out for the ceremony."

"That's nice. I'm sure your story will get people to volunteer to adopt the dogs. Well, kid, have fun and be careful, okay? Watch your back at all times."

"I'm not afraid of the inmates."

"I'm not talking about them. You'll be safer at the prison than anywhere else. I just mean keep an eye on that rear-view mirror, and if anybody is following you, call me on your cell phone. If you can't reach me, call 911 and drive to the closest precinct. Is your cell phone charged up?"

"Yes, Dad."

"Goodbye, smart ass."

●●●●●●●●●●●●●●●●●●

Nobody followed me to the women's prison, at least not that I noticed.

CHAPTER THIRTY-THREE

Of all the gin joints, in all the towns, in all the world, he had to walk into mine. It was a grocery story actually, but you get the picture. I was in such great spirits after putting up the Christmas tree with Logan the night before and enjoying Charlie being around. Charlie is one of the dogs I wrote about at the women's prison, and Logan was so inspired that he went out and adopted Charlie, a black mixed breed with a white chest and white paws. I was in a great mood today, but I had to ruin it by going to the grocery store.

There I was at Fresh Market on Union buying dog food, and I ran into Drew, my ex best friend, who also is my ex-husband, and he was with his wife, Liz, who absolutely doesn't deserve the resentment I feel toward her.

A city of 700,000 people — I live in Midtown, they live in East Memphis. There is a Fresh Market within walking distance of their house, so what are they doing in my grocery store?

We exchanged small talk about the serial killer — how strange that something like that is possible — casual conversation about a killer stalking our city. Then they felt compelled to tell me what had been going on with them and that they were shopping for ingredients to make M 'n M cookies. How dare them? That's the kind of cookies Drew and I had always made at Christmas since we were little kids. She's already got my Drew — she shouldn't be able to take my cookies, too.

I have 25 years of memories of Drew — we've been best friends since we were seven years old — and I felt like his marriage to Liz had robbed me of all of them. Not erased them, of course, but made them painful instead of happy.

Nearly everything about my childhood and adolescence is connected to Drew. We lived on the same street, our parents were friends — so close, in fact, that our families celebrated most holidays together. And the two families sometimes vacationed together at Gulf Shores, Alabama. We'd rent a gigantic old house on stilts right on the beach — their family took the second floor and ours the first, and we shared the kitchen and living room and deck. Underneath, there was room for the cars to park, a picnic table, an outdoor shower for getting the sand off before going inside and a wooden porch-style swing that Drew and I spent hours in. And we liked to sneak down to the beach late at night after everyone else was asleep.

At the beach, as everywhere else, Drew and I had that great combination of long hours of talking, balanced by periods of comfortable silence.

Not only are my memories tied to Drew, but he was important in my becoming who I am. When you have a boy for a best friend, it has an effect on you. If you cut your hair, your girlfriends will tell you it looks cute even if it doesn't. But a boy best friend isn't as willing to lie to spare your feelings. If I got a bad haircut, Drew would say, without any malice, "What did you do that for? It looked a lot better the old way."

I guess my friendship with Drew caused me to always be in touch with my male side, as the pop psych gurus say. That's probably why I have been accused of being blunt by family and friends sometimes. I call it being direct and honest. They also say I'm foolhardy. I call it courageous.

Anyhow, with the family history Drew and I have, you can imagine how thrilled both our families were when we decided impulsively to get married. Nobody seemed concerned that it was so sudden, because, like they said, we had known each other all our lives. The problem was that we weren't in love, and we found out immediately after getting married that we shouldn't have.

But I do love him in that way I always did, and I miss his friendship terribly.

• • • • • • • • • • • • • • • • • • • •

I called Jack when I got back to my car.

"Is there any way you could sneak off for dinner?" I asked him.

"Something's wrong, I can tell. Is it something to do with the killer?"

"No, it has everything to do with Drew. I just saw him at the grocery store with his wife, the lovely Liz."

"Oh, so you're in one of your snarky moods. Dr. Jack better step in and give you the cure."

We both laughed. "Well, dinner would calm the savage beast in me, I think. Italian sounds really good."

"I know just the place. Did you know one of the Grisanti family has opened a new place downtown?" I said no, I didn't. How does a busy homicide cop always seem to know about that latest restaurant openings?

"Yeah, it's called Spindini," he said. "It's on South Main and Jon Felix plays there on Sunday nights."

"Are you sure you can get away?"

"Serial killer or not, I deserve an hour or two off, don't you think? Where are you right now?"

"I'm in the parking lot of Fresh Market on Union."

"Just stay there and I'll pick you up — that'll be a good well-lighted place to leave your car."

•••••••••••••••••••

Spindini was warm and comforting. Jon was playing the great old standards on the piano and Jack was letting me talk.

"Why did they feel compelled to tell me what kind of cookies they were making? It felt like Drew was rubbing my face in the fact that Liz has replaced me. Oh, I know he didn't mean to, but it felt that way, and then when I thought it couldn't get any worse, they tell me they're going to have a baby."

"A baby? Oh, man, that's rough."

"Yeah, Merry Christmas to me."

"Do you still love him, Britt?" This was a loaded question coming from Jack, but I answered honestly with no concern whatsoever for his feelings. Everything is about me when I'm in one of these moods — not a pretty picture.

"I still love him — of course I do. He was my best friend for 25 years and then we got stupid and got married and ruined it all. It's not that I want to be married to him, and I certainly don't want to be the one pregnant, but I do want to be the one who's his friend, and I can never be that again. And their having a baby just seems to make it final."

Jack was being so sympathetic and touchy/feely that I decided to catch him off guard and see if he'd open up about his mysterious former marriage.

"Do you ever have feelings like this when you run into your ex wife?"

"I never run into her. What would you like for dinner? The menu looks good."

"How can you let me run on at the mouth like this, spilling my guts, and you've never told me one thing about your romantic past. What is this hang-up you have about talking about personal things?"

Jack sighed with annoyance. "What do you want to know? Shoot."

"Why don't you ever run into her?"

"She lives in Savannah, Georgia."

"Did y'all live there when you were married?"

"No, she moved there after the divorce?"

"Any kids?"

"No."

"How long were you married?"

"Seven years."

"What's her name?"

"Kim."

"Okay, I give up. I thought you might share your heart with me, open up about your past, but all I get is 20 questions and the shortest possible answers. Just forget it."

"Britt, I've shared my heart with you, as you put it, several times and when I do, I like to talk about my feelings for you, not something I don't feel any more for her. But you don't want to talk about you and me, so don't give me a hard time about not opening up, okay?"

"Sorry, Jack," I said, reaching across the table and putting my hand on his. "Maybe tonight's not a good time for either of us to talk about personal things. Let's just eat and talk about other stuff. I've missed you. Have you missed me?"

But I didn't give him a chance to answer. I just started telling him about Charlie.

CHAPTER THIRTY-FOUR

The Christmas season was getting stranger by the minute. Christmas parades and other public holiday events were being cancelled because of the serial killer fear that had settled over the city. On the other hand, there were holiday events that had never been staged before — like the one conceived by the Beale Street Merchants Association, which was trying desperately to get people to come downtown at night. The plan was for all the clubs on Beale to decorate for Christmas and bring in special acts for the weekend.

Somebody I know in the merchants group told me off the record that the first idea was to call it "A Blues Christmas on Beale," with the obvious double meaning of Elvis's "Blue Christmas" and Beale Street's primary musical product being blues. But after hours of debate, the decision was made that the name might have a different meaning while a serial killer was on the loose, especially with all the victims being musicians.

So, the event was simply called "A Beale Street Christmas" — not clever, but safe. And everything was about safe at the moment.

The police department had promised extra walking, bike and mounted police patrols for the weekend event, but there was another debate about how to let the public know about the safety measures without sending a message that Beale Street was unsafe now. Hearing all of that made me glad once again that I chose newspaper journalism instead of public relations.

There were jokes about the event around our newsroom, reporters being the best at gallows humor.

One reporter suggested that the press release about the event could include the promise that none of the restaurants on Beale would provide knives for those who ordered steaks. Somebody else suggested they call it, "A Bloody Beale Street Christmas." Another said the press release could say that if the musicians were willing to risk their lives to come to work, the least the public could do was come down to support them.

Jack and I decided that we'd go to the event on Friday night together — I'd do a story on it, and he would tell his commander that he was going as part of the investigation. I've always been pretty brave in my work, but these notes from the serial killer about me personally had made me a bit fearful. I liked the idea of having Jack as my personal armed bodyguard.

We started at the west end of the street and made our first stop at Blues City Café, where we ate hot tamales and listened to the Demseys, a high-energy rockabilly act that is a favorite with Memphis audiences, but since they can be seen at suburban venues as well, the audience was sparse. Then we went across the street to B.B. King's, which had a national blues act and a pretty good crowd.

I interviewed some people at both places — musicians and audience members, none of whom admitted to any fear in being on Beale Street.

We wandered down the street, stopping in at King's Palace and then on to Rum Boogie, where we took a back table and watched the crowd. We had gotten there during the band's break.

Jack and I spotted them at the same time on the other side of the room.

"There's Lettie Nolan — she must be playing here tonight," I said.

"It's interesting that she's talking to Slick Taggart," Jack said.

"That's the guy who claimed Saundra Barkley stole his song?"

161

"The very one."

"I'm surprised that Lettie is talking so friendly with a creepy old guy like Slick Taggart," I said. "Oh, my gosh, she just hugged him."

"I'm not surprised by anything any more," Jack said.

About that time, the band started back for the bandstand, and Slick Taggart started walking out of the club. We caught up with him just outside where he had stopped to light a cigarette.

"What's shakin', Slick?" Jack said as we came up behind Taggart, who turned around smiling until he saw it was Jack.

"You one of the cops they got protecting Beale this weekend?"

"Nah, I'm just here like any other music lover."

"Who's the pretty lady with you?" he said, smiling at me with teeth apparently untouched by dentistry or even a toothbrush, for that matter.

"I'm Britt Faire. I'm here writing a story for the newspaper."

Jack gave me a frown that said I was telling Taggart too much about myself.

"I know you," Taggart said, suddenly making the connection. "You're the reporter that the serial killer keeps writing to. I heard about it on TV."

"I'm the one," I said more calmly than I felt.

"I couldn't help but notice," Jack said, "that you were talking to Lettie Nolan during the band's break just now. Are you two friends?"

"Hell yeah we are. I've known Lettie for 25 or 30 years, since we were both young and starting out in the music business. She ain't a suspect in the murders, is she?"

"Everybody is a suspect until we find the killer," Jack said, "including you."

"Aw, now, detective, you don't really think me or Lettie would do something like that, do you? I mean, Saundra did me wrong, stealing my song and all, but it ain't worth killing over. And I know Lettie was a home wrecker and there was no love lost between her and Saundra, but Lettie wouldn't hurt a flea."

"A home wrecker?"

"I thought everybody knew that Saundra divorced her husband because he was getting it on with Lettie Nolan."

I was too stunned to speak.

"Are you sure, Slick?" Jack asked.

"Ask anybody who was around then, they'll tell you."

"When was that?"

"About 10 years ago. Nobody blamed Dewitt — he was a trumpet player around town, not too successful, and Saundra never let him hear the end of it. Always telling him and everybody else how she'd had a Billboard number one hit and recorded with Marvin Gay, and Dewitt couldn't hardly pay the rent with what he brought in. He worked at a factory job during the day. Lettie's real sweet and I think it just started off with her listening to him and sympathizing with him about being married to Saundra, and I guess things just went from there. Saundra hated Lettie for it and did her best to discourage club managers from hiring Lettie, but Lettie was good and it was kind of a novelty to have a woman bass player, so she got work anyhow. "

"What happened after the divorce?" I asked. "Did Dewitt and Lettie stay together?"

"Nah. Word was that he wanted to marry Lettie — he really loved that girl — but she broke it off, said she couldn't live with herself if she broke up somebody's marriage and then just married him and acted like she done nothing wrong. I told her everybody else does it, why shouldn't you, but she wouldn't have none of it. Hey, detective, can I bum a cigarette off you?"

"I don't smoke," Jack said and Slick looked toward me silently asking me the same question.

"Me either," I said scrambling in my purse for a few dollars. "But here, buy yourself a pack. Thanks for the information, Mr. Taggart."

"Hey, thanks, little lady. Well, I got to go. Some guys are waiting for me down the street."

As he walked away, Jack frowned at me.

"What's with all that Mr. Taggart stuff and thanking him for the information and buying him cigarettes? That's not the way you talk to a suspect."

"I'm not a cop, in case you've forgotten. I think you can attract more flies with honey than with vinegar."

"I've heard that old saying," said Jack, "but one thing I could never understand — why would you *want* to attract flies?"

CHAPTER THIRTY-FIVE

As Jack drove me back to Logan's, we talked about what we had learned from Slick Taggart, not failing to remind ourselves that somebody like Taggart isn't always a reliable source.

"Losers like him have always got to act like they're in the know," Jack said. "It makes them feel important. You can't believe them half the time."

"Still…" I said.

"Still, he could be telling the truth this time."

"Not that it makes Lettie guilty of murdering Saundra," I cautioned. "Even if it's all true, it happened 10 years ago. Why would Lettie suddenly decide to get revenge after all this time. Besides, Saundra had more reason to get revenge on Lettie than the other way around."

"That's true, but I've still got to go to her and ask about it. And also look into whether she had any connections with the other victims."

"Jack, you don't really think a woman is the serial killer, do you?"

"Why not? Lettie is tall and strongly built. She lifts that bass case and lugs it around everywhere, so she's probably got good strong arms. And who better to be able to walk up to one of the victims than a woman musician they know. There was no sign of a struggle with any of the victims, just a well-placed steak knife in the back. And she performs in restaurants and could easily slip some of the steak knives into her bass case."

•••••••••••••••

After Jack took me home — I mean, took me to Logan's — Lettie was all I could think of. I liked her so much. I couldn't stand to think of her as a murderer. But they say sociopaths can be quite charming. Jack had offered to let me go with him to interview Lettie again, but I declined. Her personal life was really not my business, and by going with a cop, it would seem I was accusing her, too.

Still I couldn't ignore that she was in the motor home with us on Thanksgiving. Perhaps I could imagine her hating Saundra enough to kill her, but all those other people, too? And what about those notes to me? I couldn't imagine Lettie writing those personal notes, like the one calling me a slut.

Lettie was not the serial killer, I was sure of that, and I was also sure I couldn't insult her by questioning her about the affair with Dewitt Starks. But I also needed to know if Slick was telling the truth, so I decided to go see Dewitt.

•••••••••••••••

I tracked him down through the musician's union, and he agreed to meet me for coffee at CK's.

He was on his second or third cup of coffee, judging from the torn sugar packets and empty cream containers on the table, and he was reading the newspaper when I arrived. I had seen a picture of him that was in the newspaper's morgue, which is called a library nowadays. He was handsome when the picture was taken 15 years before, and he was still nice looking, despite some middle-aged weight gain and needing a haircut, but his face was sad.

"Mr. Starks?" He looked up when I said his name and smiled politely, almost shyly.

"Sit down, Miss Faire, and tell me what I can do for you."

"Mr. Starks…"

"Call me Dewitt."

"Dewitt, Friday night I met a man named Slick Taggart, who told me that you had an affair with Lettie Nolan that broke up your marriage to Saundra Barkley. Is that true?"

"I don't know why Slick wants to go around digging up old dirt, but yeah, it's true, but it happened 10 years ago. What difference does it make now?"

"Well, it could cast some suspicion on Lettie in Saundra's murder."

That sent Dewitt Starks into orbit. He banged his fist on the table.

"So even in death, Saundra is still hurting me and Lettie. She always wins, that bitch! I loved Saundra when I married her, but the love dried up pretty quick as she just kept putting me down and just generally making my life a living hell. But I believed in commitment, so I stuck it out. I thought I could live without love, that I wasn't capable of loving anybody ever again anyhow.

"But then I met Lettie. She and I were playing a gig together and during breaks and after closing, she and I talked about everything. We were booked for several weekends, so we really got to know each other. What can I say, we fell in love. I didn't mean for it to happen and she sure didn't, but it got physical and eventually Saundra caught us. She didn't want me — we hadn't had sex for almost five years — but she was determined to punish me and Lettie.

167

She divorced me and did everything in her power to keep Lettie from getting work. But Saundra had less influence than she thought, so Lettie wasn't hurt much by Saundra's war on her, and Saundra did me a big favor by divorcing me."

"Did you and Lettie consider getting married?"

"I did. I loved Lettie. I still do. But she'd have none of it. She said she was a home wrecker, and she would always feel guilty if we got married. She said we didn't deserve happiness together after what we did. I tried everything to talk her into marrying me, but she wouldn't even see me or take my calls."

"Have you remarried?"

"I did about a year after all that happened. Big mistake. It was just a rebound thing. I feel bad about hurting her and she divorced me. Who could blame her? The marriage only lasted a year, and I've been on my own ever since. If I can't have Lettie, I don't want anybody."

"And you've never tried again to talk her into marrying you?"

"A few months ago, late September, I used her birthday as an excuse to call her and ask if I could take her out for a birthday dinner."

"Did she go?"

"She seemed reluctant, but she said yes. I've never been so excited and nervous about a dinner in my life. I was like a teenaged boy going on his first date. I took her to Café Society for dinner and then we went to her house and sat on the front porch swing. I told her I still loved her and that there would never be anybody else for me. I asked her to give me another chance."

"What happened then?"

"We kissed and held each other tight, and she told me she still loved me, too. I thought all my dreams had come true, but then she suddenly pulled away from me and stood up. 'It's too late, Dewitt,' she said while she was crying. 'It's just too late.' And she ran inside her house, and she hasn't answered my calls since. Damn caller ID."

"That's so sad, Dewitt. With so many people looking for the right person, and here are two people who found each other and now, well, now you're both alone. Did she tell you why it's too late?"

"Nope. I guess I'll never know. But I'll always think it was something Saundra did or said to Lettie. It would be so like Saundra to try to make sure I was never happy again."

•••••••••••••••

I left him at the coffee shop and drove back to the office. Why did Lettie say it was too late? Is it ever too late if both people still love each other and they're both single? I wasn't going to write a story about this — Dewitt would only agree to talk to me off the record, which was good — he gave me a perfect excuse not to drag Lettie and Dewitt's tragic love affair out in the open again.

But I did call Jack. The police needed to know that Dewitt Starks had another, more recent, motive for killing Saundra Barkley.

CHAPTER THIRTY-SIX

I knew there was a serial killer stalking Memphis musicians, but I couldn't get my mind off the first victim, Saundra Barkley and the suspects in her death before we knew there would be three other victims. Four actually, but I didn't know that yet.

Partially, I was obsessed with the first murder because I was hoping to find something to prove Lettie's innocence and now that I had heard Dewitt Stark's story, I was hoping he was innocent, too.

But it wasn't just that. Somehow it just seemed to me that the first murder might be most significant simply because it was the first. If the four victims were chosen for a reason, not just random musicians, then maybe there was a reason that Saundra Barkley was first.

I decided to talk again to Stewart Linton, the former Stax Records producer, who thought he lost his job because of her. I called him and asked if we could get together for coffee. He said he'd meet me at Java Cabana in Cooper Young.

I got there first, and the place wasn't crowded, so he was easy to spot when he walked in. For one thing, he was older than anybody else in the room, and he looked the way he sounded on the phone — intense and humorless. He had thinning brown and gray hair and round wire-rimmed glasses and wore a tweed jacket over a Stax T-shirt and jeans. A cool look ruined by his frown and cold light-blue eyes.

I started with small talk. What had he been doing since leaving Stax in the 60s?

"I was in LA for 30 years, doing studio work of various kinds, but I felt a pull back to Memphis, so here I am. My mother left me some money, so working is optional now, but I do some volunteer work down at the Stax museum and the school there. I'm sure you're not interested in my personal life. Why did you want to see me?"

"When you were at Stax, did you ever know anybody named Slick Taggart?"

"Of course, everybody knew crazy old Slick. Always hanging around trying to push his songs, which weren't any good, and claiming that his best song was "Baby Gotta Leave," which he said he gave to the Charlettes before the plane crash. Then he says Saundra Barkley claimed to have written it herself and had a huge hit with it. Went to number one on the R & B charts."

"Any truth to his claims?"

"I have no idea and don't care. Saundra and Slick were two of a kind — both always trying to work a deal in their favor, classic opportunists. Neither of them ever wrote a good song before or after "Baby Gotta Leave," so maybe neither of them wrote it. I don't know."

"Do you know a musician named Lettie Nolan?"

"Met her once at the Stax school. She came out to play the bass for the kids. Don't really know her, though."

"Did you ever hear any gossip about Lettie and Dewitt Starks?"

"I don't listen to gossip, Miss Faire, and you shouldn't either."

"Actually, Mr. Linton, I have found that gossip followed up on and substantiated can sometimes lead to important news stories."

"Good for you," he said bitterly. "If there's nothing else you need from me, I'll be going."

"Actually, I have one more question. Did you by any chance know any of the other victims of the serial killer?"

"If you're implying that I might be involved in…"

"No, not at all. I'm just asking because I know you are very involved in the music scene here in Memphis and elsewhere. Thought you might have some insight."

"Well, I knew three of the victims, and had connections to the other. I never met Mutha Boy, but he recorded his CD at the studio where I last worked in LA."

"Did you hear anything about Mutha Boy from the producers or others who worked with him?"

"Just that he was like most young rappers — arrogant and full of himself, but not a bad kid overall and easier to work with than the veteran hip hop artists."

"How did you know the other two victims, besides Saundra Barkley, of course?"

"Larry Carpenter and Churnin' Rivers were always hanging out at Stax and the other studios in town, hoping for a break. That was before Carpenter became Elvis's imaginary best friend and made a killing on the myth. Rivers — who was still called by his real name, Cleave Kelling, when I first knew him — had some real talent, unlike Carpenter. Cleave had a gift with the guitar and could sing the blues like few others, but his best friends, Jack Daniels and Mary Jane, made him stupid and lazy. It's disgusting to see somebody squander a real talent like that."

There was no pity for Cleave Kelling in Linton's voice. It sounded more like hate.

I knew my luck was running out with Stewart Linton, so I thanked him and reached out to shake his hand. He didn't offer his hand. Instead he turned and walked out, leaving me with the check, which was okay. If I could buy cigarettes for Slick, I could pick up the check for coffee for Stewart Linton.

My first thought as I watched Linton stride out the door to his beat-up old Mercury was that he was the rudest man I had ever met. My thought as I watched him drive away was that I had just spent time with a bitter, angry man, whom I hoped never to see again.

CHAPTER THIRTY-SEVEN

The next day I had trouble shaking off the gloom that Stewart Linton had left me with at Java Cabana. He didn't say it, but it was almost like he was implying that Saundra, Cleave and Larry all deserved what happened to them.

An attorney friend of mine once told me that juries in murder cases are more swayed by the character or lack of it of the victim than by the evidence for or against the defendant. In other words, did the victim deserve to die? I don't want to believe that's true, but certainly a lot of high-profile cases seem to support the idea.

But it was Saturday and I wanted to forget the serial killer for just a little while. I went to my favorite bookstore and had lunch and then browsed among the books, looking for maybe a Christmas book or something funny to distract me. Also it hit me that I needed to do some Christmas shopping.

I found the latest compilation of the satirical newspaper, *The Onion*, and bought one for myself and several for gifts. *The Onion* can always make me laugh.

Then I went to the music section of the store to look for a new Christmas CD. I love Christmas and nothing is too cornball for me at this time of year.

After picking out a Barry Manilow Christmas album — it's really good, I don't care what you say — I noticed a display labeled "Local Interest" and saw the soundtrack of *Black 'n Blue*, which I had been meaning to buy, so I did.

Driving back to Harbor Town down Poplar, I listened to the soundtrack, liking some songs and fast forwarding through others. At one traffic light, I looked at the liner notes to see who had written the songs and caught one name just as the light turned green.

I pulled into a parking lot to be sure I had read it right. Yeah, one of the songs was co-written by a Memphis rapper Donté Washington, better known as Mutha Boy.

I called Jack on my cell phone to tell him that three of the victims were connected to the movie. He said he would call the film's producer and director and talk to them about it and ask if there was any Saundra Barkley connection as well.

After that call ended and before I could drive out of the parking lot, my phone rang. It was Logan.

"My mother just called," said Logan, "to tell me that Lettie's house was broken into last night."

"Did she just come in from work and find it?"

"That's the worst part — it happened while she was there asleep. She never heard a thing, but when she woke up this morning, her house was trashed. She hasn't been able to find anything missing so far, but drawers were emptied and things pulled out of cabinets, and there was vandalism like slicing open cushions and pillows. Whoever it was even came upstairs. I can't believe none of that woke her up."

"It was probably some junkie looking for hidden money," I said.

"Then why did they open her purse, which was downstairs, and pull things out but not take the money or credit cards in it? I'm on my way over there now."

"I'll be there in 10 minutes," I said.

So much for having an uneventful Saturday of reading, listening to music and Christmas shopping.

CHAPTER THIRTY-EIGHT

When I got to Lettie's, the police had come and gone, and Logan and Maggie were standing in the living room with Lettie — the Magees looking helpful and Lettie looking angry.

"Lettie," I said as soon as I was through the front door, "I'm so sorry. You must feel violated having your things destroyed and gone through."

"I don't feel violated," she said emphatically. "I just feel pissed."

She seemed on the verge of saying something much stronger than that, but after a quick glance at Maggie, Lettie just looked around at the mess and shook her head angrily.

Not that Maggie would ever show disapproval of what Lettie or anybody else said. Maggie Magee is a very tolerant and easy-going person — I've never heard her criticize anyone personally. It's just that she is so ladylike — that's one of my mother's favorite compliments, but it fits Maggie. She always has her hair done and her make-up on, always dresses in a neat, feminine way and never uses crude language, much less profanity. So you just naturally want to be on your best behavior around Maggie.

"Lettie, do you have any idea who would do something like this?" I asked.

"No, but I wish I did know. You would not want to be around when I got a hold of him, or them."

"It's probably just a random act of vandalism," Logan said and Maggie agreed.

"Maybe," Lettie said, "or maybe it's somebody who wants to let me know they can get in my house and mess with my stuff even when I'm upstairs asleep. If they're trying to intimidate me, it ain't working."

We offered to help Lettie clean up the mess, but she said she'd rather do it herself, so we left. I started down the front steps from the porch when I remembered something, so I went back inside.

"Lettie, I hate to bother you with this right now, but it's kind of important. Do you know anybody who used to work at Stax Records who still lives in town?"

"There are several still alive and still in Memphis, but if you're looking for somebody to interview, I'd suggest Jake Sikes. He played guitar back-up on a lot of the Stax recordings and wrote a few songs, too, one that Sam & Dave did, though most of their stuff was written by Isaac Hayes and David Porter."

"Do you know how to reach him?"

"He might be in the phone book."

•••••••••••••••

And he *was* in the phone book. When am I going to learn that most people are in the phone book, even some pretty well-known people, unless they no longer have a landline.

As much as I didn't want to think about that creep Stewart Linton, I just felt like I wanted to know more about him and about Stax. I called Jake Sikes as soon as I left Lettie's, and he said he'd be glad to talk to me. He told me to come to his house at 10 the next morning.

Sikes lived in a neat, pretty little house on Alexander Street near the University of Memphis. His wife invited me in and offered me coffee, which I accepted. The three of us sat near the fireplace, Jake and Louise on the sofa and me in a cushiony armchair. Louise didn't offer to leave Jake and me alone to talk, but that was fine.

"Can you tell me about what it was like to work at Stax?"

Jake and Louise looked at each other and smiled wistfully.

"It was heaven on earth for a while," Jake said.

"You know Dr. King's speech about having a dream?" Louise said. "Well, we had that at Stax in the sixties."

"Did you work there, too?" I asked.

"That's how Jake and I met. I worked with Estelle in the record store up front. He was back in the studio."

"Estelle?"

"Estelle Axton, who founded the studio with her brother, Jim Stewart," Jake said. "They were both white and planning to do country western records, but it turned into something else, Soulsville U.S.A."

"You know, back then, Memphis and everywhere else was segregated, but at Stax it was always a mixture, and nobody paid any attention to race," Louise said.

"Stax's first hit group, Booker T. & the MGs was two black guys and two white guys," Jake said. "The Memphis Horns — they played on an unbelievable number of records over the years and not just at Stax — one of them, Wayne Jackson, was white and Andrew Love was black."

"Around the studio it was pretty much half and half black and white, but most of the hit makers were black, of course, like Rufus and Carla Thomas and Eddie Floyd and Wilson Pickett and Otis Redding," Louise said.

"And don't forget Sam & Dave and Isaac Hayes and the Staple Singers," Jake added.

"And The Charlettes and Saundra Barkley," I said.

Louise frowned and Jake shrugged his shoulders.

"The Charlettes only had one hit record before the plane crash, so they kind of get lost in the history of Stax," Jake said.

"They were sweet girls, especially the lead singer, Charlotte White," Louise said. "They were just starting to enjoy a little success, and then it was over."

"Too bad Charlotte didn't get food poisoning and miss the flight instead of Saundra," Jake said.

"Jake, shame on you," Louise said.

"I just meant if somebody had to die, I'm sorry it was Charlotte and Brenda and Evelyn."

"But Saundra wrote *Baby Gotta Leave,* and it was a big hit for her and Stax," I said.

"Yeah," said Jake, "that was a good song, I got to give her credit for that, but I guess she was a one-hit-wonder as a songwriter. Some people just have one good song in 'em."

"Do you have any idea who would want Saundra Barkley dead?"

"Everybody and nobody," Jake said. "I mean nobody I know likes her or ever did, but then again I never knew anybody to hate her enough to kill her either. They must've had to hire people to fill out the crowd at her funeral."

"Jake!" Again Louise was half shocked, half amused at her

179

husband's bluntness.

"Did you ever know a guy named Stewart Linton at Stax?" I asked.

"Sure, we all knew Stew," Jake said. Louise grimaced.

"What a nasty man," she said.

"That was my impression when I met him," I said.

"Now, I can see why you'd say that, but neither one of you knew Stew in the early days. He wasn't a bad guy then."

"Was he a musician?"

"He played a little guitar and piano, but mostly he just had an ear. He's the only producer I ever knew who wasn't much of a musician, but just had that ear, that magic touch. And in the early years, before you started working there, Lou, Stew was a pretty nice guy. Not real friendly maybe, not a jokester, but had a great dry wit and would give you the shirt off his back. A pretty good guy, all around."

"Well, I've heard you say that before, but I find it hard to believe," Louise said. "I never heard a pleasant word come out of the man's mouth."

"What happened to change him?" I asked.

"Well, I'm not sure, but it was pretty sudden."

"Did it have something to do with Saundra leaving and going to Motown?"

"Well, he wasn't happy with her, nobody was, but that's not when he changed. It was not long before the plane crash, the one in '67 when we lost Otis and the Bar-Kays. If Stew had changed after that, it would be more understandable. That nearly killed us all. Otis brought so much life and creative energy to the place. He was incredible and everybody loved him. No, it was before that. I think that was why it was so noticeable, the change in him, because everybody was riding high during that time. Before the crash, Otis was our biggest single star, but Sam & Dave were turning out hits like "Soul Man" and "Hold On, I'm Coming." The Stax Revue toured Europe with incredible response, and Otis stole the Monterey Pop Festival — everybody at Stax was so optimistic. Except Stew. Around that time, he turned bitter and became a total loner almost overnight. He went from being an okay guy and a great producer to being the man you met, Miss Faire. We never knew what happened, and he wouldn't talk to anybody about it."

"Were there any theories?"

"Sure. Some thought it was a woman, that somebody had broken his heart so bad that it made him never trust anybody again. That seemed like romantic hooey to me. I'd be more inclined to say it had something to do with work."

"Could he have been jealous of the success of the others?"

"Nah, when you work for a record label, everybody knows only a few can get the fame, but as long as you're appreciated for your work and getting a bigger paycheck, you're happy for the others' success. Besides, none of our hit makers were SOBs during that time. We really were like a family, and Stew was part of that family until he decided to be the red-headed stepchild."

CHAPTER THIRTY-NINE

Jack called the day after I talked to Jake and Louise, but before I could tell him what they said, he started asking me a question in an uncharacteristically halting way.

"Hey, Britt, would you, well, how would you feel…" He paused making me feel he was about to propose something momentous. "Hey, you want to help me decorate my Christmas tree tonight?"

"Somehow I never imagined that you'd be somebody who puts up a Christmas tree."

"What do you think I am, Scrooge or something?" he sounded genuinely indignant.

"No, no, I didn't mean it that way. It's just that you seem so busy and since your family doesn't live here, I just assumed you didn't do stuff like that."

"Just shows you don't know me as well as you think."

"I'd love to help you with your tree, Jack. Name the time. Are you feeding me, too?"

"All the pizza you can eat, kiddo. I'll pick you up after work, about 7 or 7:30. I'm leaving early tonight, regardless of who decides to take a steak knife in the back. I'm tired of having no life."

I offered to drive my own car, so he didn't have to drive me home later, but he said he'd feel better if my car stayed inside Logan's garage, and he would rather I didn't drive home that late at night.

A few hours later he picked me up at Logan's, and we got a pizza before we went to his apartment in an older complex at Poplar and Highland. We sat on the sofa and put the pizza on his coffee table.

"While we eat, let's watch some of a Christmas movie."

"Okay," I said, trying not to sound surprised that he liked Christmas movies. "Which one did you rent?"

He went to a cabinet next to the TV, a big flat-screened model like men living alone or with other men always seem to have. He pulled out four DVDs and handed them to me. He had *Christmas in Connecticut, White Christmas, Miracle on 34th Street* and *A Christmas Story.*

"Why did you rent so many?"

"I didn't rent them. I own them. I have even more on VHS. I love these old Christmas movies. I watch them all every year, but I haven't watched any this year, because of, well, you know why."

"What's your favorite?"

"I think *A Christmas Story.* It reminds me of when I was a kid."

"I can't stand that mean old father in the movie," I said.

"I was afraid of that. I've never met a woman yet who likes that movie, but guys always like it."

"So what's your second favorite?"

"Let's watch *Christmas in Connecticut.* It reminds me of you, since Elizabeth Lane is a journalist."

"Not an ethical one, but I can overlook that because I love that movie. The sailor is cute, and I love Uncle Felix."

"It's a catastrophe!" Jack said, mispronouncing it the way Uncle Felix did.

So we watched the first hour of the movie and ate and then talked about our memories of Christmas as children.

"My dad was the stereotypical military father, who wanted everything in order and by the book, but he became a total kid at Christmas," Jack said. "We went all out in my family during the holidays. It was one time that the rules were relaxed. Mom and Dad would always take us to some live Christmas production like *A Christmas Carol* or *The Nutcracker* or at least to the latest Christmas movie some time during the holidays. We always had a big tree and Santa Claus was really generous to all of us. I have a lot of happy memories of Christmas."

"My mom and dad would bring me and my two sisters up to Memphis from our hometown in North Mississippi to see the Enchanted Forest at Goldsmith's downtown every year. I was just a little kid, but my older sisters remember it more vividly."

"You mean there used to be a Goldsmith's downtown?"

"Oh, yes, it was the original location, and I loved it. It wasn't as spacious and sparkly as the suburban stores, but it felt so good. The main entrance was on the Main Street side, but there was a smaller entrance on Front Street, which I loved for some reason. I was so sad when they closed downtown Goldsmith's in the 90s.

"Well, I guess we can watch the rest of the movie after we decorate the tree," Jack said.

"Where is it, by the way? Don't tell me you have an artificial one boxed up in the closet."

"Never, but I don't have a cut one either. You're looking at my Christmas tree."

He pointed to a potted evergreen in the corner of the living room.

"I just decorate that. That box on the dining room table has the lights and decorations."

The tree was only about three feet tall and not very thick, so it only took one string of lights and a handful of ornaments to decorate it. We were finished in 10 minutes.

"Leave it to you to have Christmas lights shaped like little chili peppers," I said, laughing and poking him in the stomach.

"Okay, the tree's done, so we can watch the rest of the movie," he said like a kid turning on cartoons on Saturday morning.

As we watched, Jack put his arm around me and I cuddled next to him, but that was as far as it went. I appreciated his respecting my request to back off of romance (not that there had ever been more than a few kisses between us) for a while and at the same time, I kind of wished he'd disregard my request.

After the movie, Jack drove me back to Logan's and hugged me at the door.

"I hope I didn't keep you out past curfew," he said with mild sarcasm. "If I did, Logan may be waiting up for you and decide to ground you."

I poked him in the ribs again and gave him a kiss on the cheek before going inside, where Charlie was waiting at the door for me, wagging not just his tail but his whole body. Logan had tied a red ribbon and a Christmas bell around Charlie's neck.

With only an unspoken pledge by both of us not to mention the serial killer at all, Jack and I had managed to put aside death and fear for one night and just enjoy Christmas.

CHAPTER FORTY

The only problem with a lovely night like the Christmas movie night at Jack's apartment and the fun evening with Logan and Charlie, decorating Logan's tree, is that those nights were so normal, so like Christmas ought to be, and reminded us just how abnormal this Christmas season was.

I love Christmas so much — not that I'm one of those people who starts shopping in July and puts up the Christmas tree the day after Thanksgiving. No, I confine my Christmas celebration to the month of December. The first couple of days of the month, I let myself break out the Christmas music, but I just dole out a little of it for a while, so I won't be burned out on holiday music by the time the real day comes along.

I do a little shopping early in the month, but mostly I look for any opportunity to entertain or celebrate with friends and family. Since I'm not much of a cook, I don't give parties in the traditional sense of the word, but I organize holiday get-togethers. Like saying to one friend, "You've got such a nice, big house, why don't we have a party there a week or two before Christmas. Everybody can bring something, so nobody has to do all the cooking." Or to a group of my closest friends, "Let's go out somewhere special for dinner and then ride around and look at Christmas lights." I act more as cruise director than hostess, I guess.

But none of that this year. I wasn't even planning to go to my parents' house in Florida for Christmas unless this serial killer had been caught by then.

Not that I felt the most sympathy for people like Jack and me. Reporters and cops, and I would assume doctors, get used to compartmentalizing, so that we almost forget what should be happening at any given moment and just concentrate on the problem at hand. But at Christmas, it's hard not to feel sorry for yourself when you're working overtime and wondering when the next person will die.

But I mostly felt sorry for the city as a whole, for the ordinary folks who aren't cops or reporters or musicians. When the word "serial killer" first started creeping into our minds, there was an air of morbid excitement in the city — it was all anybody could talk about. Everyone felt like they were living in a movie or TV show. It didn't seem real. This couldn't really happen here, not to us. Pretty quickly the excitement turned to active fear, and then more to a dull sadness and dread, more than anything else.

By two weeks before Christmas, most people in the Memphis area had long since had their self-protection plans in place (We'd always walk to our cars in groups after work; we wouldn't go out after dark unless we absolutely had to; and we'd get a big dog or a new alarm system or a taller fence at home).

Part of the sadness was that this killer was isolating people, making them stay inside their homes and lock the doors at times when they normally would have been at home with friends or going out for reasons ordinary and special. Holiday parades and performances were mostly cancelled, and merchants struggled to stay in business by promising extra security guards and better lighting. I would love to see statistics on how much online shopping was done that Christmas by Memphians. Nobody I knew was having a party or even just casually having friends over.

Instead we were all just huddled inside our homes or workplaces with a siege mentality — I was no braver than the rest with my encampment at Fort Logan. Everyone was waiting for it to be over. But would it ever be over? Most people I know, outside of the news media or police department, would talk and act as if this was just temporary, that the cops would catch the killer soon and we would all go back to normal, maybe even before Christmas. The attitude reminded me of what the English thought during the first six months of World War I — "Home by Christmas," they'd said, not knowing that four of the bloodiest years in their history were ahead.

But some of us had the courage to face the truth: that this might never be over. Some serial killers are never caught and others continue killing for 20 or more years before they are caught. If the killer wasn't caught soon, I wondered, would we all just stay locked in our houses in fear for years, avoiding any activity that made us feel vulnerable? Can you indefinitely cancel normal living like you cancel a parade or a *Nutcracker* performance?

More alarming perhaps, if the killer weren't caught soon, would we become blasé about yet one more death of a human being, one of our fellow Memphians? I hated most of all the thought that we might all become casual about murder.

"Did you hear that another musician was stabbed last night?"

"That's too bad. What movie should we see tonight?"

As for me, I was caught up in all those scenarios. At work, I was shockingly unemotional about the serial killings. I laughed when cops or other reporters made serial-killer jokes. I discussed the murders and the investigation with clinical cool. Back at Logan's, I was a little bit more of a human being, but I found myself lying in bed every night, trying to put the pieces of the puzzle together until I finally fell asleep mentally exhausted.

But then sometimes, something, usually something random, would hit me hard, and I would be overcome with the emotion of it all. Sometimes it was interviewing somebody connected to the victims, like Churnin Rivers' daughter. Other times I was struck by fear for my own safety after a sudden realization that I was more personally involved in this thing than I wanted to be.

When somebody would ask me if it scared me to know that a serial killer was writing me letters and knew where I lived and might even be stalking me, I would laugh it off, tell them I wasn't worried. Then something less obvious would be said, like somebody mentioning the Metal Museum, not even in connection with the killer, and I would suddenly remember that I was casually enjoying a picnic with Jack while Churnin Rivers was being murdered just across the street. And that maybe it was my fault. That's when that cliché about blood running cold became very real to me.

•••••••••••••••

On Sunday, while I was still enjoying the temporary illusion of normalcy, I decided to pay a visit to Shannon, the woman who trained and loved Charlie in prison, to wish her a Merry Christmas and to bring her a photo of Logan and Charlie during one of their walks by the river. I found her surprisingly upbeat.

"It's funny, but I feel a lot safer in here than out there," she said. "I figure this is one place that the serial killer is not."

I laughed. "That's one way of looking at it."

"You know, Miss Faire…"

I stopped her. "I told you, call me Britt. Please. It embarrasses me when you call me Miss Faire."

"Okay," she said with a sweet smile. "I'll tell you a little secret. Since you came out and did that newspaper story about this dog program, I've been telling some of the girls in here that you and I are friends. I hope you don't mind me exaggerating like that."

"It's not an exaggeration. Charlie has brought us together, that makes us friends, for sure. That reminds me, I brought you a Christmas present. I put it in a gift bag, so the guards could search it," I said, stating the obvious. "I wanted to frame it, but I didn't think that would be allowed."

When Shannon pulled the photo from the tissue paper in the

bag, tears popped into her eyes.

"Oh, Charlie, my sweet Charlie," she said, touching Charlie's image. "I miss him so much, but it makes me feel better knowing he's with your friend. Is this him? Is this Charlie's owner?"

"Yep, that's Logan. He and Charlie take a walk every day down by the river. Charlie loves it."

Now, Shannon's eyes weren't teary, but glowing with admiration.

"Damn! You didn't tell me this Logan was such a hotty."

"I guess he is pretty cute."

"You guess? Honey, if you have to guess that he's cute, you need your eyes examined. Are you and him dating?" she asked, winking at me.

"Well, not exactly, but I am staying at his house while all this serial killer stuff is going on, just to be safe, since he has a good house alarm and a garage that you can walk straight into the house from." Why on earth was I telling this woman I barely know all this personal stuff?

"Just a hook-up, huh?"

"No, not a hook-up. Honestly, I stay in one of his guest bedrooms."

"Whatever you say, sweetie. I'm just glad you and Charlie are some place safe. Speaking of the serial killer, I got a letter from my boyfriend, who's serving time for the same ID theft thing I am, and he said that when all this stuff came out on TV about Churnin Rivers and Mutha Boy, the guys told my boyfriend that Mutha Boy's brother, Q.T., who's a rapper, too, was serving time in the same lock-up with Churnin Rivers last year. How's that for a weird coincidence?"

I thought about what Jack would say: "I don't believe in coincidences."

CHAPTER FORTY-ONE

It was 10 days before Christmas when my friend, Elizabeth, called to say that she wanted me to talk to her neighbor.

"Britten, (she's always called me the formal version of my name) this is important. I was talking to Lena in the driveway last night as we were both coming home, and we were talking about being frightened by the serial killer being on the loose, and Lena, who's a cocktail waitress at one of the casinos down in Tunica, told me she knew that Elvis impersonator, what's his name?

"Larry Carpenter?"

"Yeah, the one who was murdered. You've got to talk to her."

'But, Elizabeth, there are a lot of people who knew all the victims. So unless she knows something pertaining to the murder..."

"She does, she does. Why do you think I want you to talk to her?"

"Has she been questioned by the police?"

"No, she's scared to talk to the police, but I talked her into telling you what she knows."

"Okay, well, when can we get together?"

"Come to my house now. She's right here, and she doesn't have to go to work until 5 this afternoon."

●●●●●●●●●●●●●●●●●●●

When I got to Elizabeth's, her neighbor was sitting at the kitchen table with a cup of coffee in front of her that she didn't appear to be drinking. She looked up at me anxiously as we were introduced. Elizabeth said she was late for some kind of appointment but gave me a key to her house and told me how to turn on the alarm system. I poured myself a cup of coffee as she was leaving.

"Lena, why were you afraid to go to the police?"

"I'm afraid to talk about this to anyone, but Elizabeth told me I could trust you to not use my name."

Elizabeth had no right to make such a bargain, but I didn't say anything.

"What are you afraid of?"

"Getting murdered, for one thing, but also losing my job. One of the cocktail waitresses talked to a reporter about how business is off at the casino since the murders began. I mean anybody would know that by just looking around at all the empty chairs, but they fired her for talking to the newspaper. The management doesn't like any kind of bad publicity."

"Why do you fear being murdered?"

"Well, they could snuff me out like they did Larry."

I wanted to say she'd been watching too many mafia movies, but I just looked sympathetic.

"Why don't you tell me what you know about Larry Carpenter."

"He's a pretty nice guy, well, he was, but I didn't know him real well, but he'd say hi and pass the time of day with me sometimes. I first noticed him when he did his Elvis show last August during Dead Elvis Week, I mean Elvis Tribute Week — the management gets real mad when we call it Dead Elvis Week like everybody in Memphis does. Anyhow, he came from his show, still wearing his wig and costume and all, and he started playing at the black jack table. I swear he played all night and he almost never won a hand."

"Was he a regular at the casino?"

"Well, I never noticed him before that night, but I did after that, even when he wasn't in his costume. Sometimes he had his wife with him — I guess she was his wife — I don't think a girlfriend would get that mad at you for losing, but mostly he came alone."

"Was he always playing black jack?"

"He tried everything and lost at almost everything. Several times I saw him go back to the office and come out and play again. Then one night, about a week before he got murdered, a big, stern-looking guy came over and sat at the slot machine next to him and started talking to him. When they finished their conversation, the guy got up and walked out."

"What happened after that?"

"Larry got murdered."

"Do you have any reason to believe the man threatened Larry or wanted to hurt him?"

"Well, the conversation didn't look too pleasant. I'd bet anything that it was some goon sent to whack Larry for gambling debts."

Again, too many movies and TV. Still, it was worth looking into.

•••••••••••••••••

As soon as I left Lena and secured Elizabeth's fortress of a house, I went straight to 201 to talk to Jack.

"Sounds like this dealer has an overly active imagination," he said.

"I agree, but what if she's right?"

"Well, in the first place, if Larry had a lot of gambling debt and owed it to the wrong people, I still don't think they would kill him. You don't kill somebody who owes you money, especially when they have a good income and a house in Germantown. They'd be more likely to threaten to kill him if he didn't sell the house and give them the money. But I'll look into it."

"Maybe you should also look into whether any of the other victims were gambling addicts, too."

•••••••••••••••••

It was just two days later that Jack got back to me. He said he'd found out that Carpenter was a gambling addict for sure. He was well known around the casinos, all of them, and he bought lottery tickets every day at the convenience store near his house. He was a sports gambler, too, of course. His wife, who Jack called in Sweden, said Larry would bet on anything.

"He even bet online on whether Oprah would hug or shake hands with Stephen Colbert when she went on his show. Larry bet they'd shake hands, but it was a hug, so Larry lost again. She said when he won occasionally that was all he would remember even though she constantly reminded him that he lost much, much more than he won."

"I assume he was majorly in debt."

"Yeah, second mortgage on the house, lots and lots of credit cards, all maxed out, but no evidence that he was in debt to anybody dangerous. Seems like a better candidate for suicide than murder."

"What about the others? Did any of them have gambling problems?"

"Churnin Rivers seemed to spend all his money on drugs and booze, and Saundra Barkley was one of those really self-controlled gamblers. Her friends said she'd go to Tunica about once a month, take no more than $200 and leave her ATM card at home, and she often won."

"What about Mutha Boy?"

"Well, nobody described him as a gambling addict, but they said he loved the casinos. He liked to go down there and throw a lot of money around, and he always got a lot of attention from other gamblers. Some of them would ask for his autograph and stuff like that. I heard that sometimes he would actually give money away to strangers if somebody was losing bad."

"Nice guy," I said.

"Yeah, when he wasn't molesting under-aged girls and making girls in wheelchairs cry."

CHAPTER FORTY-TWO

My parents, who called about twice a week to check on me, had been very supportive of the Memphis cops' efforts to catch the serial killer — until they found out I wasn't coming for Christmas. Suddenly, they were all criticism.

It was a week before Christmas when I finally got up the nerve to call them and break the news. I had warned them all along that I might not be able to get away, but I guess they always thought either the killer would be caught or that I'd want to go to Florida to escape the danger.

"I just can't believe you're not coming home, Sweet Pea," Mom said, her voice breaking a tiny bit. "Jill and Libby and Ryan will be here. It won't be the same without you."

"Well, in the first place, Mom, it's not that I'm not coming home for Christmas. You live in a gated community in Fort Myers, for goodness sake. Memphis is more home to all of us than there."

"Home is where the heart is," my father cleverly interjected.

"Libby didn't come for Thanksgiving, and we still had fun," I said, trying a different strategy. "So y'all will have fun without me this time."

"But Christmas is a more important family holiday than Thanksgiving," Mom said.

"Don't you think I want to be with y'all for Christmas? Come on, don't guilt trip me about this. I just can't help it. I need to be here in case, something else happens."

Making them feel sorry for me probably wasn't a good idea, because then I had to listen to a diatribe about how incompetent the Memphis police were. It seemed they were saying that the Memphis police had ruined my Christmas.

"Well, I can tell you that Robert Goren would have this thing solved in no time," my dad said, referring, I think, to one of the characters on one of the Law & Order shows. My parents watch syndicated episodes of all of the CSI series, in addition to Law & Order, Monk, Matlock and Diagnosis Murder. It's caused them to be like the rest of the public who have trouble separating reality from fantasy.

Those shows are great entertainment, but they have given the public unrealistic expectations for a criminal investigation. When I was still covering courts, the judges had to start giving instructions to the jury that they could not judge the state's case on CSI TV standards. They had had some acquittals where the jury said the state didn't make a case because all kinds of fancy techniques had not been used at the crime scene.

In reality, crime scene investigation is very important and usually very boring. A crime scene investigator might spend two hours on the stand testifying and showing pictures documenting the size and angle of dozens of bullet holes in fences and walls near where the victim was shot or telling which fingerprints were found where.

In fact, I have rarely heard crime scene testimony that was not a snoozer. The public doesn't realize how many criminal cases involve little or no significant physical evidence. Most cases are solved with good old-fashioned shoe leather — interviewing witnesses and dozens of people who might know something, checking alibis, questioning suspects, looking for motive and opportunity — most of all, applying experience-honed intuition, logic and plain old common sense.

Sure, technology helps. DNA occasionally makes or breaks a case, but not often. Fingerprints are sometimes helpful, but anybody who watches TV knows to wear gloves or wipe down weapons if you're going to kill somebody premeditatedly. National databases of fingerprints have helped solve crimes, but they only help if the criminal has been arrested for a previous crime or had some other reason to be fingerprinted. People like my dad think that everybody in the world's fingerprints and DNA are just magically on file with the cops or FBI, waiting to be matched.

Of course, with a serial killer on the loose, the cops are definitely using every forensic and technological technique available to them, but a case like this doesn't yield much physical evidence. Memphis has a nationally recognized blood-splatter expert on the medical examiner's staff, which has helped the cops know where the victims were killed and what angle the knife entered the body and other helpful information.

But I explained to my parents that since all the victims have been stabbed in the back and died without a struggle, there is no skin or blood of the killer under the fingernails of the victims and no hair or other forensic evidence to follow. The medical examiner, of course, has looked for that kind of physical evidence, but nothing has turned up so far.

"A murder planned by a clever person is harder to solve than a crime of passion or expediency, where the killers do careless things that get them caught," I told my parents.

They were having none of it.

"Well, all I know is that somebody like Adrian Monk would have this serial killer caught in a matter of days," my mom said.

I started to say something smart-ass like, "Well, if you run into Monk, tell him to come up to Memphis and help out." Instead, I just gave up.

"Well, I'll call y'all on Christmas Eve, and don't worry about me. I'm still safely tucked away in Logan's fortress of a house."

"But, Bitsy," my dad said sadly, "what will you do for Christmas, sit around the newsroom or the police department?" My dad calls me Bitsy, not because I was an unusually small child, which I was, but because I could never get my fill of my father singing "Itsy Bitsy Spider" and walking his fingers up my arm as he sang. When the walking fingers got to my neck, he would tickle me, and I would giggle until I could hardly catch my breath.

"Oh, Daddy, I'll be fine, I promise," I said affectionately. "I'm sure Maggie will cook Christmas dinner and invite me. I'll miss all of you, but I'll make the most of a bad situation."

As I was saying goodbye to my folks, I was surprised by a sting of tears in my eyes. It was going to hurt not getting to spend Christmas with my family. They, as usual, would all gather around, with big bowls of Mom's famous homemade caramel popcorn, to watch *White Christmas* on Christmas Eve in the warmth of Ft. Meyers, while I stayed in Memphis shivering and waiting for a serial killer to strike again.

CHAPTER FORTY-THREE

The killer hadn't struck in nearly three weeks now, and there was a touch of hope in the air in Memphis. I heard various people, including my dentist, say they thought this was the end of it, that the killer was finished.

"It's just a matter of time before he gets caught. He's killed his last musician," Dr. Delmar said with authority as he looked into my mouth with a little mirror to see if the hygienist did her job.

He then asked me a couple of questions, which, of course, I could only answer with a grunt since his hands were in my mouth. Why do dentists do that? I can only assume they don't really want an answer and are only asking a question to make sure the patient knows the dentist is nothing like the one who tortured Dustin Hoffman in *Marathon Man*. Come to think of it, Dr. Delmar does look a little like a shaggy haired Sir Laurence Olivier.

When I was able to talk again, I asked him if he knew Dr. Kendelman, the dentist who had a falling out with Mutha Boy over the diamond-studded mouth grills.

"I've met him, but can't say I really know him. Though I did hear that his wife is divorcing him. Don't know why."

"What was your impression of Dr. Kendelman?"

"My impression? Is that a dental joke?" he said, laughing at his own joke about the joke I didn't know I had made. "Well, he was pretty arrogant, I thought, really full of himself. He was bragging about how he didn't need to put in 40-hour weeks like we guys in regular practice do. Said he had a deal going with some rap singers, who he made that mouth jewelry for and that he was making so much money that he was able to give up his practice.

"I remember him saying, 'No more staring all day into people's nasty mouths,'" Dr. Delmar said, and then he suddenly made the connection. "Don't tell me that rap singer who got murdered was one of his clients."

There was no point in denying it, but I didn't tell him about the conflict between Mutha Boy and Kendelman, and I resisted the temptation to reassure Dr. Delmar and all the other regular dentists that Kendelman was back to the daily grind of looking into the mouths of those who didn't floss or use fluoride rinse.

Speaking of floss, I once pulled up beside Dr. Delmar at a traffic light, and he was actually flossing his teeth while waiting for the light to turn green. He didn't look my way, fortunately, so he didn't see me laughing.

•••••••••••••••

When I left the dentist's office, I was feeling a bit hopeful myself, for no other reason than that everyone around me seemed a little hopeful. So I determined that I would spend the rest of the afternoon Christmas shopping and then meet a friend for dinner.

Phyllis was available, so we met at Paulette's, figuring we should treat ourselves to something nice in honor of the holidays. The restaurant was decorated very tastefully for Christmas, and a pianist played Christmas songs and other music. Phyl and I joked about how wasted the romantic atmosphere was on us. As we were looking at our menus, I glanced around the room and was surprised to see Jack, who never seemed like the Paulette's type to me. I was even more surprised to see that he was with a woman, a really pretty blonde woman. She wasn't wearing a lot of makeup and her hair, which was either naturally blonde or a really expensive dye-job, was pinned on top of her head in that way that looks like it was just done spur of the moment, with sexy tendrils of hair falling around her face and neck. Actually, it probably took an hour to achieve that look of careless disregard for hairstyling. It was the kind of hair that in movies, with the removal of one hairpin, falls beautifully to the actress' shoulders. And usually a man is pulling that pin.

The woman was wearing a silky, pale pink blouse that was unbuttoned one button too many, and none of this fetching picture was lost on Jack. They were too far away for me to catch any of their conversation, but he was smiling, and she seemed to find his every word fascinating. At one point she said something and looked sad, and Jack touched her arm in sympathy.

I was really tempted to walk over and say casually, "Hi, Jack. Who's your friend?" but then I remembered the time that my friend Beth had broken up with her longtime boyfriend, and Beth and I were having lunch with Drew in a restaurant. Beth's ex came over to our table — we never knew if he was there coincidentally or if he was stalking her — but he came over and said, "Hi, Beth. Who's your friend?" or words to that effect while staring hard at Drew. It was a horribly uncomfortable moment for all of us, especially Drew, who had no idea what was going on or why.

No, I definitely didn't want to come off as jealous or like a stalker. In fact, I suddenly wished I were invisible. I slid down further in my seat and disciplined myself not to look over at them again, for fear Jack and I would make eye contact.

The only thing that saved me was that they had finished dinner and were almost ready to leave when we arrived. Out of the corner of my eye, I saw them walking toward the door, and once they had their backs to us, I let myself take a long look. She had a gorgeous figure — round in all the right places and flat in all the right places, and her black skirt was form-fitting and short without being vulgar (my mother's favorite word). She wore heels just high enough to make her legs look great — though they would probably look great in fuzzy house slippers, to be honest — but not high enough to look like a tramp (another of my mother's favorite words).

Jack placed his hand lightly on her back to guide her out the door, and I suddenly lost my appetite. At least until the food came.

I still wasn't sure I wanted Jack as more than a friend and ally, but I was sure I didn't want someone else to have him before I decided.

CHAPTER FORTY-FOUR

The next morning I woke up thinking about Jack and the blonde, but I was able to block it out when I went downstairs and as I walked down the hall, saw Logan sitting at the kitchen table reading the New York Times, which was lying open on the table. He was eating cereal with his right hand and petting Charlie with his left. He was dressed in jeans and a yellow crew-neck sweater. I look terrible in yellow — it makes my skin look sallow, but Logan seems to look good in every color.

He was off for the winter semester break, so he could linger over breakfast. When I first came down the hall toward the kitchen, Logan didn't notice me, but Charlie ran toward me and playfully jumped up on me. Logan looked up and smiled that smile of his. I won't even try to describe it, but it makes you feel that there is nobody else in the world he would rather see than you. Not that I'm saying it's only directed at me. I've seen him smile that way at his mom and other friends, too, including Lettie.

"What are you up to today?" he asked and then ate another spoonful of cereal.

"I thought I'd spend some time at my house today, maybe wrap some gifts there."

"Do you think that's safe? I've got paper and ribbon here."

"Thanks, Mom, but I'll be fine."

He smiled. "Okay, I forgot, I promised not to smother you while you were here."

"I miss my house, humble though it is. I need to spend a Saturday just toodling around the house."

"Understandable," Logan said, "but don't you think it would be fun to have Charlie there with you."

"Maybe it would," I said, pouring myself a bowl of cereal. I took part of the newspaper, and we read in silence, except for the crunch of eating cereal and an occasional comment on something in the paper. Once again I felt that confusing emotion that I often have with Logan — is this comfortable warmth the kind you feel with a beloved brother or with someone you love romantically?

•••••••••••••••

After breakfast, Charlie and I got in my car and set out for Cooper Young. I hadn't picked up my mail for a couple of days, so there was tons in the mailbox, but thankfully no notes from the killer. I'm not sure I'll ever go through my mail again without feeling anxiety.

After opening the mail and tossing most of it, I walked room to room, as if re-familiarizing myself with my own home. I pretended I was giving Charlie the grand tour. He ran ahead of me like a kid exploring a new playground.

Then I went to the kitchen and got out my few recipes. I'm not much of a cook, day-to-day, but I do like to make some goodies at Christmas and give them to friends.

I thought about making mom's caramel popcorn, but that would make me feel sad. No, it had to be a recipe I didn't connect with my family. I decided on "Jimmy Carter's Favorite Peanut

Brittle," which I had clipped out of the food column in the newspaper.

I'd do that and my neighbor's sugar cookie recipe with butter cream icing and sprinkles. So, Charlie and I went to the grocery store to buy the ingredients and stopped by Dollar General to get some cookie tins for giving away. Since it was not really cold and certainly not hot, I thought it was okay to leave Charlie in the car while I went inside. I knew it was silly, but I felt like he might not be safe at my house alone.

We got back to my house, and he ran ahead of me to the door, straining at the leash. He slept on the floor of the kitchen most of the time while I was cooking. I pulled the peanut brittle and let it cool and then started the cookies. I didn't cut the cookies in little shapes because I don't have any cookie cutters and because it would remind me too much of Christmas cookie making with my sisters when we were kids. I just used an upside down juice glass to cut out circles.

While the cookies were cooling, waiting to be frosted, I went to the hall closet to get out my wrapping paper and ribbon. Charlie stayed behind snoozing in the kitchen.

I listened to Christmas music and wrapped gifts and before I knew it, it was five o'clock and getting dark. I was just about to go back to the kitchen to ice the cookies when Charlie in the kitchen started barking, barking ferociously and growling. I guess my day of Christmas normalcy had made me forget that the rules had changed, that I wasn't supposed to be brave to the point of stupidity any more, that a serial killer knew where I lived.

So I just walked into the kitchen to see what Charlie was barking at. My first thought was that maybe Logan had decided to drop by, but as I walked down the hall, I realized that Charlie would never growl at Logan. An excited bark, yes, but a growl, no.

Someone was knocking on the back door. I don't have curtains or shades in my kitchen, another thing that never seemed like a big deal before, and suddenly I felt naked and vulnerable standing in the light of the kitchen with whoever was outside able to see me, but me not able to see him. I turned off the lights and stepped back into the hall. I called Charlie, but he wouldn't come and wouldn't stop barking.

I ran down the hall toward the back bedroom, turned the light off and went to the bedroom window to see if I could see who was at the backdoor. As I drew back the curtain slowly, instead of a distant view of someone at the back door, I found myself face to face with a man outside my window. I dropped the curtain and screamed and Charlie came to the bedroom and was barking and growling at the window.

The man began banging on the window and saying something. I was fumbling with my phone trying to dial 911, but my hands were shaking so much I couldn't manage it. My vision was blurred from abject fear. Then I realized the man was calling my name, and I was even more afraid. But then I recognized the voice. It was Freddy, my yardman.

"Miss Britt, don't be afraid. It's just me. It's just me, Freddy," he said, and he sounded as afraid as I was.

I pulled back the curtain. "Freddy, what in the world are you doing outside my window? You scared me to death. I thought you were the serial killer. Come back to the door, I'll let you in."

I went to the back door and opened it, and he came in. Charlie sensed it was okay to stop growling, but he still barked several times as Freddy came inside.

"I saw your car outside, and it hasn't been here for such a long time, so I thought I'd say hi and see if you need me to do any yard work before your folks come for Christmas."

"They're not coming this year," I said, trying to stop shaking. "Here, let me give you some of this peanut brittle I just made. I'll put it in a tin for you, and I want to give you a little money gift, too."

While I did that, Freddy told me which football game he and his brothers planned to watch on Christmas Eve and that they were going to order "real pizza" instead of buying frozen ones. He also told me that he'd been keeping an eye on the house for me while I was gone. That's when I noticed a piece of folded notebook paper sticking out of his shirt pocket.

"Freddy, if you don't mind my asking, what's that in your shirt pocket?"

He looked down as if he'd never seen the paper before and then he smiled.

"Oh, this?" he said, pulling the paper from his pocket. "Somebody had left it stuffed into the edge of your back screen door, so I was bringing it in for you."

He handed it to me, and I opened it with the dread that had become all too common in my life. I went to the phone and called Jack after I read the brief note:

"I'll have a blue Christmas without you" was its only message.

CHAPTER FORTY-FIVE

On the Sunday morning before Christmas, I had planned to go to church with Logan and his mother for the traditional Nine Lessons and Carols program at Maggie's Presbyterian church. Instead, I spent the day with the Memphis police and the editors of my paper, all of us trying to figure out if the killer planned to kill me.

Speaking of religion — churches, synagogues and other places of worship were the only public places that saw an upswing in attendance during the serial killer's run. So many holiday civic events were cancelled because people were afraid to get out at night and because some musicians, especially the amateur ones, were afraid of being the next victim, but places of worship seemed determined not to be bullied.

And fear and sadness drove more people than ever to attend services and seek counseling. Hope and comfort were hot commodities that fall and winter. But that Sunday morning, I was not able to avail myself of that.

At 201 Poplar, the debate was heated. Jack was angry that the MPD hadn't already been conducting a 24-hour still watch of my house. He had wanted it all along, but those above him had ruled that during a serial killer investigation, that would be a waste of manpower. Even without surveillance, they argued, the killer hadn't left me a note for three weeks. Were they supposed to have one patrolman a shift, three shifts a day every day, just watch my house when every cop in the city was already working overtime?

Jack was livid, but I agreed with his bosses. I even disagreed when Jack suggested I be given 24-hour police protection.

"For how long, the rest of my life?" I argued.

"Only until we catch the son of a bitch," Jack said.

"Which could be the rest of my life."

"Britt, he's planning to kill you," Jack said in a quiet, worried way that scared me more than the yelling.

"Now, wait a minute, Trent," the police director said to Jack. "The profiler in Nashville, Eileen, Irene…"

"Irene Ringold," the head of homicide, Walter Raines, said.

"We talked to her this morning," the director continued, "and she said that the note could mean that another musician is being targeted. The killer has made his predictions through Miss Faire before — this may just be another such communication."

"The note does say, "you," and it was delivered to Britt," Raines said, "so I don't think we can assume the killer is referring to someone else."

"Certainly Miss Faire needs to exercise extreme caution, and we need to give her all the help we can, but I think the killer is just using another music themed threat, and Blue Christmas is just too good to pass up, I would imagine," the police director said.

"Blue Christmas is an Elvis song," I said. "Do you think he's going to kill another Elvis impersonator or somebody connected to Elvis?"

"Highly unlikely," Raines said. "I mean, who would that be? Lisa Marie and Priscilla aren't in town, and most of the musicians connected to Elvis are dead or not here. Still we need to look into that possibility."

"Irene said there seems to be a pattern of the killer choosing victims from different musical genres," Jack said. "The first, Saundra Barkley, was an R & B

girl-group singer; Mutha Boy, a rapper; Carpenter, an Elvis impersonator, which could represent rock 'n roll; and Churnin Rivers, a blues singer. What does that leave? Jazz? Gospel? C & W?"

"You'd have a hard time finding a professional country musician around here, don't you think?" I said.

"Good, maybe the killer will move over to Nashville and leave us alone," Jack said, and everyone laughed.

"If the killer is spreading it around like this," Raines said, "we'd better get the word out to the churches that have gospel choirs to be extra careful during Christmas programs and services this week. And don't forget that Al Green is a minister now, but also a singer, so somebody needs to warn him."

"Are we sure that we haven't already got the killer in custody?" the police director asked. "This yardman could be seen in Miss Faire's yard without arousing suspicion, and he did have that note in his pocket. Maybe he was delivering it, instead of finding it."

"Freddy? He wouldn't hurt anybody or anything," I said vehemently.

"We took him in for questioning last night," Jack said, "and while he doesn't have an alibi for any of the killings, my gut tells me he's not a killer. He's not the brightest bulb on the tree, and I just can't see him planning and carrying out all these murders, leaving no evidence behind, never slipping up. I tried to talk him into having a lawyer present during the interrogation, but he said he didn't need a lawyer, he just wanted to help make sure nobody hurt Britt."

"I watched the interrogation," Raines said, "and I agree with Trent. I don't think this kid is the killer, even though he fits the demographic of typical serial killers — 20something and white. I just don't buy it, but we'll keep an eye on him anyhow."

"Speaking of keeping an eye on somebody," Jack said, "what

about police protection for Britt?"

"I've got an idea," I said, "instead of wasting essential police manpower to watch me, I'll get my newspaper to hire a body guard."

Everybody said that would be a good compromise, Jack agreeing reluctantly.

•••••••••••••

Next stop was the newspaper. The police director went with me, so he could try to persuade the editors not to run a story on the note I received. If we didn't publish news of the new note, the director argued, it might flush the killer out to try to deliver another note.

The editors finally agreed, with the understanding that in exchange for their cooperation, the MPD would give us the story first when there was a break in the case. Fortunately, the director never mentioned my idea about the newspaper hiring a bodyguard for me. If Jack had been there, he certainly would have.

I had no intentions of putting myself under 24-hour protection, police or otherwise. I wasn't going to do anything stupid, but neither was I going to be on a leash. I was a big girl and could take care of myself.

•••••••••••••

I got back to Logan's mid afternoon, and believe it or not, I worked on my cookie tins. Even with all the hubbub at my house last night, before Charlie and I left to go back to Logan's, I gathered up my unfrosted sugar cookies, peanut brittle and dollar-store Santa Claus tins. I don't cook often enough to just leave all that behind at the house I now didn't intend to return to for a while. I told you I'm not stupid.

At Logan's kitchen table, I spread the butter cream icing on the cookies and Logan did the sprinkles. It's important to get them on while the icing is still moist on the surface. Then I broke up the pieces of the peanut brittle and divided them into little baggies and tied each one with a piece of ribbon.

I was going to put a little bag of brittle and several cookies in each tin and later in the week give them to my friends and a few co-workers. While I was filling the goody tins, Logan went upstairs and came back about 10 minutes later. He helped me for a while and then when he saw the headlights of a car pulling into the driveway, he told me to put on my coat. When I looked puzzled, he said, "You'll see," and smiled that smile of his.

He opened the front door, and there were Maggie and Lettie, carrying her bass. Outside, another car pulled up, and Ben and Caroline got out. Ben was carrying a tambourine, of all things.

"Are you having a party?" I asked. "I'm not really in the mood for a big Christmas party, but I can just go upstairs to my room."

"It's not a party," Logan said. "Trust me on this, Britt. Just put on your coat."

So I did. And without telling me what was going on, everybody and everything left the house, including Charlie and the bass. We went to the house next door, and Lettie unzipped her bass and started to play in the front yard.

"We're going to go Christmas caroling," Logan said, and before I could protest, they all started singing *We Wish You a Merry Christmas* until the neighbors came to the windows and peeped out. When they recognized Logan, they came out on the porch and joined us on *Come All Ye Faithful.*

At the next house, they not only came out on the porch, they joined us as we moved down the street singing. If there were children at a particular house, we made sure we sang *Santa Claus Is Coming to*

Town and *Jingle Bells*, to which Ben played his tambourine.

The family in the fourth house brought out some candles for everyone to carry. There were a couple of houses where the people only listened from behind locked doors and windows, but most of Logan's Harbor Town neighbors, even the ones who didn't know any of us, joined in the caroling. I guess some figured there was safety in numbers while others, like me, didn't mind taking a little risk for the sake of feeling normal for a change.

There was a lot of laughter, but there were also somber times when we sang about Christmases we used to know, about being together through the years and about sleeping in heavenly peace.

Still there was joy and empowerment in knowing it would take more than one sick, evil person to silence the music.

CHAPTER FORTY-SIX

After the emotional high of our Christmas caroling adventure, I actually slept well that one night. The other nights during the past two months, I had had trouble sleeping. It was not usually out of fear — except on nights I received notes from the killer, when I definitely was kept awake by fear. But most of the time, I didn't sleep well because I couldn't stop trying to figure this whole serial killer thing out. It was like a puzzle I couldn't stop trying to solve.

If I had been convinced 100 percent that this was a typical serial killer picking musicians at random to kill, I think I would have felt less compelled to try to solve the puzzle. But I couldn't let go of the idea that the killer was choosing these people for a personal reason and that would mean the killer knew them and was probably living among us. So I often lay awake trying to connect the dots.

The day after the Christmas caroling, I called Jack and asked if we could get together to talk about the case. He said to come on over to his office at 201, but I wanted to talk where there were no interruptions. I didn't want to get together at Logan's either, so Jack said he'd pick me up about 8 when he left work, and we'd go to his apartment.

When he picked me up, I came armed with several sheets of 11 by 17 paper I had taken from the copy machine at work. We stopped and got barbecue sandwiches to eat at his place. We drank Diet Cokes instead of beer for maximum alertness. After we ate, I spread out one of the large blank sheets of paper.

"When I saw you come out with that paper, I was hoping you had something written on them that would give us a breakthrough on the case," Jack said, "and now I find it's blank."

I told him it wouldn't be blank for long.

"I don't have any new information for you, but I wanted us to put our heads together and sort some things out. Jack, let's just for the heck of it assume that these killings have not been random, that somebody had a reason for killing all four musicians."

"Okay, kid, I'm game," he said. "What's the paper for?"

"Most of the time when you write a news story, you just sit down at your computer with your notes and write, and it's done in an hour or two. But whenever I'm doing a big story, something really long with lots of sources, I sometimes sit down and spread my notes out and just organize my information on a big sheet of paper before I write. I want us to do that with this case."

"Where do we start?"

"Well, let's list the victims on the left first."

So I started at the top left with Saundra Barkley, skipped a lot of space, and put Mutha Boy below that; skipped more space and wrote Larry Carpenter; more space and Churnin Rivers near the bottom. I labeled that column "Victims" and the next column "Suspects."

"I think it's important to list the suspects in each murder and possible motive as if it's not connected to the other murders and think about the connections later," I said.

Under suspects in the Saundra Barkley murder, we put her ex-husband, DeWitt Starks, whose motive would be hating Saundra for her treatment of him and for breaking up his relationship with Lettie Nolan. Reluctantly, I put Lettie on the list, too, so Jack would know I was being objective, but I knew in my heart that the woman I Christmas caroled with the night before was not a killer.

"I know we have to consider Lettie as a suspect," I said to

Jack, "but it doesn't make sense. If she felt so guilty about her affair with DeWitt that she refused to marry him or even see him, wouldn't she have even more moral reluctance about killing Saundra, especially all these years later?"

"On the surface, yes," Jack said, "but we may not know all that has gone on. Maybe Saundra inflicted one more act of professional vengeance on Lettie, and Lettie couldn't take any more from this woman who was determined to ruin her life."

"It's possible," I said, not convinced.

"And we also have to consider that Lettie and DeWitt conspired to kill Saundra since she had hurt them both and that they are just staying away from each other to allay suspicion."

Then we added Ray "Slick" Taggart to the list of suspects, even though Jack reminded me that Slick had opportunity to kill Saundra, Larry and Churnin Rivers, but that he was in police custody when Mutha Boy was murdered. Still, since he had been claiming for 30 years that Saundra stole his song and ruined his life, you had to put him on the list.

Lastly, we put Stewart Linton on the list of suspects in the Barkley murder. We hadn't discovered a solid motive for him to kill any of them, but he was open about his disdain, perhaps even hate, for Saundra and the others.

"I've never seen a person who just radiated hate and loathing like he does," I said. "I don't know why he would kill any of them, except maybe Saundra, who he blames for his losing his job at Stax, but I think he's cold blooded enough to be a murderer."

"A real sociopath, if you ask me," Jack said.

So we moved on to the suspects in the Mutha Boy murder.

"Well," said Jack, "you got to top the list with some rival rapper, name unknown."

"Except," I corrected, "you've never found any evidence, none whatsoever, of a hateful rivalry that might lead to murder, LA or New York-style. But okay, we'll put that down on the list."

Then we wrote down William and Jason Brownell, the father and brother of the teenaged girl, who Mutha Boy "auditioned" for his video.

"Jack, what was your gut reaction when you interviewed them?"

"They were both still mad and didn't pretend to be sorry the rapper was dead, but they were also scared of being considered suspects in his death — a totally normal, expected reaction on their part."

"Did anybody remember seeing them at the Plush Club the night of the murder?"

"No, but the Brownells don't normally hang out at places like that, so if they were there, probably nobody would know who they were or remember them."

"The daughter isn't in a wheelchair, by any chance, is she? Remember somebody telling you that Mutha Boy refused to give an autograph to a girl in a wheelchair and made her cry?"

"Yeah, but the girl in the wheelchair was white with dishwater blonde hair, and the father and son are medium-skinned black men. Still I checked, and Brownell only has that one daughter, and she's not in a wheelchair."

"Did you talk to the daughter?"

"Yeah, her name's Erica, and she was very upset about the rapper's death, but kept assuring me that her dad and brother would never kill him."

"Did the Brownells ever get to confront Mutha Boy or did they file any charges for molesting a minor?"

"They tried their best to get to him, so they could tell him off and threaten to take action if he ever got near Erica again, but Mutha Boy always refused to see them."

"Which," I said, "probably made them angrier. Isn't it possible that the only way they could get near him was to hang around the Plush Club after the show?"

"These guys, Mr. Brownell and Jason, they seem like real quality people," Jack said. "I can't imagine them stabbing somebody in the back with a steak knife."

"Well, I don't know for sure, since I'm not a parent," I said, "but my parents and sister and other people with kids tell me that parents are like bears who go on the attack when they feel their cubs are in danger. Maybe a good, upstanding father would be even more likely to strike out at somebody who tried to sexually exploit his beloved daughter."

"Yeah, a bad father and brother would probably try to get in on the deal, get their share of the money from the video, not caring how it affects the girl. Even after all these years, it still shocks me and sickens me when I hear about a crime where a parent has sold out their own kid."

Then we wrote down the final suspect in the death of Donté Washington, which was Dr. Kendelman.

"Yeah, the guy who gave up his practice to become the Hip Hop dentist," Jack said. "I talked to him, and he was still pissed at the rapper for 'betraying' him, as he put it, but he was totally shocked that we would suspect him. 'Kill somebody over teeth?' I remember him saying, and he would have a point, except that it wasn't about teeth, it was about money. Like the bible says, 'The love of money is the root of all evil.' More people have killed over money than over love or hate."

"I would never have expected you to quote the bible," I said, and immediately regretted it when I saw his look of genuine offense.

"Why, cause I'm a cop? My folks took me to Sunday school and church at the Baptist Church every Sunday morning of my life and back again on Sunday night and Wednesday night for prayer meeting. You think I'm a heathen just because I'm a cop? When was the last time you went to church, Miss Self Righteous?"

"Good point. I take it back and apologize. Let's go onto Larry Carpenter," I said quickly, anxious to change the subject.

"We don't really have any suspects in Carpenter's murder, except his ex-wife, because wives and husbands are always suspects. But she was in Sweden at the time and would have to have hired a killer, and you can't just look in the Yellow Pages for those."

"No suspects at all?"

"Nobody in particular. Most people didn't like him, but in a vague sort of way. Nobody really seemed to hate him, but then nobody loved him either, except the Elvis fans who didn't really know him. Larry Carpenter's murder is the best evidence in favor of this really being a serial killer choosing musicians at random."

"Does Churnin Rivers fall into that category, too?" I asked.

"Yeah, nobody much liked him, and by all accounts he was a very unpleasant guy to be around, to say the least, but like the old saying goes, 'He wasn't worth killing.' I guess one of his kids, who hated him for killing their mother would be the only suspects in his murder."

"But why wait so long?"

"Because, Britt, they didn't know where he was all those years after he deserted them and changed his name. And when they did find out where he was, he had a little money and a little fame, which he didn't deserve, and he hurt the sister again by rejecting her when she wrote to him. That might have pushed one of the brothers over the edge."

"You got any ice cream?" I asked.

"Yeah, chocolate chip."

"Good, let's have dessert before we try to make sense of all this."

CHAPTER FORTY-SEVEN

After two bowls of ice cream each, we sat down with our chart again and tried to write down all the connections between the various suspects and victims.

"Before we get started on the connections, remind me about who of the suspects had an alibi when the murders happened," I said.

"Well, nobody on this list had a good alibi for all the murders, and they didn't even have iron-clad alibis for any of the murders, except for Slick Taggart, who was in police custody. A lot of them said they were at home asleep or doing something alone. But I don't put much stake in alibis, anyhow, except when it is rock solid. When it comes to friends or family saying you were with them, I take it with a grain of salt."

"Yeah, you can always find some friend or family member who will lie for you," I said. "Okay, let's talk about the connections now."

"Yes, Detective Faire. Well, the first and most obvious connection is that three of the four victims were in this movie, *Black 'n Blue*. That seems too much of a coincidence to me."

"I agree. I keep thinking Saundra must have something to do with the movie, too, but what?"

"The movie's producer said he never thought of using her. Her kind of music just didn't fit in a movie about hip hop and blues cultures, but I asked him to ask the casting director anyhow if she auditioned, and he got back to me with a no."

"Still, it would be so unlike Saundra Barkley — egomaniac opportunist that she was — to pass up a chance like this to be in a movie made right here in Memphis. Of course, a lot of movies have been made here in recent years…"

That's when it came to me.

"Why didn't I think of that before," I said. "We've had tunnel vision, Jack. She was in *Walk the Line*."

"The Johnny Cash movie? I don't remember her in that?"

"It was a bit part. I think she had one line, maybe two. It was the part about June and Johnny and Elvis on tour."

"I didn't pick up on that, but for what it's worth, let's put it on our connections list," Jack said and wrote under the word, "Connections," that all four victims were in a movie made in Memphis.

I then pointed out that Stewart Linton knew Saundra, Larry and Churnin and had worked at the studio in LA where Mutha Boy recorded his last CD.

"What did he say about the rapper when you talked to him?"

"Said he didn't know him personally, but that he was arrogant like all the young rappers," I said. "But he did say he had heard he was basically a good kid."

"Maybe something happened to make him hate Mutha Boy that he's not telling us because it would put too much suspicion on him. Why did he say he hated Rivers and Carpenter?"

"He didn't exactly say he hated them," I said. "He just acted hateful when he talked about them. Said Churnin had talent and wasted it, and Larry didn't have talent, but thought he did. They both hung out a lot at Stax and Sun and Hi, hoping to get on recording sessions, Stewart said."

So Jack wrote down on our chart that Stewart Linton had a connection to all four victims.

"What about the height of all these suspects?" I asked. "Are any of them shorter or taller than that range the medical examiner came up with?"

"Actually, they are all between five nine and six feet. I'll put that down here, too," Jack said. "Another connection between the victims is gambling, though I'm not inclined to think it's significant."

"We know Larry was a gambling addict, and Saundra was a self-controlled casino gambler, and Mutha Boy liked to show off his money at the casinos, but I thought you said Churnin cared more about drugs and booze."

"Yeah," Jack said, "but I found out later that Rivers liked to shoot craps in backrooms and alleys. So all four victims liked to gamble in one form or another, but it's far-fetched that all of them would be murdered because of that."

"What about suspects who worked at restaurants that use steak knives like the ones used for the murders? I know DeWitt Starks was one of them, but can't remember the others."

"Yeah, Starks has worked as a cook at a couple of Beale restaurants, and Slick Taggart washed dishes at three different restaurants over the last few years," Jack said. "And Jason Brownell has worked at a couple of restaurants as a waiter, like half the college kids in town."

"Then we have a couple of random connections, like Mutha Boy's brother being in prison with Churnin Rivers last year."

"And don't forget," Jack just had to remind me, "the romantic connection between Lettie Nolan and DeWitt Starks."

"You know, Jack, I just keep coming back to Saundra Barkley. Maybe it's because she was first or maybe it's because she was the most hated of the four victims, but I just keep coming back to her."

"In my mind, she seems more significant, too, but I can't pinpoint why really, except that she had her fingers in so many pies and *tried* to have her fingers in all pies."

"Ambitious opportunists like Saundra Barkley know a lot of people and make a lot of enemies," I said. "Still I can't figure out how her murder could have led to the other three."

"The movie connection seems like it could be a breakthrough now that we know that Saundra was in *Walk the Line*, and the other three were connected to *Black 'n Blue*, either through acting or the soundtrack," Jack said standing up. "Come on, kiddo, I need to take you home. I got to get up early tomorrow. I'm going to start asking around about the movies and the victims."

As we drove back to Logan's, I tried to keep the conversation personal, hoping Jack would tell me who the mysterious blonde was that I saw him with at Paulette's. But he was his usual unforthcoming self.

CHAPTER FORTY-EIGHT

The next day while Jack was questioning everybody who we knew had anything to do with *Black 'n Blue* and *Walk the Line*, I was broadening the search to all movies made in Memphis. I found a list on the website of the Memphis and Shelby County Film and Television Commission and was surprised to find there were more than 40 feature films and TV movies that had been made entirely or partially here since 1985.

When I called a woman I know who works at the commission, Chloe Richardson, and asked if I could get a list of all local people cast in those movies, she laughed. She said that kind of information on all 40 movies wasn't at her fingertips, and she just didn't have time to put together a comprehensive list for me of extras and speaking roles filled by locals over the last 30 plus years.

"What about a list of all the locals in the most recent films made here?"

"That would be more doable," she said. "I can probably get it for you later today, if it's as important as you say, Britt."

"Thanks, Chloe, can you e-mail them to me?"

•••••••••••••••••

When the list came, I first looked at the movies that involved music, thinking that was my best bet — *Hustle & Flow, Walk the Line, Black Snake Moan, Black 'n Blue*. As I remembered, Saundra Barkley did have a bit part in *Walk the Line*, but I was surprised to see that Mutha Boy, then just called Donté Washington, was an extra in *Hustle & Flow*.

The next familiar name I came across stunned me. A bit part in *Hustle & Flow* was played by Lettie Nolan. Until now, we thought she knew Saundra, Larry and Churnin, but not Mutha Boy. That meant she knew all the murder victims. I still didn't think Lettie was a murderer, but I felt sick thinking that this would make her a more viable suspect. And I felt even sicker knowing that a seed of doubt had even been planted in my own mind.

I moved on to the other films made in Memphis in the last five or six years and saw lots of familiar names — locally prominent actors, a University of Memphis dean, a well-known restaurateur. Fred Smith, the founder and CEO of FedEx, even had a bit part in Cast Away when Tom Hanks' character returns to FedEx and Memphis after being stranded on an island for years.

But there was another possibly significant name on the list of extras and bit parts in Cast Away — Vanja Carpenter. Could that possibly be Larry's Swedish wife?

I called Jack to tell him about Donté and Lettie being in *Hustle & Flow* and to ask if he had found out anything. The answer was no, but he said he would be contacting Lettie to ask about the movie connection.

"One more name caught my eye on the list," I said. "Jack, what is Larry Carpenter's wife's first name?"

"It's Vanja, spelled with a j, but sounds like a y," he said.

"Vanja Carpenter had a small speaking role in Cast Away," I said. "She was one of the FedEx people Tom Hanks' character talked to in Russia or whatever foreign country it was. I guess they thought a Swedish accent could pass for a Russian accent."

"Well, none of the others were in that movie, but it still connects her to Memphis movies, if that means anything."

"Jack, when are you going to talk to Lettie?"

"Immediately. Sorry, kid, I know you hated to see that name on the list."

CHAPTER FORTY-NINE

Do you know the difference between false security and danger? There is really no difference, except that false security is more dangerous than danger, and false security makes you feel stupid when you find out it's false.

Why did we think it was all over? What kind of fools were we to think that serial killers stop killing because it's Christmas and Hanukkah and Kwanzaa and whatever else is celebrated this time of year — all the occasions that generate good will toward men among us non-homicidal folks and have no positive effects whatsoever on psychopathic killers.

I don't care what the profilers say about serial killers not usually being insane, I think you have to be a certifiable psycho to go around killing strangers or even people you hate, especially three days before Christmas.

Considering the note I had gotten a few days ago from the killer, my only solace was that the victim wasn't me. Not so fortunate was Rusty Grasslie, an on-his-way-down country singer, who was in town for just one night to sing at some dump on Brooks Road, just a couple of miles from Graceland.

When Jack called to tell me that Grasslie was the latest victim — stabbed behind the roadhouse where he was playing — he already knew that the victim lived in Nashville, was born in Cuba, Alabama, and grew up in Pickens, Mississippi. In other words, he was the first victim with no strong connection to Memphis.

Grasslie hadn't even performed in Memphis much over his career, because Memphis is not a big country music city. However, when Grasslie was hot in the 90s — he actually had a couple of hits on the C & W charts — he did play the Pyramid, which was Memphis' primo sports and entertainment venue before the FedEx Forum was built.

In fact, Jack said, Grasslie had only been back to Memphis once since then, according to his manager, and that was to play the same seedy joint he was playing the night he was killed.

"Why was he out behind the club alone?" I asked.

"Supposedly a smoke break, but why would he need to go outside to smoke when smoking's still allowed in bars that only allow in people over 21? More likely it was a snort break or a shoot-up break."

"Ten or 15 years ago, even I had heard of Rusty Grasslie, but he's really dropped off the radar screen."

"For good reason," Jack said. "There have been rumors for years that he has every nasty addiction you can think of — booze, drugs, tobacco, porn, gambling, all of which contributed to his meteoric fall from fame and fortune."

"It's sad when somebody is that self-destructive."

"From the look of the guy's body and teeth, I'd guess meth was his drug of choice," Jack said. "If you wanted that guy dead, all you had to do was wait a few months, and Rusty would take care of it himself."

"But that would ruin the fun for the serial killer, I guess."

•••••••••••••••

Jack had only had time for a short conversation with me on the phone earlier in the day, but that evening I sat at the kitchen table with Logan, drinking coffee, eating Christmas cookies Maggie had made and talking about the events of the day.

"It apparently happened about 3 this morning when Rusty went outside between sets," I told Logan. "Jack thinks he was going out there to get a drug hit of some kind, probably meth."

Then I told him about all the other addictions Jack had heard about.

"Yeah, I think I read about that on the cover of one of the tabloids in the line at the grocery store," Logan said. "I guess he was one of those people who was in and out of rehab all the time."

"I don't think so. From what Jack said, I think Rusty skipped the rehab and went straight to the relapse."

"Cutting out the middle man, huh?" Logan said and then looked guilty. "What's happening to me? I've been hanging out too much with reporters and cops — I'm starting to make jokes about people getting murdered."

"Now you see it's the only way you can keep your sanity sometimes."

"No witnesses, I'm assuming."

"No, he went outside behind the club. When he was hot, he always had bodyguards and hangers-on with him everywhere he went, but nowadays, Jack says, his manager doesn't even travel with him. He just phones it in. And no roadies. Rusty has to carry in his own stuff and set up with the club people."

"How quickly the mighty doth fall. Any physical evidence this time?"

"Nothing obvious, and it's too soon to know about the autopsy or lab work. No sign of a struggle once again, so it's doubtful they'll come up with much."

"What does Jack make of all this?"

"That we're at another dead end because this guy is not even from Memphis, and as far as we know, he didn't know or have any connection to the other victims or suspects. He's starting to think, and so am I, that this really is a serial killer choosing his victims at random from the music community."

We let Charlie in from the fenced backyard and went up to bed. I had just put on my nightgown when I heard the phone ring next door in Logan's room. A few seconds later, Logan knocked on my door.

"Britt, it's Lettie, she wants to talk to you. She didn't have your cell number."

I opened the door and took Logan's phone as if it were something dangerous. I could see from Logan's expression that I wouldn't like what I was about to hear.

"Baby Doll, can I get that homicide detective's phone number from you? I've been fretting all day about what to do, but I finally decided it was better if I told him instead of waiting for him to find out on his on."

"Find out what, Lettie?"

"That I know Rusty Grasslie, too. When he played the Pyramid in '95, they hired extra local musicians to play with his usual band, so they'd have a fuller sound for that big venue. I was one of them, and I was even invited to party with them after the concert. I didn't stay long. I'm no goody-goody, but they were drinking and drugging too much for my taste, and Rusty was a mean son-of-a-bitch when he was high."

I gave Lettie Jack's cell number. I wasn't sure what else to say.

"The detective came by and talked to me yesterday before this happened and asked me about why I hadn't told anybody about me being in the movie, and I said I didn't like to brag, and he asked why I never told the police I knew all the victims, and I told him all the local musicians knew Saundra and Churnin and even Larry, but I knew Mutha Boy, too, and I didn't even know it. There were a lot of young kids in the movie I didn't know. He wasn't famous then, so I didn't pay any attention to him.

"I swear, Britt, I wasn't hiding it. But when I heard on TV today that Rusty had been murdered, I felt sick because I realized that meant that I knew all five of the victims and that doesn't look too good for me. I didn't even know Rusty was in town last night."

"Just call Jack, Lettie, and tell him the truth. Call him tonight. It's not too late. Jack's a fair guy. Your volunteering that you knew Rusty will help him to see that you didn't do anything wrong. He'll probably have to bring you in for questioning, but that doesn't mean he believes you did anything."

I kept using vague terms like "you didn't do anything wrong" and "doesn't believe you did anything," because I could not bare to use the words "you" and "killer" in the same sentence.

We said goodbye, and I handed the phone back to Logan. Charlie was sitting at our feet trying to figure out what was wrong.

CHAPTER FIFTY

I went into work the next morning, December 23, and was reminded of previous Christmases when everybody was busy doing holiday stories and most were looking forward to getting off for Christmas. Of course, large city newspapers don't close down for holidays, but they always try to get by with a skeleton staff, so that most people are home with their families.

I thought of Christmas Eve my first year at this paper. I was working as one of the general assignment reporters and hoping nothing caught fire, nobody got murdered, nothing at all would happen in the last three hours I had to work on December 24. I was scheduled to be off on Christmas Day, thanks to the generosity of an older Jewish reporter, who volunteered to work in my place. I still thank him every year for that.

Anyhow, I was sitting there on that Christmas Eve, anxious to get home to celebrate with my parents and sisters and grandmother, but into the newsroom walked an old man with rosy cheeks and a sweet smile, not unlike the actor who played Kris Kringle in *Miracle on 34th Street*. The next thing I knew I was being told "to interview Santa Claus," as the city editor put it, and to write a story for the Christmas Day issue.

His name was Allan J. Rawlinford, a retired postal worker from Chicago, who told me he had lost his wife and adult son to cancer the same year and almost grieved himself to death. But finally, he decided to stop crying, take early retirement and travel the world, using his postal pension to "pamper children who never got pampered."

Mr. Rawlinford showed me clippings from Mexican newspapers, which labeled him "The Santa Claus of Acapulco." By the time I met him, he had moved to Israel, where he was "spoiling" terminally ill children in a Tel Aviv hospital. One of them loved Elvis, who was long since dead by then, but Mr. Rawlinford had promised to go to Memphis and get Elvis gifts for the little girl, whose photo he showed me.

He planned to spend the night in a cheap hotel downtown and wait for the paper to come out, in hopes that someone would see the story and offer a special gift for Mr. Rawlinford's special little girl. And somebody did, though I can't remember what it was.

It was such an honor to meet Mr. Rawlinford, but I will always regret that I let him spend Christmas Eve alone in that old hotel instead of bringing him home to spend Christmas with my family.

Sitting at my desk on this December 23 looking around the newsroom and then out the window at the Memphis skyline, I wished that another inspirational, quirky character would walk through the door — someone to make us smile and distract us from the serial killer terrorizing our city.

CHAPTER FIFTY-ONE

My memories of Mr. Rawlinford were shattered by the ring of the phone on my desk. It was Jack telling me that they had released Lettie, even though she certainly hadn't been cleared of involvement in the murders.

"But you know, Britt, I have a gut feeling she didn't do it or have any involvement with it."

"What's softened your attitude toward Lettie?" I asked, thinking, but certainly not saying, how ironic it was that just as I start to have doubts about Lettie, Jack starts to believe in her.

"Well, for one thing, she absolutely has no motive to kill anyone except Saundra, and really not even Saundra, considering that Saundra's ex wanted to marry Lettie, and marrying him could have been the best revenge."

"I'm glad you don't suspect Lettie as much anymore, Jack, but just to play devil's advocate, what difference does motive make if this is truly a serial killer choosing musicians at random or picking them from the different genres of Memphis music?"

"Yeah, but I just don't think it's like that. I really think they're all connected, that somebody hated them all enough to kill them."

I agreed with him, and then he told me his other reason for

not suspecting Lettie much anymore.

"We questioned her for several hours last night and she was very cooperative, not at all quick to turn to her lawyer to see what she should say. In fact, she told him to shut up several times when he tried to advise her not to answer certain questions. No matter how we rephrased questions or turned things around, she never tripped herself up. And she wasn't too smooth, either. It is always suspicious, you know, when somebody seems to be answering from a script. But Lettie Nolan at times just said she couldn't remember or she wasn't sure, which is far more believable than someone who has a quick answer for everything."

Jack said he and several other detectives were working that morning on the movie angle. He had called the film and TV commission and told them he had to have a list of every Memphian involved in all the movies made here in the last few years and that he would also need casting directors' names and contact info. along with the same information on producers and directors. They were going to be calling these people throughout the day and in future days until all leads had been exhausted.

After we hung up, I started my own research, but not on the movie angle. The cops seemed to have that well under control. Instead, I decided to find out everything I could about the latest victim, Rusty Grasslie, so I started with my favorite starting spot, Google.

First I searched the words, "Rusty Grasslie," and got a lot of non-famous Rusty's, so I narrowed it to "Rusty Grasslie Memphis music," which brought up 32,200 entries. Of course, they weren't nearly all about Rusty Grasslie.

However, one article from a music magazine said that Rusty Grasslie's uncle was a studio musician at American Sound Studios in Memphis. I was shocked to find out that American Sound Studios was a Memphis studio. I had never heard of it, and yet according to many entries, the studio did 122 chart records in one five-year period in the late 1960s and early 70s, which no other studio has ever matched. How could I not know about this bit of music history?

I had heard of Chips Moman, a record producer who helped start Stax and started American, but I had no idea his studio had produced rock hits like Dusty Springfield's "Son of a Preacher Man," Neil Diamond's "Sweet Caroline," B.J. Thomas' "Hooked on a Feeling," Elvis Presley's "Suspicious Minds" and so many more.

I called Jack and asked if he'd ever heard of American Sound Studios.

"No," Jack said, "and to tell you the truth, kid, I don't have time for casual conversation today."

So I told him what I had found out about Rusty Grasslie's uncle being a studio musician on all those hits.

"Don't you see, Jack, this means that Rusty does have a Memphis music connection after all."

CHAPTER FIFTY-TWO

I got to the paper early on Christmas Eve, even though I had stayed up half the night reading hundreds of Google entries on Rusty Grasslie, getting personal information on him and most of all searching for anything that might connect him to our victims and suspects.

I could have kept searching at home, but I was so tired I was afraid I would fall asleep at the computer if I stayed at Logan's. At the office it would be much more stimulating.

The night before I had found out some interesting background on Rusty Grasslie. He was college-educated and he played football — defensive end.

After college, he began playing music around Nashville and caught the attention of a record producer. His rise to fame was as sudden as his fall a few years later. All of that came from legitimate newspaper and magazine stories.

If you can believe the blogs, and I'm not sure you always can, somebody who claimed to have gone to school with Rusty said he always drank heavily, like many college students do, but that he added drugs to the mix his senior year and never graduated. I made a mental note to try to verify that.

In the late morning, I finally found what I had hoped to find.

There was an old article from the Memphis Flyer, the alternative weekly in Memphis, about an auto accident that occurred in downtown Memphis in the 90s when Rusty was playing The Pyramid.

About 2 a.m., after the concert, apparently there was an incident at Main and Auction in which a teenaged waitress was hit by a car being driven by Corky Krandale of Nashville. She had just gotten off work and was walking home when Krandale's rental car jumped the curb and hit her on the sidewalk.

The waitress, Brandy Wilerstin, 19, was taken to the Med and had to have emergency surgery on her left hip and left leg. Krandale was charged with failure to maintain control and reckless endangerment. He had been drinking, but his blood alcohol levels were well below the legal limit.

All of that information I later found in my own paper's story, a small item that ran the next day after the accident. But the Flyer story, which ran some time later, had more information. According to the Flyer, Krandale, while he didn't tell police this, was in Memphis because he was road manager for Rusty Grasslie, and The Flyer quoted "an unnamed source close to the singer" as saying that he believed Rusty Grasslie himself may have been driving the car, instead of Krandale.

"Rusty and Corky left the Pyramid together," the unnamed source said, "and Rusty was pretty wasted by that time. As they were walking out to the car, they were arguing over who was going to drive. Corky kept saying that Rusty was too wasted to drive, but well, Rusty, was the boss, and he always got his way."

The unnamed source said that those waiting at the hotel for Grasslie and Krandale were surprised when Grasslie came back alone. When they asked where Corky was, Rusty said he didn't know.

"And instead of partying with us at the suite, Rusty told us to get out, that he was going to bed," the source said. "We were pretty freaked out, because Rusty seemed like he had sobered up pretty fast, and it was almost like he was scared more than mad or sleepy."

The source told the Flyer that he didn't know until the next morning that Krandale had been involved in the accident and had spent the night in jail. He hadn't called any of them after he was arrested, but instead called his lawyer in Nashville to help him make bail.

"Hell, I wouldn't have expected Corky to even have a lawyer — he wasn't the type," the source said. "Everybody was surprised when the accident didn't make the TV news the next day, but Corky said he didn't tell them he worked for Rusty, because he knew the reporters would blow it all up."

The Flyer said Corky Krandale, because he had no previous record, wasn't drunk and because the victim survived, got a suspended sentence.

The final quote from the anonymous source was, "I don't know if Corky was taking the rap for Rusty or not, but if he did, he shouldn't have, because Rusty sure wouldn't have done the same for Corky."

Brandy Wilerstin, according to the Flyer story, sustained permanent injuries in the accident but declined to be interviewed. Could she be the girl in the wheelchair, the one who cried when Mutha Boy wouldn't give her an autograph?

CHAPTER FIFTY-THREE

I looked online and in the Memphis phone book hoping to find a Brandy Wilerstin or at least hoping not to find 18 Wilerstins. Thankfully there was only one, though it wasn't Brandy. There was a Riley Wilerstin at an address I knew was in a run-down neighborhood north of downtown.

I started dialing Jack and then hung up. I hated to sic the police on poor disabled Brandy Wilerstin until I had some hint that we were barking up the right tree. For example, I might get to her house and find she was African American, which would mean that she couldn't be the mysterious girl in the wheelchair at the scene of Mutha Boy's murder. That girl had been described as white with dirty blonde hair.

Besides, just because she was injured by Rusty Grasslie or his road manager, doesn't mean she had anything to do with the murder of Rusty or any of the others.

I thought about calling the Wilerstins first, but I decided to just drop in. If Brandy refused to be interviewed by the Flyer, why would she talk to me? I decided to go to their door and take my chances. In my years as a reporter, I've found it's harder to turn away a friendly face at your door than to hang up on some strange reporter on the phone.

I didn't think for a minute that this wheel-chair-bound young woman was the serial killer, but an interview with her would make a great story just after the Rusty Grasslie murder and might help the police find the killer.

As I used GPS to find the Wilerstin house, I was struck by what a sad neighborhood this was, not just because the people who lived there were obviously poor, but also because so many of the houses were once lovely Victorian homes that were now either abandoned and falling in on themselves or in such a state of disrepair that it must be a constant struggle for the inhabitants to keep rain from coming through the roofs and to avoid falling on rotting steps and floors.

Then I spotted a rare exception, a pretty Queen Anne cottage with a fresh coat of paint and a neat yard. Burglar bars and an iron security door were the only indications the house was in a high-crime neighborhood. A sweet-faced, elderly African American woman was sitting on the front porch swing, her coat wrapped tightly around her, as if waiting for someone to pick her up. I looked at the address, hoping it was the Wilerstins' house, but theirs was next door, a bedraggled one-story frame house that appeared to have been yellow at one time.

As I walked across the porch to the front door, I dodged a rotted hole in the porch. There was no doorbell, so I knocked. At first, no response, so I knocked again louder. Someone peeped from behind a yellowed white curtain in the window beside the door.

I heard several locks unlatched before the door opened and before me stood a frail-looking woman about my age wearing a hot pink velour jogging suit. She was white, but she wasn't in a wheelchair and her hair, instead of dirty blonde, was bright red, that unnatural shade of red favored by some young people and never found on the Lady Clairol shelf at the drugstore.

At first I was disappointed that she didn't match the description of the Mutha Boy suspect, but then I felt relieved. And I felt pity, especially when she looked so glad to see me, as if she had been waiting for me. She must have been confusing me with someone else or she wouldn't have opened the door so readily. Or maybe she was just lonely.

"Merry Christmas," I said weakly. "Are you Brandy?"

She nodded yes and pulled the door open wider, as if to usher me in, and said, "You're that lady I seen on TV." Several TV reporters had ambushed me when it first came out that I had received notes from the serial killer.

Well, so much for figuring out how to broach the subject of my wanting to interview her for the paper. This was getting easier by the moment, although there might be a protective parent inside to usher me back out.

As if to read my mind, she said, "Come on in. Daddy's not home right now. He's at work. He don't get off 'til four."

She led me into the living room, which was stiflingly hot and fumey from the gas space heater. It was furnished with shabby, mismatched furniture. Brandy walked with a decided limp, but nothing that would require a wheelchair.

"Sit down," she said and headed for the kitchen. "I made some cookies. It's Christmas Eve, you know." She sounded like a child waiting for Santa Claus.

"Sounds like you like Christmas as much as I do."

"I love Christmas," she shouted from the kitchen as she clattered china. "When Mama was alive, we'd go to my aunt's house in Arkansas for Christmas, and we'd have us a big old time."

When she came back with a plate of iced sugar cookies, I ate one and complimented her baking ability and then asked when her mother had died. She said she was 14 — a terrible time for a girl to lose her mother, I thought, if there is a time that is not terrible to lose your mother. She said she was 42 now, but she seemed to me much younger.

"Why did you come to see me or did you come to see Daddy?" she asked.

"I came to see you, Brandy. I was wondering if you would mind telling me about the accident you had, when the car hit you?"

"That was when I worked as a waitress. I got good tips, too, but I haven't been able to work since then, so Daddy has to work two jobs. I'm a terrible burden on him," she said matter-of-factly.

"I'm sure you're not."

"He says I am. I think I could work, but he says I'm too handicapped. He says we need my disability check."

"That night of the accident were you just walking home on the sidewalk? Did you see the car coming?"

"It came up behind me, so I didn't see it coming, so I couldn't jump out of the way or anything. I just heard it and the next thing I knew I was being pushed up in the air and throwed against the wall of a building."

"Was anybody there to help you?"

"They said there weren't no witnesses, but I remember two men yelling."

"Yelling for help?"

"One of them was yelling at me, calling me stupid and saying why didn't I get out of the way, and the other one was yelling at the other man and saying he had killed me. Then I blacked out, I guess, and I didn't come to until I was at the hospital."

"Who called the police and the paramedics?"

"I guess Mr. Krandale, the man who ran over me. Daddy came along too, because he had been supposed to pick me up at work and forgot, so I started walking home, but then he remembered and came along."

"How do you know the man who hit you was named Mr. Krandale?"

"Because he came to see me in the hospital and brought me a teddy bear and some pink roses. I was in the hospital for a long time. My hip was crushed and my leg got broke. He was a real nice man and said over and over how sorry he was I got hurt."

"When was the last time you saw him?"

"When I was in the hospital. I still have the teddy bear. I named him Rusty."

I nearly dropped my Christmas cookie.

"Rusty? Why Rusty?"

"Daddy said I should name him Rusty, because Rusty was going to make us rich. I never did know how a teddy bear could make us rich."

I asked Brandy if she and her dad had more money to spend after the accident, but she said no, it was just the opposite — they had less. Then tears came to her eyes.

"Sometimes on payday," she said, "he goes down to Tunica to the casino with his paycheck and loses the whole thing in one night, and then all we have to live on is my disability check and what Granddaddy gives us."

Then tears began to flow down her cheeks, and I looked around for tissues. Seeing none, I rushed to the bathroom for toilet paper. Coming out of the bathroom with a roll of toilet paper in hand, I looked across the hall into the bedroom and saw a large wheel protruding out of a closet.

I walked into the bedroom to see if it was a bicycle, but it was a wheelchair, a battered wheelchair

.

CHAPTER FIFTY-FOUR

I stood there in the bedroom for a few seconds trying to compose myself and trying to figure out what to do. Now I regretted not calling Jack and telling him where I was going. I wanted to call him now, but my cell phone was in my purse in the living room. But there was no reason to panic, I reasoned. I certainly wasn't afraid of Brandy, and her father after all was at work. She said he got off at four, and it was only 2:15 now.

Brandy's father was obviously an opportunist, who had tried to blackmail or at least get an under-the-table settlement from Rusty Grasslie, but that didn't make him a murderer. And the wheelchair might link Brandy to the Plush Club the night of the Mutha Boy murder, but not necessarily. Why would a serial killer set out to kill someone with his wheelchair-bound daughter in tow? That absolutely made no sense.

I went back into the living room and gave Brandy the roll of toilet paper. She tore off a section and blew her nose loudly.

"Brandy, I wasn't trying to snoop, but when I went to the bathroom, I saw a wheel sticking out of a closet. Is that your wheelchair?"

"Yessum, but I only use it when we go out. We don't have a car anymore, so unless we can use my granddaddy's car, Daddy has to push me in the wheelchair if I have to go somewhere. But I don't go out that much. I can walk around here okay, but it's hard to walk very far without a bunch of pain."

"Brandy, I have a very important question to ask you, and I need you to tell me the truth."

"Mama always said I should never lie."

"That's good. Brandy, did your daddy or anybody else take you to the Plush Club on the night that the rapper Mutha Boy was murdered?"

She fell into my arms, sobbing so hard I could hardly understand her words.

"I've been so scared that Daddy was the one who killed him. I don't think he would kill nobody, but it was just so…" and she trailed off into more sobs. I sat her up and wiped away the tears on her face and gave her another wad of toilet paper to blow her nose.

"Tell me about that night from the beginning. What did your daddy tell y'all were leaving home to do?"

"In the afternoon, I asked him if he would take me to the Plush Club to see the show. I loved Mutha Boy and I had heard some of the kids in the neighborhood talking about there being a big show on Beale Street. At first Daddy laughed and said some mean things about Mutha Boy and all rappers and said no, he wouldn't take me. He said it with cuss words."

"What happened to change his mind?"

"Well, he had planned to use Granddaddy's car to go down to Tunica, but when Granddaddy called and said he wasn't coming home that night, Daddy changed his mind. He said I didn't get out enough and that he was going to push my chair down to Beale Street. That was the nicest thing he's ever done for me. I was so happy."

"So he pushed your wheelchair down to Beale Street. Did you go to the show?"

"When he got there and found out how much it cost, he said

we weren't going in, but we'd wait outside and I could get autographs from Mutha Boy or one of the other rappers. I was disappointed, but it was still fun to think I might get to see them up close. We waited a long time, and finally Mutha Boy and some other people came out. I stuck out my paper and pen and asked him for an autograph, but he pushed it away and laughed at me. It made me cry."

"Did you and your dad leave then?"

"I wanted to. I felt embarrassed, like people were making fun of me. Daddy pushed my chair over to the sidewalk across the street, and then he went back, but he didn't tell me why. I saw him go to the back of the building. Then after a few minutes, he came back, not running exactly, but walking real fast and he started pushing me home. He didn't say anything the whole way home, and he made me go to bed as soon as we got home."

"Why are you afraid your daddy might have killed Mutha Boy?"

"I wasn't that night, but the next day when I heard all about it on TV, it started to scare me. And when I was watching it on TV, Daddy came into the room and turned off the TV and started cussing about me watching TV too much. I've been scared ever since that my daddy might be a murderer. Then when I heard about the other ones, I really got scared."

"Did you tell anyone about your fears?"

"I told Granddaddy, but he hugged me and said not to worry, that my daddy would never kill anybody unless it was accidental or in a fight or something. He said Daddy wouldn't kill a bunch of strangers for no good reason, so I stopped worrying so much. Granddaddy doesn't lie to me like Daddy does sometimes."

I heard the heavy footsteps on the front porch and the key turn in the lock before I had a chance to run or grab my cell phone.

Riley Wilerstin, thin with a gaunt, dissipated face, just starred at us for a moment and then demanded, "What the hell are you doing here?"

Brandy looked terrified. She grabbed my arm and held on for dear life. Her father saw her reaction and rushed toward us, his face exploding with anger.

"What have you done, girl? What did you tell her?"

Then he turned his wrath on me. "You had no right to come into my house like this and mess with my girl. She's retarded, she don't know what she's talking about. She's messed up in the brain because of that S.O.B. Grasslie. I'm glad he's dead, but that don't mean I killed him."

His anger seemed to be escalating. I considered trying to run, but I knew he'd catch me, so I decided to try to convince him I was on his side.

"I wouldn't blame you if you did kill Rusty after what he did to Brandy and then just leaving her there for dead, letting his road manager take the blame."

"How do you know that? I was the only one who saw him running away. I recognized him from his record albums."

"I talked to Corky yesterday," I lied, "and he confessed that Rusty was the one who really was driving, not him. He said Rusty paid him to take the blame."

Wilerstin exploded again. "That son of a bitch paid Corky off, but he wouldn't give me a penny?"

"I'm surprised you didn't sue him for all he was worth, considering what he did to Brandy, robbing her of a normal life," I said, trying hard to convince him I was sympathetic to whatever he had done.

"I tried to, but the lawyer said no jury or judge would believe me because I had waited so long and didn't tell the police that I saw Grasslie running away from the wreck."

"You probably didn't trust the cops to do the right thing, since Rusty is famous and rich."

"Damn right, I didn't trust the cops. I just figured me and the singer would settle it between the two of us, so I contacted him a few days later. He should've been willing to shell out some major money just to keep it out of the papers and TV. It was the least he could do for the girl he hurt, but that bastard laughed in my face, said nobody was going to believe me over him."

If Brandy had stayed quiet, I think I might have somehow convinced Riley that I didn't think he had killed Rusty, much less the others. I might have been able to say my goodbyes and walk calmly out of the house. But Brandy didn't stay quiet.

She blurted out, "Daddy, did you kill Mutha Boy? Why did you kill Mutha Boy? He didn't do nothing to me except laugh at me. That's no reason to kill somebody."

Riley flew toward Brandy in a rage and began hitting her and screaming at her to shut up. I wanted to run, but I was afraid he would kill her before I could get help.

Suddenly the door flew open and to my utter amazement, it was somebody I knew.

CHAPTER FIFTY-FIVE

"You take your filthy hands off that girl or I'll kill you," he shouted, rushing toward Riley and a screaming, terrified Brandy.

Slick Taggart acted like he didn't even see me. Riley kept hitting Brandy, whose mouth and nose were bleeding now.

"Granddaddy, help me!" she wailed.

"I'll kill you, I swear, Riley," Slick screamed, as he tried to pull what I found out later was his son-in-law off the girl.

Riley stopped and turned his anger on Slick.

"Yeah, you gonna kill me like you did Saundra Barkley, old man?"

Riley lunged toward Slick, and I knew this was my chance to run, but I stumbled over the coffee table as I tried to make for the door. Before I could get up, Riley grabbed my arm and threw me down on the sofa.

"No, you don't. You'll go to the cops," Riley said. I tried kicking him in the groin, like I've heard you should do if a man attacks you, but I hardly touched him, and that made him even angrier, of course. He grabbed me with both hands and began to shake me. His face was purple with rage.

Slick jumped Riley from behind, and I bit Riley's right arm as hard as I could. He howled in pain and then slapped me across the face. Our three-way struggle was long enough for Brandy to scramble across the room and pull a handgun from the drawer.

"Stop," she screamed. "I'll shoot you, Daddy. I swear I will."

Riley just sneered and let go of me. "Baby, you ain't gonna shoot your own Daddy, you know you ain't." He moved toward Brandy, but I grabbed the gun from her hand.

"No, she probably wouldn't shoot you, but I will," I said, though I was all bluff. I had the nerve to shoot him, but not the ability. I had never fired a gun in my life. In my nervousness, I dropped the gun. But before Riley could pick it up, Slick jumped Riley from the back again, and Brandy and I piled on to seal the deal. It probably looked comical — two women and an old man piling on, pinching, hitting, biting, whatever it took to subdue this serial killer. By the time Jack and the other cops came swarming in, we had Riley locked in the windowless storeroom.

When we had called 911, the operator told us that someone else had already called and the police would be there any second. We later found out the elderly lady sitting on her porch next door had called the police when she heard all of the screaming.

During those few minutes while we waited for the police, Slick told Brandy what he didn't want her to hear from the TV news or from somebody else. He said he was working as a dishwasher in one of the clubs on Beale the night Saundra was murdered.

"Saundra was there that night and was acting like a big shot as usual, and somebody even asked her to sing "Baby Gotta Leave" with the band," Slick said to Brandy, occasionally glancing over at me. "I had gotten some bad news that day from the doctor."

Brandy looked alarmed. She obviously loved her grandfather. "You're sick?"

"I'm afraid so, Baby. They told me I got stage four lung cancer, so I had been drinking on the sly all night when nobody was looking. I had a bottle hid in the kitchen. So when Saundra left the club, I followed her and took a steak knife from the kitchen. I caught up with her about a block away, and nobody was around. I didn't intend on hurting her. I was just going to threaten her with the knife.

"I told her I had cancer and I deserved to live my last months without having to wash dishes and that the least she could do for me was pay me for my song, cause she knew as well as I did that I wrote it, not her. But she just said I was lying about the cancer and she turned away and started walking again. And I just did it, just stabbed her with that knife and ran off. I didn't know she had died until I heard it on the news the next day. Riley was with me when I heard, and he remembered I had blood on my shirt when I came home and he put two and two together, but said he wouldn't tell anybody."

Slick said the police took him in for questioning a few days later and kept him overnight, and when he called home to tell Riley he wouldn't be home and why, Riley just said, "Don't worry about it. I'll take care of it."

"I had no idea what he meant by that until they released me and I went home, and Riley told me, real proud-like, that he had stabbed that rapper so it would look like a serial killer and that would clear me since I was in custody. He said he went over there with a knife, intending to do it, but then lost his nerve. But when the guy was mean to Brandy, Riley went back into the club and stabbed him."

"Oh, no, Daddy did kill Mutha Boy," Brandy whimpered. "I was hoping he didn't."

Slick took her hands and said gently, "He was trying to help me, but I wouldn't never have wanted him to do that. I didn't even mean to kill Saundra, but at least she was somebody who done me wrong. But that kid didn't do nothing to deserve to be stabbed."

Jack and the others stormed in the door, guns drawn, about that time. We told them where we'd locked Riley up.

"You'll need to take me, too," Slick told the cops. Jack looked at me for confirmation and I nodded yes.

"Granddaddy, before you go, I need to ask you, is my daddy the serial killer they talk about on TV?"

"The police will have to figure that out, Baby, but I got a bad feeling he is."

Before they took Slick and Riley away, I asked if there was any family member we could call to come for Brandy, once the police had taken her statement. Slick gave me a name and number of his other daughter, who lived in Arkansas.

I told Brandy that she would have to go to the police station and tell the police what she knew, but that she was not under arrest and that she'd be with her aunt soon.

Jack told the cops who were taking in Riley and Slick that he'd bring Brandy and me down to 201 in a few minutes. Since Brandy was disabled, a guardian ad litem would have to be appointed for her, I knew, before they would interrogate her, so there was no hurry. Slick looked at Brandy one more time and said, "I love you, baby. I'm sorry for what I'm putting you through. Your Aunt Evie will take a sight better care of you than me and your daddy ever did."

After they left and a patrolman had been told to wait for the crime scene people who would swarm the house soon looking for evidence, Jack came toward me, and I flew into his arms.

"Thank God you're okay," was all he said. The lecture on how foolish I was to come over here alone could wait until later.

CHAPTER FIFTY-SIX

Jack drove us in his car to 201 Poplar, and I sat on the backseat with Brandy, comforting her and reassuring her that she would not be put in jail. I also told her she'd probably be released in time to go home for Christmas with her aunt, whom Jack called on his cell phone from the car.

The aunt, who was married and had two daughters younger than Brandy, lived in Jonesboro, Arkansas, which is just an hour or two away. She told Jack that she had been wanting Brandy to come live with her ever since Brandy's mother died, and especially after the accident, but that Riley wouldn't allow it. She was in tears at the thought that her father was a murderer and her brother-in-law a possible serial killer, but she promised that she and her husband would leave immediately for Memphis.

"See, Brandy, I told you your aunt would come get you and you'd get to spend Christmas with them like you used to," I said, patting her back.

"Except Mama won't be there, and Daddy and Granddaddy will be spending Christmas in jail."

I had no answer for that.

•••••••••••••••••

Another detective took my statement, and by the time I left 201, Brandy's aunt and uncle had arrived and were able to be with her while she waited to be questioned. I called Logan to pick me up and take me to my car, and Jack told me he'd call me later.

As Logan drove me back to the Wilerstin house, I told him everything that had happened. He said the radio and TV stations were reporting rumors that the serial killer had been caught, but the police had not officially confirmed it yet.

"Yeah, I got to get to the paper quick, so we can get the story online before anybody else."

The police director had kept his word to me about letting us have it first, since the newspaper had cooperated in several ways during the investigation, like holding back details of the killer's notes. He said he wouldn't hold a press conference until I got a story put up on our web site, but he could only give me a couple of hours lead time. He also promised to give us some exclusive information for tomorrow morning's print edition. It was going to be a strange Christmas Day issue of the paper, but read by everyone in the county. They would need an extended press run.

"I've already called my editor, and at first they wanted me to do a first person story, but I said no," I told Logan. "I'd rather have one of the other reporters do the story and just interview me about my experience. I'm too deeply involved to do the story myself."

"I can't believe how calm you are," Logan said and reached over to take my hand. "That guy could have killed you, like all the others. I mean, you just got through physically wrestling a serial killer, and you're cool as can be."

"It will hit me later and I'll fall apart when I realize what a close call that was and how stupid I was to go over there alone, not even telling anybody where I was going. Thanks for not telling me what a fool I was."

Logan looked at me with that grin that said, *I was just about to tell you how dumb that was.*

"Believe me, Logan, if I had known Riley Wilerstin was going to get off two hours early from work because it was Christmas Eve, I wouldn't have hung around — that dumb I am not. I just thought I had some time, and I thought Brandy would open up to me better than to the police. Then once that creep came back and started hitting Brandy, I couldn't run away and let him kill her. Then when Slick came and all hell broke loose, it didn't even feel like I was dealing with two murderers — it seemed like I was jumping on the school bully with some of the other kids to stop him from picking on some poor kid. That's the way it felt, honestly."

Logan laughed. "I believe you, Britt, really I do. It wasn't smart to go there alone, but after you got there, well, you did what you thought best, and I admire your courage. I want to be you when I grow up. Well, either you or Spiderman."

Logan leaned over and gave me a little kiss on top of the head as I opened the car door to get out.

"I'm just glad you didn't get hurt," he said. "After you get through at the paper, are you coming back to my house? Mom is cooking Christmas Eve dinner at my place for all of us. Invite Jack, too."

"He probably won't be able to get away, but I'll tell him, and yeah, I'll see you and your mom a little later."

•••••••••••••••••

Driving back to the paper, I had to do one thing before I forgot. This Christmas Eve I wouldn't be thinking much about my family in Florida, but I knew they'd be thinking of me and worrying as soon as they got the news. So I had to get to them first.

I called them on my cell phone, and Daddy answered.

"Hey, Bitsy! Merry Christmas! We thought you'd call later, so everybody's not here to talk to you. Mom and ..."

"This isn't my Merry Christmas call, Daddy," I interrupted. "I guess you haven't heard — they caught the serial killer today, and I was involved in the capture."

"Are you okay? Are you hurt?"

"No, no, I'm fine, and I've got to get back to the paper to help with the story, but I just wanted to make sure you all knew I was okay."

I gave him the Cliffs Notes version of what had happened that day.

"So my little girl single-handedly captured a serial killer," Daddy said proudly.

"You should work for the National Inquirer," I said with a laugh.

"Well, I'm glad I answered the phone instead of Mom. She'd have had a heart attack."

"Well, break it to her gently, starting with the words, 'Britt is fine, absolutely fine.' I know how you love to drag out a story and give it a big finish, but don't leave her and Jill and Libby hanging about whether I'm okay or not. Do you promise?"

"I promise, and can I tell them you'll call again later or on Christmas day?"

I promised I would call on Christmas day and hung up just as I was pulling into the newspaper parking lot. I parked in a visitor spot. No way I was walking from the regular lot on a day like this.

When I walked into the newsroom, everyone applauded and I took an exaggerated bow. They were all patting me on the back and saying good job, but the editors wanted me to quickly get to work with Josh, who was going to write the story for the web, which would be updated throughout the night until an expanded story came out in the print edition early in the morning.

The police director had given our reporter a quote saying that the department was hopeful that the serial killer had been apprehended, but at the moment, two suspects were being questioned in connection with the murders of Saundra Barkley, Donté Washington, Larry Carpenter, Churnin Rivers and Rusty Grasslie .

So I just told him my story and let him put it all together, leaving out some details until the police had had a chance to decide whom to charge with what. The reporter asked me if I was scared during all this.

"I guess I was afraid," I told him, "but when all of that stuff is going on, you can't be paralyzed by fear. You have to react first and be afraid afterward."

"Good quote," he said and turned to his computer to get started on the story.

And I left the newspaper, not sure what to do next.

CHAPTER FIFTY-SEVEN

As I drove across the little bridge to Harbor Town and turned right onto Island Drive, I felt a little shaky for the first time today. I pulled into Logan's driveway and opened the garage doors with the electronic device Logan gave me the night I found the note on my car outside Molly's LaCasita.

A note from a killer who now had a name. Just like George Howard Putt, Memphis' last serial killer — whose name was known to many people who didn't even live in Memphis or weren't born yet when he was doing his killing. Riley Wilerstin and to a lesser degree Slick Taggart would be remembered. Remembered for a terrible reason. And very few of their victims' names will be remembered.

It seems wrong that serial killers' names are remembered for years, decades, centuries. Jack the Ripper, Charles Manson, Ted Bundy, Richard Speck, John Wayne Gacy, Jeffrey Dahmer. They kill multiple people for perverse and usually random reasons, and in return they get a certain immortality in the public mind. It isn't right, but it's reality. And we in the press are the ones who keep the names alive. Did I today, by stopping Riley Wilerstin, make up for that a little?

After what had happened earlier in the day, it seemed odd to see the Christmas tree lighted in the window of Logan's house and to smell Maggie's wonderful cooking in the kitchen. And in houses around the city, Santa Claus would come tonight, just like always.

When I saw that Maggie, Logan and Charlie weren't in the kitchen, I took the opportunity to sneak up the back stairs and go to my room for a while. I wanted a hot shower and a little time alone.

After I dried my hair, but still wearing the thick terry cloth robe provided me by Logan for my stay, I went out on the balcony to sit for a while. It was cold, but I didn't care. It was 8:15 now, and I knew they were probably holding dinner for me, but I needed to breath fresh, cold air and stare at the lighted bridge over the Mississippi River and know that this time, I didn't have to fear that someone out there might be watching me.

And that's when it hit me, just how close I had come to being Riley Wilerstin's fifth victim. I burst into tears and cried until my sobs became a whimper and then I just sat there on the balcony hugging myself to stay warm. I heard the ringing of the cell phone in my room. It was Jack.

"Am I still invited for Christmas Eve?"

I cleared my throat and tried not to sound like I had been crying.

"Of course, but I never dreamed you'd be able to get away."

"I'll have to come back, but we got our confessions, so some of us can take a dinner break. I'll be there in 10 minutes."

After I hung up, I put on charcoal gray pants and a black velvet pullover like I might wear on a normal Christmas, and I packed my suitcase since I'd be returning to my own house after dinner.

•••••••••••••••••

The doorbell was ringing as I came down the front stairs. Logan was standing at the foot of the stairs, smiling up at me, and

Maggie opened the door to Lettie and Jack, who arrived separately but at the same time.

"I brought you a cop for Christmas," Lettie said. "I hope you like it."

We all laughed and Charlie barked with excitement at all the activity.

"Are we going to eat first or try to drag information out of Jack first?" I asked.

"Well," said Jack, taking off his coat, "I haven't eaten since a breakfast of two doughnuts and bad coffee, so if you'll feed me well, I'll tell all. And before you ask, Britt, I already called your reporter and told him most of what I'll tell y'all over dinner."

"It's a deal," Maggie said scurrying into the kitchen to serve the food. Everyone followed her and helped. Jack sliced the beef brisket while I helped Maggie put the vegetables into serving bowls. Logan carried the heavy casserole dish of garlic cheese potatoes to the dining room, and Lettie put ice in the drinking glasses and poured the water. Logan had already opened two bottles of merlot.

At first we just ate — we were all famished — and talked about my experience with Brandy and family, but over our second glasses of wine, Jack told us the whole story.

"First of all, let me say that our foolhardy little friend, Britten Faire, I hate to admit, made our job easy," Jack said. "Knowing what Britt had already heard at the house and that Slick had already told us all he had done and knew, Riley was easy to get a full confession from."

"I don't know Riley," Lettie said, "but I got to tell you, I've known Slick Taggart for 25 years and never in a thousand years would I think he'd be capable of murder, and I sure never believed him when he went on about Saundra stealing his song. So, Slick Taggart actually wrote a number one hit song."

"It would seem that way," Jack said. "And Lettie, sorry about suspecting you were the murderer."

"Hey, Jackie Boy, you were just doing your job. You wouldn't ask me not to play my bass, and I wouldn't ask you not to investigate a murder."

"So, Jack, did this Riley guy confess to all the murders except Saundra Barkley? Logan asked.

"Yep, eventually. At first he just admitted to killing the rapper, since he had confessed that one to Slick, but as he said why he didn't kill the others, he started tripping himself up, and over a couple of hours, he confessed to them all."

"When I saw Slick and Riley together today," I said, "there didn't seem to be any great love between them. Why on earth would Riley kill Mutha Boy just to cover up for Slick killing Saundra?

"Apparently, Riley didn't like living with Slick, because Slick was always throwing it in Riley's face that he blew all his money on gambling, and Slick never stopped reminding him that without Slick's help, Brandy would be too much for Riley. Which might lead you to expect him to be glad if Slick got arrested for Saundra's murder, but Riley needed Slick's financial help and help with Brandy and he also wanted to help Slick so Slick would owe him. And he hated all rappers because he didn't consider them real musicians and thought they didn't deserve the money they were making."

Jack explained that Riley's original plan was to just kill Mutha Boy and nobody else.

"But then his basic deviant nature took over," Jack said, "and, by the way, Britt, Slick told us that Riley had been abused by his old drunk of a father and abandoned by his mother when he was 5, so the profile of the serial killer as abused child holds up here.

"After the rapper's murder," Jack continued, "Riley found that he felt important, empowered, invincible, and he began sending the notes to you after he read your story about Mutha Boy. He said when he delivered a note to your house, he would just carry a rake with him so that he'd look like one of those guys who goes around door to door asking for yard work. I guess that's why nobody noticed him. He's a pretty non-descript guy. And at Molly's he followed you there and then just stood around the back door like he was taking a smoke break and put the note on your car when nobody was around."

"What I want to know most," Logan said, "is how he knew what went on in the motor home when we went to Ole Miss on Thanksgiving. How in the world did he pull that off?"

"You know how they say you can find out how to build an atomic bomb on the Internet? Well, Riley was just watching TV one night, one of those true crime reality shows on cable, and they had a story about a man who stalked and later killed his ex-wife, and the way he kept up with her was he put a cell phone with a GPS under the lower part of the dashboard and tracked her and simply listened to what was said. So Riley did that to the motor home, only his phone was old and less sophisticated, no GPS. Apparently, your dad didn't lock the motor home the night before Thanksgiving or after you returned from Oxford. Guess you all must have talked about where you were going and the sweet potato casserole and of course he could hear you singing. And then that night, he took the phone out of the motor home, and that's why they didn't find it in Florida."

"Clever, but creepy," Maggie said. I was speechless.

Lettie asked how Riley picked the other victims. Jack turned to me.

"Britt, you know how we thought the movie connection was significant? Well, it was, but not in the way we thought. After Mutha Boy's death, Riley and Brandy rented *Black 'n Blue*, and Brandy said her father got furious and started turning over furniture and cussing when he realized that a couple of no-count dead beats like Larry Carpenter and Churnin Rivers got to be in the movie and make money from the film and from gigs they got because of the movie. Seems Riley was a frustrated musician himself."

"So he killed them," I said. "And were you able to confirm that he killed Rusty because he refused to pay Riley off after the accident."

"Yep, we asked the Nashville police to question Corky this

afternoon, and he admitted that he took the rap for Rusty, who was really driving the car. He said Rusty was drunk and had been drugging and already had a couple of possession arrests, so Rusty convinced him to take the rap or they would all lose their meal ticket in Rusty. And he promised Corky a big payday for taking the rap, which he delivered on."

So when Riley heard that Rusty was coming to town to play, he decided to make Rusty his next victim, Jack told us.

"One of the things that has puzzled me during all this," Logan said, "is how has the killer always been able to place the knife in just the right place to cause instant death without a struggle?"

"I had the same question, Logan," Jack said. "It seems that Slick just got lucky when he stabbed Saundra and remember, she didn't die immediately. But Riley apparently knew exactly where to place the knife. He said he learned it when he was in Vietnam and his squad usually got the reconnaissance duty. He said his squad leader had some advanced hand-to-hand combat training and showed the guys how to sneak up on a Vietcong and take him out with one well-placed stab of the bayonet or with a knife."

That left us all silent until Maggie said, "Who wants dessert?" We laughed and helped her serve the chocolate cake with praline icing. Soon afterward, Jack said he needed to head back to work. There were plenty of loose ends to tie up. The arraignment of the two men would be the day after Christmas, and he predicted they'd be held without bond — Riley because he's a serial killer and Slick because a man with Stage 4 lung cancer who's a professed murderer is a flight risk.

I walked Jack out to his car, and we gave each other a long hug. When he got in his car, he said, "So, kiddo, I guess we did pretty good today, huh?"

"Yeah, Jack, we did pretty good. I guess we make a good team."

"I'm not sure if I should become a reporter or you should become a cop," he said and smiled.

"How about we just stay the way we are." I didn't mean that as a negative pronouncement on our possible romantic future, but I thought I saw a flicker of sadness on his face, or was it agreement? I thought of the blonde at Paulette's.

Jack started to drive off and then stopped and leaned out the window.

"If you ever, and I mean ever, do anything so stupid again, going alone to the house of somebody who might be a killer, I'll...well, anyhow, I'm glad you're okay."

I just smiled, blew him a kiss, pulled my coat tighter around me and waved to him. As he drove off, Jack shouted out the window at me, "Merry Christmas, kiddo!"

Inside, Logan was trying to convince Maggie and Lettie to spend the night, since it was so late and tomorrow was Christmas.

"Okay, but I need to leave after breakfast," Lettie said. "I'm thinking about seeing Dewitt some time tomorrow."

When we all got excited, she put up her hand. "Hold your horses, I said I'm *thinking* about it, didn't say I was for sure."

Logan turned to me. "How about you, Britt? Will you stay one more night?"

"It's tempting, but no. However, I will borrow Charlie just for one night, if you don't mind. I'll bring him back when I come for Christmas breakfast."

"I'm sure he'd be delighted to go home with you, and when Santa gets here, I'll tell him Charlie hung up his stocking at your house. I'll walk you two to your car."

And he did. Logan opened the back car door and put Charlie in, along with my suitcase, and then took me in his arms and kissed me, not a long, passionate kiss, but not like you would kiss your sister either.

When we pulled apart, he buttoned my coat for me, like I was his little girl.

"The circumstances have been horrendous, Britt, but I've got to say, it has been so great having you here for these weeks. I'll miss you a lot."

I started to do my Lauren Bacall to Bogey imitation and say something about whistling if he needed me, but instead I just said, "I'll miss you, too, Logan. Thank you for being my place of safety."

I gave him his garage door opener back and drove away. As I crossed over the little Harbor Town bridge back into downtown Memphis, I decided to take the long way home. I rolled down my window, put in a Christmas CD, and Charlie and I breathed in the clean, cold air as we drove along Riverside Drive. While Frank Sinatra promised that through the years we all would be together, if the fates allowed.

ABOUT THE AUTHOR

Candy Justice is a former newspaper reporter and columnist who now is an award-winning journalism professor at the University of Memphis.

Made in the USA
Coppell, TX
01 November 2019